**She was staring down at her hands, fingers knotted together, in her lap. She was no longer shaking, but he suspected that was a conscious effort on her part.**

"If you hadn't been here," she began.

"Annalise, you saved yourself."

"He would have caught up with me. Stupid shoes. Impossible to run in."

Brett glanced at the heels she'd had on, kicked off when she'd sat down on the couch. Strappy summery things that looked indeed impossible to run in. Hell, to him they looked impossible to walk in. He didn't know how women did it.

But he knew why. "But sexy," he said, and regretted it the instant the words were out. She gave him a startled look, and that alone told him he'd strayed into inappropriate territory. What was it about her that had him not just thinking dangerous things, but saying them?

\* \* \*

**The Coltons of Grave Gulch: Falling in love is the most dangerous thing of all...**

\* \* \*

**If you're on Twitter, tell us what you think of Harlequin Romantic Suspense! #harlequinromsuspense**

Dear Reader,

Every book I write is special to me in one way or another. But I felt a particular affinity for this one because of the setting. I was born about three hundred miles from the fictional town of Braxville, Kansas, albeit in Iowa. True, we had moved before I was a year old, but we went back to visit family every year (by car, mind you, an endless trip when you're a kid), and it frequently involved a stop in Kansas. And I remember those trips vividly, the vast distances, the real, true amber waves of grain and the flat of it all. Sometimes I think that's why now I'm not truly happy unless I can see mountains. Probably why I now live where I see them every day. But I digress.

What I remember most about those trips through the heartland is the people. When we got a flat tire, a man driving down the road in a tractor stopped and helped my dad change it. When we encountered some major road construction and ended up having to ask for directions to the interstate (yes, there was a time before Google Maps), we didn't just get directions—the gentleman actually drove out of his way to lead us to it. And I remember once we had an overheating problem, and the owner of the gas station we stopped at let me watch TV in his home behind the station while he and my dad fixed it. Because that's who they are, these people of the heartland.

It was a pleasure to revisit them in this story. Happy reading!

*Justine*

# COLTON K-9 TARGET

---

**Justine Davis**

Special thanks and acknowledgment are given to Justine Davis
for her contribution to The Coltons of Grave Gulch miniseries.

**HARLEQUIN**®
**ROMANTIC SUSPENSE**™

Recycling programs
for this product may
not exist in your area.

ISBN-13: 978-1-335-75938-2

Colton K-9 Target

Copyright © 2021 by Harlequin Books S.A.

This edition published by arrangement with Harlequin Books S.A.

For questions and comments about the quality of this book,
please contact us at CustomerService@Harlequin.com.

Harlequin Enterprises ULC
22 Adelaide St. West, 40th Floor
Toronto, Ontario M5H 4E3, Canada
www.Harlequin.com

**Printed in U.S.A.**

**Justine Davis** lives on Puget Sound in Washington State, watching big ships and the occasional submarine go by and sharing the neighborhood with assorted wildlife, including a pair of bald eagles, deer, a bear or two, and a tailless raccoon. In the few hours when she's not planning, plotting or writing her next book, her favorite things are photography, knitting her way through a huge yarn stash and driving her restored 1967 Corvette roadster—top down, of course.

Connect with Justine on her website, justinedavis.com, at Twitter.com/justine_d_davis or on Facebook at Facebook.com/justinedaredavis.

### Books by Justine Davis

### Harlequin Romantic Suspense

### *The Coltons of Grave Gulch*

*Colton K-9 Target*

### *Cutter's Code*

*Operation Midnight*
*Operation Reunion*
*Operation Blind Date*
*Operation Unleashed*
*Operation Power Play*
*Operation Homecoming*
*Operation Soldier Next Door*
*Operation Alpha*
*Operation Notorious*
*Operation Hero's Watch*
*Operation Second Chance*
*Operation Mountain Recovery*

Visit the Author Profile page at Harlequin.com, or justinedavis.com, for more titles.

# Chapter 1

Annalise Colton knew how nervous she was because of how much she was talking to herself. Enough that she couldn't even pretend that she was really talking to the dogs at her feet.

"Stop it," she said in her best police K-9 trainer voice. "You're even making them nervous."

And now she was giving herself orders. Out loud.

She sighed and made herself turn away from the mirror. She'd done her best, and it would have to do; if she tweaked her makeup any further, she'd be doing more harm than good. She'd already gone from having her long blond hair up, back, then down three times, before finally giving up and just letting it fall loosely.

After Bennett had unceremoniously dumped her in public, it had taken her months to even think about dating again, despite wishing for a settled life and someone to share it with more than almost anything. But when she had finally steeled herself to try again, she had vowed there would be nothing but nice guys from here on out. They might not have Bennett's flash, but they wouldn't have his cruel streak, either.

"Nope," she said to Jack and Apple, the shaggy canine duo she was fostering, "nothing but Mr. Nice Guy for me from here on out."

The two dogs danced at her feet, tails wagging madly. They'd come a long way in the weeks since she'd brought them home, after some wrangling with her landlord. At first they'd been skittish, afraid of everything and nothing. Their true personalities—Jack goofy and bold, Apple quieter and more sensitive—were emerging. Soon potential adopters would be able to see that, instead of the fearful, cringing creatures they'd been when they'd come into the shelter. She only hoped they would be adopted together; hard times had bonded the two deeply.

*That's what I want. That kind of bond. The kind that says I'm there for you, no matter what.*

"Dream on," she muttered as she checked their food and water. If it went well tonight, she might be late. And it certainly seemed like it should go well; Sam was exactly what she'd been looking for.

Or at least he seemed to be, online. She'd been a little wary of using the popular Grave Gulch Singles app, but some of her friends swore by it. She'd trod carefully, and for some reason the fact that there were awful profiles as well as interesting and appealing ones made it seem more genuine to her. She'd messaged with a few guys who seemed nice, but then Sam Rivers had popped up.

That he was an ER doctor here in Grave Gulch—along with her sister Desiree's fiancé, Stavros, also a doctor there, and she kept meaning to ask him about Sam—was what had caught her attention initially, and that he was warm, funny and kind had kept her messaging with him. And eventually chatting on the phone, where his nice voice and self-effacing charm had won her over. The man checked all the boxes, even a few she was embarrassed to admit to, like chiseled good looks and an even more chiseled body; that photo of him at the lake had taken her breath away. It was probably just as well hospital rules prevented him from video chatting; she'd probably get tongue-tied just looking at his handsome face.

But for her, it wasn't just his looks. No, the icing on the cake was Charlie. The picture of Sam with his adorable beagle lovingly licking his cheek had melted her heart. Surely anyone dedicated to saving lives, anyone who could make a dog love him, had to be a nice guy, right?

And wouldn't it be funny if she and Desiree both ended up with doctors? They could share experiences, commiserate on the downsides, and laugh at the weirdness of life together.

She shouldn't have started getting ready so early, because now she had time to kill. Too much time to kill. And she would absolutely not change clothes yet again; this was a very nice—but not too nice—outfit, suitable for the Grill. Not that they'd throw her out if she showed up in rags, given her father owned the place.

Her phone signaled an incoming text, and the distinctive chime, a short riff from her little sister's favorite song, told her Grace was checking in. They'd agreed when Annalise had first started using the app that she would always send Grace the details on any actual dates. She thought Grace was being a bit overly cautious, but wrote it off to her sister being a rookie cop. Yet another Colton in the Grave Gulch PD.

Ready?

As I can be.

Still on for the Grill?

Yes. She would have preferred this first face to face with the yummy Sam Rivers be somewhere else, but it seemed his heart was set on taking her to the most popular restaurant in town.

Just talked to Mom. She's keeping Dad home, as promised.

She smiled at that. I owe her flowers.

Because Sam didn't yet know it was her father's place. As a Colton in Grave Gulch she knew people sometimes made assumptions simply based on the name, so she'd held that back. Just as, while chatting about her work as a dog trainer, she'd omitted exactly who she trained them for; time enough to get into that when they were together in reality instead of cyberspace.

I hope he's everything he seems to be, Grace sent.

I think he will be.

She did think so, although she was mentally prepared for a certain amount of disappointment. No one was perfect. And dating a doctor would be intense—there would no doubt be lots of times his work had to take precedence—but she could handle that. She could always ask Desiree for advice on how she managed.

She gave a shake of her head as she signed off with Grace. She hadn't even met the guy in person yet, but here she was fantasizing about a long-term future with him. Maybe in person there would be no chemistry, no spark. Maybe he'd hate her on sight; maybe her streak of rotten dating luck was destined to continue.

Desperate for distraction, she called up her work schedule for tomorrow. Frowned at the reminder that progress reports were due this week; she loved working with the dogs, but she could do without the paperwork. But they would have to be done, because Robert Kenwood ran a tight ship. A former police K-9 handler himself, the man many still called "Sarge," even though he'd retired from the actual force to become the director of the training unit some time ago, was pretty by the book. But she could put up with his meticulousness, because he loved the dogs just as she did.

Just as Sam did. The thought made her smile. And she kept smiling, until she noticed what she'd forgotten until now; she had a scheduled session with Ember tomorrow morning. The lovable black Lab seemed to have a knack for scenting explosives in particular, and Sarge wanted to find out how solid it was. Which would so not please her handler.

Brett Shea.

The man who had saved the now-fiancée of her brother Troy by dismantling a bomb. Troy had told her Brett had sworn to leave such skills behind when he'd left the military. Something he'd never, ever wanted to do again, and yet he had. Because someone had to, and he had the knowledge and skill.

She felt a little flutter of nerves when she thought about that. Thought about him. Tried to quash it, but it persisted. She grimaced at herself. What was wrong with her? Readying for the first in-person meeting with the man who could be exactly what she was looking for, and here she was feeling butterflies over another, entirely unsuitable, unattainable, uninterested guy?

Of course, any woman would probably find the tall, rugged, intensely masculine K-9 officer attractive. Any woman with a pulse, anyway. Funny, she wouldn't have thought she'd be attracted to a redhead, but combined with his startlingly blue, sometimes uncomfortably intense, eyes it was a potent combination. And seemed utterly right. Now she couldn't imagine him without that thick shock of auburn hair.

*You look Irish.*

*And what does an Irishman look like?*

*You.*

That silly exchange when they'd first met, shortly after he'd laterally transferred in from Lansing, had ended with him adopting a very exaggerated brogue and speech pattern she suspected was a clichéd version of the real thing. And when he did, she too easily imagined him in green. Something else she had never spent much time thinking about before he'd walked into the training center.

*Sure, and I am. And you are a Colton, aren't ye?*

*I am.*

Back to his ordinary—although she couldn't think of the deep, rough timbre of it as ordinary—voice, and a very flat tone, he'd ended it then. *Safe bet around here, it seems.*

She remembered watching him walk off with Ember, thinking he'd sounded unhappy. At the least wary. She supposed she couldn't blame him. There were a lot of Coltons on the force. And when one of them, her cousin Melissa, was the chief, it made it difficult to make real connections with people sometimes. Which is why she'd sworn off ever dating a Grave Gulch cop. A decision she was content with.

Or had been, until Brett Shea had turned that brilliant

blue gaze on her. And started her mind down paths she'd sworn never to travel.

And wasn't going to start now. She had a date, with a sexy, handsome, exciting guy, and it was going to go fabulously.

She was sure of it.

# Chapter 2

Detective Brett Shea smiled when Ember's tail started to wag. The clever black Lab knew she was on home turf the minute they walked into the sprawling old stone building that housed the Grave Gulch Police Department. She hung on to her beloved knotted rope tug-of-war toy though. And he let her; she'd earned it after finding that missing kid so quickly this morning.

The building felt normal to him now, too. And much more welcoming than the big, multistory glass-and-concrete box he'd been used to in Lansing, where he'd transferred from. And every face he passed in the hallway was familiar, which had been one of his main goals in coming here. He knew each name and something about them and was working on learning enough to judge their reactions in any given situation, because someday his life or someone else's might depend on it.

Brett headed for his desk to finish his report on a recovered child, who had in fact only wandered a bit far from home and fallen—thankfully without injury—into a gully that hid him from the street above. Ember followed happily, and after he gave her a good solid pat of approval for a job well done, she settled down on the flat pad near his chair, contentedly chewing on the toy.

He frowned as he wrote the disposition on the case. There seemed to be a lot of kid-related stuff going on in Grave Gulch lately. He didn't like that. Dealing with adult problems was bad enough. First there'd been Mary Suzuki's wedding, when sketch artist Desiree Colton's toddler had been grabbed, then just last month, Soledad de la Vega, the owner of Dream Bakes downtown, had gotten caught up in that ugly case that resulted in the horrible death of her best friend and her getting custody of that friend's baby.

*And ending up engaged to Palmer Colton. Don't forget that part.*

It wasn't enough that he was practically surrounded by Coltons here at the department and in Grave Gulch. It also seemed all of them were on a binge, getting engaged one after the other.

He'd left the big PD in Lansing for many reasons, one of which had been the size of the department. It seemed too big to him; he'd wanted to know his colleagues, know who he could trust to have his back. A holdover from his military days, he supposed.

So here he was now at a department with fewer than thirty sworn officers, which he'd wanted. What he hadn't counted on was that every other one of them seemed to be a Colton, from the chief on down. He knew it wasn't true; it just felt like it. And it seemed lately the town wasn't too happy with that either, but right now the town wasn't happy with a lot of things, and with good reason. Randall Bowe chief among them.

By manipulating evidence, the corrupt forensic scientist had ruined many cases and lives, and cast a long shadow over the department in the process. Especially over the Coltons, because of how many of them there were on the force. Brett had seen more than one sign at the organized protests that bore sentiments such as Nepotism Brings Corruption.

He understood the feeling. He'd certainly dealt with certain people getting special treatment enough in Lansing, although he suspected that was endemic to any capital city. And it wasn't that he didn't like the Coltons he worked with. In fact, his frequent partner, Troy Colton, was one of the best cops he'd ever worked with. He was no slacker or stranger to long hours. It was part of the reason they worked well together. And Desiree was really talented at capturing suspects from descriptions, better than any computer program he'd used; her sketches were uncannily accurate. Even rookie officer Grace Colton showed great promise.

Another Colton, CSI Jillian, had been under a dark cloud with the whole forensics and manipulated-evidence mess. But it appeared she'd been exonerated, though he was withholding judgment on that, or on her at least; there were too many unknowns.

But it still worked out that—he did the math in his head—a good percentage of the department carried the Colton name. And that wasn't including Annalise.

*The K-9-trainer Colton.*

He made the mental correction automatically. That, at least, had become habit. Now if he could only get it to happen *before* her name popped into his head. He needed to think of her as just that, the police K-9 trainer, and nothing more. She was Ember's trainer, that's all. Not a lovely, blue-eyed blonde with dimples that lit up a room. Not a graceful, caring woman whom dogs seemed to love on sight, dogs whose instincts about people he trusted completely. Because thinking about her that way could only lead to trouble, and he'd had enough of that in his life.

No, it would be much—*much*—better to think of her as…as a kid sister. Yeah, right, that'd do it. It had better. Because getting involved with a Colton would be riskier than most of the bombs he'd disarmed, back in the day in a different uniform. Not only because her cousin was the chief, but because every one of the Coltons was like a bulldog in protecting the other Coltons. The last thing he needed was one—or all—of them coming after him.

And he didn't miss the irony that he'd come here to work at a department small enough to know everyone, hoping it would feel more like a law-enforcement family than a government entity tied to the politics of the capitol, and instead had ended up in the middle of an actual family. A family he wasn't and would never be part of. And in the back of his mind was still the thought that if it ever came down to one of them saving his ass or a Colton's, there was only one way it would go.

He finished up the report and leaned back in his chair. It would be nice to go home on an up note for a change. Maybe he'd finish up that bookcase project. If he could wear Ember out with a tennis-ball session in the huge backyard… The outdoor space had been the main reason he'd chosen the older house. To call the house itself dated would be an understatement, but the exterior, with big trees, shrubs that bloomed without much attention and expansive spaces for Ember, was ideal.

A sudden jab from his empty stomach reminded him food was in order. He'd been running a little lean lately, judging by the fact that he'd had to take his belt in a notch. But he'd been so consumed by this damned Bowe case that eating had fallen a bit on the priority list. For him, anyway—Ember, as always, ate heartily and well. And the dog literally glowed in the dark these days, her coat so shiny it caught and reflected even moonlight on a clear night, ever since Annalise had given him a supplement to add to her food.

*Trainer. Ember's trainer.*

Disgusted with himself, he shut down his computer and stood up. *Focus on food*, he told himself.

He was in certainly no mood for the flash of the Grill tonight. The Grave Gulch Grill, owned by Annalise's— *Ember's trainer's*—father, Geoff Colton. Nor did he want the bustle and required social interaction at Howlin' Eddie's bar, even if the appetizers were a meal in themselves. He could stop at Mae's, except he didn't really want to go into the diner and sit down while Ember waited in the vehicle, although the dog could be very patient when necessary.

Pizza. That was it. He could call Paola's now and it should be almost ready by the time he got there. Besides, they always threw in a little side of sausage for Ember, too, which he carefully rationed out to her. And carefully didn't mention to Annalise.

*Trainer!*

"Shea!"

The yell came from the doorway, and he turned to see Chief Colton in the doorway. She was in civilian clothes, obviously on her way out of the station. "Chief?" Brett answered.

"Patrol's working a possible Bowe sighting five minutes ago. Probably nothing again, but thought you'd want to know."

The hunger ratcheted down as adrenaline spiked. Technically he was off duty. Technically he should wait until they called him in, if they found anything. Technically, technically, technically…

But damn it, he wanted this guy. Wanted him bad. If there was anything that chapped him, it was a miscarriage of justice. It had about killed him when his buddy and fellow cop Mitch had been arrested and gone through such hell in Lansing. The man he'd served beside, who had been one of those who had always had his back, had sworn he was innocent of taking bribes. Brett had known he was, but he hadn't been able to do a damned thing about it. Had been unable to find enough evidence to convince anyone otherwise, in a city too big to care about one single officer's certainty. Had been unable to get anyone to listen; no one seemed to care that he knew the man down to the bone, with the kind of knowledge gained under fire.

That Mitch had later been exonerated didn't erase either what he'd gone through, or Brett's feeling of utter helplessness. It was not something he cared for, and one he'd do just about anything to avoid experiencing again. And the best way to insure that was to find the slimy Randall Bowe, who had contaminated dozens of cases, perverting justice according to his own twisted views.

Yes, he wanted the guy. So, he'd swing by the location, and just say he'd been in the area. Grave Gulch was small enough that could be true no matter where he was. Well, compared to Lansing, anyway.

And small was what he'd wanted. He just hadn't counted on dealing with a family like the Coltons.

Hadn't counted on one of them being a woman like Annalise.

"Ready for another game, girl?" he said to Ember, needing the distraction.

The dog was on her feet in an instant, the toy abandoned without thought at the prospect of what she seemed to love most: seeking what he wanted her to find.

# Chapter 3

When Annalise saw Sam's face light up her phone—she'd picked the shot of him with his dog Charlie for her contacts, because it made her smile—her first thought was she'd somehow lost track of time and was late.

Had she done it again? Had she slipped into silly ruminations about Brett Shea and lost track of time? All because his dog happened to be on her schedule for tomorrow?

Sure, she was attracted; with those eyes, that tall, lean but muscular body, that way of moving that had her picturing him striding across wild Irish hills somewhere, who wouldn't be? And as far as she knew, he was single, uninvolved. But he was also incredibly intense and focused, and that could be a warning sign. Maybe he was single because there was no room in his life for anything but the job. She knew a lot of those types. Heck, she'd dated a few of them.

But Ember adored him. And Ember was a very smart

girl. Annalise had worked with enough K-9s and their handlers to recognize a genuine and deep bond when she saw one, and Brett and the slick-coated black Labrador had that. It was easy, for her at least, to see that he was devoted to the dog and she to him. And that spoke volumes, in Annalise's eyes.

But being a cop hadn't stopped Troy from finding the love of his life. Grace had joked that all the Coltons had better stop drinking the water, because they all seemed to be getting locked into permanent relationships. Annalise had laughed, but her heart hadn't really been in it, because it was true. Most of her siblings and her cousins had done just that, and she felt pretty left out.

*Poor, pitiful you.*

Even thinking about Brett Shea—too much—was better than whining.

She gave herself an inward shake.

*You're not getting involved with a GGPD cop. You. Are. Not. You're going on a date with a great guy, it will go wonderfully and your long trek through the dating desert will be over. And you'll no longer be one of the last Coltons without her soul mate. Your mother will stop trying to set you up, and your father will quit asking when you're going to settle down.*

She caught the incoming call in the moment before it would have gone to voice mail, and her hello was no doubt embarrassed because she'd done it again, slipped into pondering Brett Shea instead of focusing on the charming, handsome doctor who wanted to be with her tonight. Sam was exactly what she'd been looking for, hoping for, so why was she standing here mooning over another man?

*Maybe all your dating problems aren't men, but you!*

"Honey," Sam began, giving her a little thrill. He'd slipped into the endearment quickly, shortly after they'd started actually talking a few days ago, telling her he'd known the moment he'd seen her profile photo with her foster dogs that she was the one he'd been waiting for. "I'm so sorry. We're slammed in the ER, and there was a big crash and lots of injuries."

"Oh, no! Do you have enough staff? Is Stavros there?"

"Who's Stav— Look, I don't have time. I just wanted to tell you I'm so disappointed I have to postpone. I've been looking forward to tonight all week."

"Oh." *Well, that sounded lame.* Even as she thought it, she was wondering why he hadn't seemed to know who Stavros was. Maybe because he was new, he only knew him as Dr. Makris. "I'm sorry, too," she said.

She was more than sorry. All her anticipation about tonight drained away, leaving her feeling…she wasn't sure exactly what. She had the sour thought that she'd somehow brought this on by all her meanderings about Brett Shea. She dismissed that silly idea and tried to focus. "But I understand," she said.

After all, hadn't she just acknowledged to herself that dating a doctor, especially an emergency-room doctor, would have its downside? It was things exactly like this that she'd been thinking of. So how could she really complain? The man took care of people who needed him. So dating him would be complicated, just like…dating a cop.

"I'll make it up to you. We'll reschedule. But I don't want you to miss out, so I'm sending dinner to you."

"What?"

"There's a waiter from the Grave Gulch Grill on the way, with the dinner we were supposed to have. He should be there any moment now."

Her brow furrowed. She knew she'd never given him her address, but had she ever even told him where in town she lived? "But how did you—"

"Sorry, honey, I have to run. Two more patients just arrived. Later. Love you."

The silence was undeniable, he was gone. *Love you?*

Dr. Samuel Rivers had just said he loved her.

Of course he'd said it in haste, in that casual way that didn't mean anything. It certainly didn't mean he'd meant it in the way she was thinking. But still—

Jack and Apple burst into a cacophony of barking and raced over to the front door. Her first instinct was to smile; the two were already acting like guard dogs. That told her they were starting to feel comfortable here, which made her feel good. It would make it easier to transition them to another, forever home. And she had the thought that she would just keep them until someone came along who was willing to take the pair, keeping the devoted friends together.

Her second thought was to wonder if the waiter could already—

The doorbell cut off her wondering. Sam hadn't been kidding when he'd said any moment now. She walked over to where the dogs were, setting her phone down on the table by the door as she leaned in to peer through the peephole. Sure enough, the man standing there—or kid, he looked awfully small—was wearing the black-and-silver apron from the Grill, had a cart holding dishes covered with the standard silver lids, and…a bouquet of pink roses in a vase.

She couldn't help smiling happily. Sure, she was disappointed Sam had had to cancel, but she'd been cancelled on before. It was another indication of her lousy dating history. But no one had ever gone to such lengths to make up for it. If he'd intended to blow her away, he'd succeeded.

"Hush, now," she said to the dogs, and scooted them away from the door. "Sit." They sat, their gazes fastened on her, and her smile widened. "Stay," she added. That command, and the subtext of *Until I say otherwise*, wasn't quite ingrained yet, but it should hold long enough to get the door open for the kid.

Except it wasn't a kid at all. To her surprise, once she had the door open and could see clearly, the waiter was not that young, but merely short and very thin. So thin the apron he wore wrapped around his back and nearly came to the front again. She could only see part of the silver lettering across the front, *rave Gulch Gri,* and she had the inane thought the phrase sounded like some underground party site or something. Then she felt bad; it wasn't his fault he was so thin.

"Hello, Annalise," he said.

He sounded oddly familiar, although she didn't remember ever having seen him before, at the Grill or elsewhere. And it seemed odd he'd addressed her by her first name, but maybe Sam had given him instructions.

She said hello, only then realizing he wasn't wearing the usual name tag. Maybe he'd been in a rush and hadn't had time to grab it. She wondered what Sam had said to explain what he'd wanted done. Home delivery wasn't something the Grill normally did, so it must have been good. Maybe she'd ask. She'd like to hear what he'd said.

Then again, if it was something like *I gotta miss a date and she hasn't put out yet, so I need to keep up the charming*, she'd pass. She'd been through that one before, too.

"Come in," she said, backing out of the way.

The stay hold on the dogs broke, and they darted over to the waiter, not quite growling but making the low sounds that indicated they were not totally pleased with the situation. The man looked down at them warily. Funny, they seemed much bigger next to him, because he was so short.

"It's all right," she hastened to assure him. "They don't bite, but they're kind of new here so a little nervous."

He muttered something she couldn't hear and she wondered if she should be glad. He wheeled the cart past her into the living room, pushing it rather awkwardly, almost crookedly, as if he wasn't used to this at all. But this was how meals were brought to larger groups inside the Grill, so he should be familiar with it. Maybe one of the wheels was off, like a wobbly grocery cart. Or the white tablecloth that covered it had slipped and gotten tangled.

Belatedly she realized the reason was that he wasn't gripping the cart's handle fully with his right hand, but only had his thumb and forefinger wrapped around it. His other three fingers were curled back, as if he was holding something else. Her mind took off, wondering if Sam had sent a note or card along with the meal, to be presented to her in his absence. But then why wouldn't it just be on the table? Or on the plastic clip she could see sticking up out of the bouquet?

"Doesn't it smell wonderful?" the waiter said with a smile. "You're going to really love this."

She frowned. In fact, she couldn't smell anything. But, she reasoned, she hadn't been closed up in a car with it, either. As soon as the silver lids came off the plates, she was sure she would.

He wheeled the cart over to where her small dining table sat, she presumed so he could set the plates on it. She followed, curious now about what Sam had ordered up for the meal. Wondered if he had remembered their chat about their favorite foods.

You love shrimp scampi? I knew you were the one for me.

It had been the first time he'd said that, about her being the one. It had startled her, since it had only been the second time they'd messaged each other. But he'd instantly made it a joke by sending, Too fast? plus an adorable, google-eyed emoji.

She stopped as the waiter positioned the cart. She still couldn't smell anything. Surely if it was scampi she would at least smell the garlic. She glanced at him, about to ask. He was letting go of the cart and turning toward her. His right hand moved, and as he took a step toward her she saw what he held.

She knew what it was. She'd seen tranquilizer darts before, in Dr. Foreman's office. The vet who worked with the police K-9s also handled other animals the force encountered on occasion, and more than once when the officers had had to take action, the creatures had come in with this exact thing embedded in their flesh. A very cranky badger she remembered in particular.

It took a split second to get past the incongruity of it. Her first thought was for the dogs, after the way he'd looked at them. Did he carry it because he was afraid of them? Were they in danger of being tranquilized because they were still not-quite-growling at him?

And then he took another step toward her. And he raised that hand with the dart.

Far too late it hit her. The dart wasn't for the dogs.

It was for her.

# Chapter 4

Brett trusted that Ember knew what she was doing. But then, he trusted her more than he did anyone these days. And certainly more than he did any other female, of any species. So he followed as silently as he could as the dog moved along, questing, searching, for Randall Bowe.

They were on a quiet residential street, lined with small, neat little cottage-type houses. He couldn't imagine what Bowe would be doing here, unless it was looking for someplace to hide.

They were one house down from the corner when he heard the scream from the next house. A very frightened scream. A woman. Ember's head came up sharply. Dogs were barking furiously, smaller ones judging by the pitch of the sound.

It wasn't a tough call. Given how long he'd been after Bowe he wasn't really optimistic that some random maybe sighting was going to yield anything—and a crisis was in progress now, with a woman possibly in danger. He snapped out the command to Ember and headed for the house.

There was a lit window on the side nearest them. He went for it at a run; he needed an assessment before he charged in there. Wouldn't do to get the woman killed in the process.

Things hit him in rapid succession. He noticed two people. A room away from the front, so he could only see in pieces. Little guy. No sign of a gun in his hand. Woman, blonde, fighting back. With something large, round, silver, metallic. He even heard the sound as she connected.

The guy reeled back a little. Probably hadn't expected the fight. *Good for her.*

Brett ran for the front door. Got there just as it was yanked open. Someone barreled into him, and they both staggered back. He grabbed at the other person. The porch light was dim, but in a split second he registered curves, blonde and a familiar scent. The woman. For an instant he felt something crazy, something that had no place in this scenario. *Heat. A special kind of heat.*

He shook it off. Shifted his hold from containment to support. Ember gave an oddly welcoming bark but he had no time to ponder that. The guy was already out the door behind them and running.

He swore silently, trying to disentangle himself. The woman's back was to him, and Ember was oddly close, unusual for her. He dropped the leash and snapped out the command to track. Labs weren't much on attacking, but he'd pit his girl's nose against any dog's for following a scent.

A scent.

It hit him in that instant, before he'd even gotten a good look at the woman.

It was the same sweet, flowery scent Annalise wore.

He pulled back a little as the woman got her feet under her. But she was shaking, so he didn't let go. He heard her take in a big gulp of air. And then she turned around.

Crap. It *was* Annalise.

Well, that explained the moment of unexpected physical response. His brain might not have known yet it was her, but his body had known instantly. He wanted to back off, feeling more than a little singed, but she was clearly still very rattled, and almost clinging to him. And he was certain she still hadn't registered who he was; she hadn't even really looked at him.

He heard a car start and the bark of tires on asphalt as it left at high speed. In the distance he could see what looked like a midsize silver sedan racing through the halo of a street light. Great. The most ubiquitous kind of vehicle in the universe. And halfway down the block he could see— barely, since she was the color of the night—Ember sitting at the edge of the street, her signal that the trail had ended. No doubt that was where that sedan had been parked.

He freed one hand and grabbed his phone to call it in. And then he let out a piercing whistle to call Ember back to him. Ember, who, contrary to her idiot handler, had immediately known Annalise. The dog started their way, dragging her lead and looking dejected, as she always did after a fruitless search.

"How could I be so stupid?"

Annalise's words were barely a whisper and clearly distressed. And suddenly he didn't want to back off at all, he wanted to hold, to comfort. And that, even odder, scared him more than the realization of who it was he had his arms around.

And then Ember barked. He looked up, saw her again sitting, but this time on the grassy area next to the sidewalk. And the dejection had vanished. Which meant she'd found something, something connected. That familiar tension of the hunt shot through him, and he wanted to go to the dog, see what she'd found. But he didn't want to leave the victim—*damn, Annalise*—here alone and still shaken. So he called out to Ember to hold.

Then he heard a siren. The sound seemed to shake her out of her distress. Annalise's head came up. And immediately her eyes widened. "Brett."

"Yeah," he said, rather inanely. And belatedly let go of her at last. And felt a sudden chill entirely inexplicable, given it had to still be hovering around seventy degrees after a day that had nearly hit eighty.

She let out a soft sigh. "No wonder I felt—"

She broke off, and even in the faint illumination of the porch light he saw her cheeks darken.

*You will not ask her to finish that sentence.*

He snapped the order at himself fiercely. Get to business, that was what he needed to do. First things first.

"Are you all right? Did he hurt you?"

"I… Yes. He never really touched me."

One corner of his mouth quirked. "Probably because you startled him, wailing on him with that—what was that?"

"A cloche. A plate cover."

This time his mouth twisted wryly. When he ordered in, it didn't usually involve actual plates, covers and a tablecloth. More like paper bags and ketchup in little containers. "Sometimes you have to use what's handy," he said. "Good job." She'd earned that, at least.

"I… I think he grabbed my purse on the way out. He had something in his hand. And he'd already dropped the dart."

Brett went still. "The what?"

"He had a tranquilizer dart. Like you use for wild animals."

All his bemusement at how he'd happened to end up here, of all places, at this perfect time, vanished. A rather fierce anger started to build. "He was going to tranq you?"

"God, I was so stupid. I let him in because I thought he was—"

She stopped as a marked unit slammed to a halt in the driveway. The siren shut off and two uniforms jumped out.

"You're all right? I need to go see what Ember found."

He could almost feel her gathering her composure. Saw her draw herself up, steady herself. "Go. See what that smart girl of yours found."

Once the officers were there, he left her to explain, now that she was calmer, and headed for his dog. Well trained—mostly by the woman he'd just left—she held position as she watched him come. She was sitting just outside the circle of light from the streetlamp, but just inside that circle was a small, oblong object that caught the beam in an odd way. It wasn't until Brett got closer he realized it was a small purse with beads on it, which explained the sparkle effect.

"Good girl," he told the dog, and she wiggled happily. But he hadn't released her from that last command, and she held. She was amazing, Ember was.

He pulled out his phone and took a couple of photos of where the purse lay from different angles, then got out one of the latex gloves he always carried, pulled it on and picked up the small bag. It apparently closed with a magnet, so he couldn't be sure if the guy had had time to rifle through it. It wasn't empty in any case, so Annalise—just thinking her name made him suck in a breath at how close she'd come to being hurt, or worse—would have to tell them what if anything was missing.

He grabbed up Ember's lead and headed back to the house. The house he'd carefully avoided knowing anything about, not just the address but even the neighborhood. Annalise was in the front yard, her arms wrapped around herself as if it was winter and snow was blowing in.

At his request one of the officers who'd arrived got him an evidence bag out of the trunk of their unit. Then Brett walked over to Annalise, who was clearly startled to see her purse.

"Ember found it."

"Of course she did." She managed a smile and a "Good girl," for the dog. "He dropped it?"

Brett nodded. "Whether accidentally or intentionally, I don't know. But it's not empty, so I need you to look and see if anything's missing. Without taking anything out, if you can."

She nodded. With his gloved hand he held it open for her to look. She leaned in, and he realized there wasn't much light. He pulled the penlight he also always carried out and flicked it on to shine into the bag's interior.

"Thanks," she murmured, still focused on the small purse. "He opened it," she said after a moment. "The cash I had is gone."

"How much?"

"Not a lot. Ride-home money. Just in case." Careful, he thought. Not surprising. "My driver's license is there."

"Phone?"

"I had taken it out to answer…" Her voice broke for a moment. Then she seemed to steady herself. "To answer the call that started this mess."

He wanted to know more about that, would need to for the report, but for now he stuck to the matter at hand. "Wallet?"

She shook her head. "It's doesn't fit in this bag, so I took the license out. Just for tonight."

"Special night?" he asked neutrally.

"It was supposed to be," she said, sounding more humiliated than anything.

"I gathered," he said, his tone dryer than he'd meant it to be.

She looked up at him then, as if puzzled. Then looked back into the purse. And once more he saw her cheeks redden, and knew she'd realized the edge of a small foil packet was visible. "That's…another just in case."

"Always wise to be prepared," he said, and was proud he'd managed a more neutral tone this time. Especially when he was trying to deny that the idea of Annalise Colton going on a date with a condom in her purse unsettled him.

But he had no more time to think about it, because three vehicles pulled up in rapid succession. And out of them poured…Coltons. Troy didn't surprise him. That he had his sister Desiree with him did, a little, although neither was a problem. He and Troy worked well together, and Desiree never failed to thank him for his part in searching for her little boy when he'd been kidnapped in an effort to force the department to reopen an old case. He supposed Grace's arrival shouldn't surprise him either; he knew the sisters were close. Word had obviously spread through the PD that the incident involved one of their own. He wondered if anything else could have gotten them to respond like this.

And then a tall redhead got out of the last car, and he groaned inwardly. The woman strode toward them with as much command presence as any officer he'd worked with. As well she should.

*So even the chief of police rolls out after hours—for another Colton.*

He understood, sort of, even though this kind of family closeness wasn't something he'd ever had. The Coltons were a tight-knit bunch, and lately they'd been under siege. It was only natural that they'd pull together, knowing they could trust each other but not sure about anyone else.

Including him. He was still an outsider, even after all these months. And he felt it more than ever as Chief Melissa Colton came to a halt beside them. And in that moment, if she'd ordered him to hand everything over to Troy to investigate, he'd do it without a qualm.

Hell, he'd do it gratefully. And take Ember, the only female in his life at the moment, home for a well-earned treat and a tennis ball session. And forget all about this… whatever it was.

And the way Annalise Colton had felt in his arms.

# Chapter 5

"You want this?"

Annalise looked up at Brett's words, but saw he was talking to Troy. Who was looking at Brett rather oddly. Did Troy want *what*? Apparently her brother was puzzled too, because his brows lowered as he answered.

"You want to hand this case off?"

Brett shrugged. "Your call. She's your sister."

Troy looked at Brett as Annalise watched them both, curious. Or maybe in desperate need of distraction.

"Some would say that's exactly why I shouldn't take it," Troy said, his voice inflectionless in that way she knew meant he was testing, that he wanted to know how Brett would answer.

"Some would," Brett agreed.

Something in his expression made Annalise think that Brett would be one who would think exactly that—that Troy would have a conflict of interest. Which didn't surprise her—she'd known he had a solid, ethical core when it came to the job. She suspected that was one of the reasons he'd left the big city department to come here; too many there didn't have the same ethics.

*And now he thinks...what? That GGPD is a Colton-family-run organization? Maybe even worse than the big city?*

Sure, there were a lot of them working for the department in various capacities, but it wasn't like that. It wasn't anything like that. No matter what the media and the protesters said.

Another thought hit her. He didn't believe all the awful stories going around, did he? That the Colton family was somehow at fault for Bowe's actions? That the mishandling of evidence that had resulted in wrongful convictions and acquittals was the fault of her family? He'd never said much about it, but then, they didn't have long, involved chats when she was working with Ember, or when they were doing so together. *Because you don't dare.*

But Troy had ethics, just like Brett had. And he proved it now by saying, "Now that we know she's okay, I'll get everybody out of your way." And a moment later he made good on the promise, shooing everyone away, saying, "Let the man do his job."

Annalise saw Brett watching, assessing, as the Coltons backed off. Including the chief. Then, at Brett's suggestion they stay out of the way of the CSIs, she led him—and the three dogs now present—down the hall to the second bedroom that served her as an office.

She realized she'd been focusing on recent troubles to keep from focusing on what had actually happened tonight. And now she was going to have to explain. To the person she least wanted to explain to.

She wasn't sure she understood exactly what was going

on in the first place. After she'd told him the details of what had happened tonight and Brett started asking questions and taking notes, she knew she was watching the detective he was at work. It was a strange feeling, to see this side of him.

"You've never seen this guy before?"

"No. But he had on the Grill apron. I thought he must be new."

His mouth quirked. She'd always liked the way he did that. "Your sister Grace already called your father. Nobody new hired in the last three months. And no one matching this description."

"Oh."

"Did you notice anything else about him?"

Her brow furrowed. "His voice seemed familiar, but I couldn't place it. But nothing else other than he was short and thin and had a scraggly sort of beard… I'm afraid when I saw that dart I freaked and struck out."

"That may well have saved you from much worse. We'll have you do a sketch as soon as…your sister can get set up. While the details are fresh."

She nodded. She knew Desiree was very good at what she did, and she'd at least feel comfortable with her. More than she could say for being with Brett Shea.

"What about the date you were supposed to have tonight?"

A little jolt went through her. *Sam.* She'd have to tell Sam what had happened, that the waiter had tried to attack her. And her father, who would be furious that one of his employees—

"You met this guy online? On a dating app?"

When he said it out loud like that it sounded…pitying. Or maybe it was just that it was him saying it. And that made her feel a bit snippy. "Yes. You have a problem with that?"

"Not for me to judge."

She wasn't sure why she felt the need to prod. "But you'd never do it?"

He looked up from his notepad then. "Not an issue. I'm not looking." He glanced downward to where Ember had plopped on the floor to patiently wait. Unlike her two fosters, who were clearly overstimulated by all the excitement. "Ember's the only girl in my life."

She looked down at the sleek black Lab who was one of the easiest dogs she'd ever had to train. Then she looked back at her master and said with the smile the animal always brought to her, "She'll never let you down."

"I know," he said softly.

His love for Ember was so clear in his voice it made the last of the edginess that had made her push at him drain away and she answered him. "My friends were nagging me to try the app, and—"

He waved that off. Obviously he didn't care about the sorry state of her love life. Or the lack thereof.

"Who started it?"

"Contact, you mean?" He nodded in turn. "He texted me first. He loves dogs—he has an adorable beagle named Charlie—and when he saw I was a dog trainer he reached out. I didn't say who I trained for though. Some people get spooked if I say I train for the PD."

"Might have been better if you had." He grimaced, as if he regretted the words. "Never mind. So how long before you actually spoke?"

She thought, although she didn't quite see why it mattered. "It was a while. He's an ER doctor at the hospital here, and always busy, so texts were more convenient for him."

He looked a little puzzled then, as if he didn't quite get what she was saying.

"Did you ever initiate a call to him?"

"No, I couldn't because it might interrupt him in the middle of an urgent case." She gave him a smile. Somehow talking to Brett about the man in her life made her feel...something. She wasn't sure what to call it. "He's very dedicated to his work."

"Right," he muttered. And before she could point out that so was he, he asked, "Did you ever do a video call?"

"No. He can't do that at the hospital, for privacy reasons, and he's there so much..." She shrugged. Surely he must understand, being a cop, a job that was as consuming as being a doctor. "Besides, he said he needed a new phone because the front-facing camera doesn't work well, keeps dropping out."

His expression was unreadable now. And his voice became utterly neutral and businesslike. Somehow that was unsettling. "So you've never actually seen him."

What was he getting at? "Oh, I've seen a ton of photos," she said, pulling the phone she'd grabbed up before they'd come in here. She called up the shot with Charlie first and showed him, then swiped through several others. Sam was a truly handsome man—he looked great in even casual photos—and she felt a little burst of satisfaction as Brett looked; at least he'd know a good-looking, successful guy wanted to date her. Why that mattered she wasn't sure, but it did.

"And tonight was the first time you were going to meet in person?"

She nodded. "But they had a rush at the emergency room and he couldn't leave. He's very dedicated."

His expression never changed, but the questions came

faster now. "Did you check his other social media? Does he have a lot of friends there?"

"Look, I don't see what this has to do with—"

"Does he?"

This was definitely Brett the cop. He was acting like Troy who, as their father said, was fierce once he got his teeth into a case. *Just answer, then you can call Sam. He'll make you feel better.*

"Not really," she said. "He doesn't have much of a presence. No time."

"Where does he live?"

"I...don't know, exactly. He's rooming with a fellow doctor until he finds his own place." She was starting to get very uneasy. Somehow all these things she'd accepted as they'd gradually happened, when strung together like this, sounded...wrong.

"Did he ever ask where you lived? Maybe under the guise of looking for that place for himself?"

*Under the guise?* "Yes, but I only told him the street. But the Grill would have access to my address, too, for the delivery because my father has it."

Brett's jaw tightened. Because she had mentioned her father? Troy had told her once Brett was wary of being surrounded by Coltons. But this was different. Wasn't it?

He excused himself to make a couple of phone calls. She watched him walk away. When she realized she was admiring the way he moved—again—she chastised herself inwardly. Tried to focus on something else. Like being grateful her parents were out of town, or they would have already descended on her. Like what she was going to say to Sam when she called to tell him what had happened. He'd be upset, obviously. He'd probably feel—

Brett came back. And she didn't like his expression. He drew in a deep breath. "We'll need your phone."

"What?"

"We'll need to pull the texts and those photos."

Annalise stared at him. "Of Sam? Why?"

"The Grill didn't send anyone, and no one matching the description you gave works there."

"But Sam—"

"Annalise." Something in the way he said her name made her go silent. And then, rather gently for the usually businesslike detective, he said, "There is no Dr. Sam Rivers at Grave Gulch Hospital."

She gaped at him. "What?"

"In fact, there's no Dr. Sam or Samuel Rivers registered in the state of Michigan."

This was bizarre. Of course there was; she'd been in touch with him dozens of times. "I...don't understand."

"I had Desiree check with her fiancé. Stavros confirmed it. No such person at the hospital."

"What are you saying?"

"I'm saying," he said, his tone even more gentle now, which made her conversely more edgy, "you've been catfished."

# Chapter 6

Annalise supposed she could be more embarrassed, although she wasn't quite sure how. What she did know was that she had never felt so stupid, so played in her entire life. And that Brett Shea knew it—knew it all—was just the sour frosting on a bitter cake.

She wanted nothing more than for him to leave, so she could hole up in her room and feel nauseated at her own stupidity. When she walked back out into her living room—at least having the presence of mind to leave Jack and Apple in the office—and saw the cart, this time she really did feel nauseous. She suddenly realized she'd never had quite enough empathy for what crime victims had to go through afterward.

But Brett was like Troy; once he had his teeth in a case, he wouldn't let go until it was done. And that's what she was now. A case.

Sam didn't exist. It wasn't even that he was a player, or

a liar, a phony, a faker, maybe an orderly claiming to be a dedicated doctor to gain her interest and trust. He did not exist. He never had.

When Desiree had finished the sketch from Annalise's description plus some input from Brett, Annalise practically recoiled from looking at it. Not only because she knew she'd had a lucky escape, but because mentally she was comparing the decidedly unattractive image with the string of photos "Sam" had sent her. At the beach, in the gym, in hospital scrubs, he'd been beautiful in them all. This man was anything but.

And Brett Shea knew it all. Including how stupid she'd been. In fact, he had her phone right now, although it was now in a plastic evidence bag.

She glanced over at him, standing across the room—she wished they'd move that damned reminder of a cart out of her dining room —on his phone again. She'd watched numbly as he had taken hers—which was now prime evidence— and sent the photos of…whoever it really was, to someone else at the department. But now he was still holding hers up to look at.

Oh, God, what if Brett was reading the texts? He probably was. He probably had to, to see if there were any clues there. He'd see her sappy writings, the silly stuff she'd written when…Sam had texted late at night, saying he'd just gotten home off a rough shift and needed some sunlight in his life. She'd been charmed. She'd been captivated.

She'd been fooled. Utterly and completely. And Brett would now see every facet of her idiocy. She felt color flooding her cheeks again at just the thought, although she was a little amazed she had the energy to even be embarrassed any longer.

One of the CSIs on scene looked up at him and asked if

he was on with Ellie and Brett nodded. GGPD's tech expert, Ellie Bloomberg, was probably looking into the app.

*Great. I can just imagine how that conversation went. "Hey, Ellie, got an idiot woman here who got herself catfished. Best part? She's a Colton."*

She wished she'd never heard of the word. Wished it only applied to rather ugly, bottom-feeding fish.

Only then did it strike her how appropriate the word was. Bottom feeders. And ugly.

She didn't know how long she'd been standing there staring at the delivery cart she'd so blithely let into her house when she sensed a warmth behind her. It felt good, because she was feeling chilly. Which was strange because it had been a typically warm August day and after she was ready she'd turned off the air conditioning because she'd been going out.

She knew how out of it she was when she belatedly realized the warmth behind her was a person.

"Oh!" She managed to keep her balance despite her startled spin, but barely.

Brett. Of course. Prove to him even more you're an oblivious fool.

"You okay?"

Did he have to sound so…gentle? *Of course he did. He thinks he's dealing with an oblivious fool.* But that didn't mean she had to like it. She crossed her arms in front of her and glared at him. "Don't patronize me."

He blinked, drew back. "What?"

"I know I was laughably stupid, a complete fool. I don't need you treating me like a child to remind me."

He was silent for a long moment and she kept hearing, not her words but her tone, echoing in the air. She hadn't meant to sound quite so belligerent. But she was so embarrassed about everything, she couldn't seem to help it.

"Given the circumstances," he said finally, "if I had walked in here and found you dead on the floor it would not have been a surprise. That I didn't is nothing to do with me happening to be here. It was you. You're the one who fought back, with the only weapon you had at hand. That's not something I laugh at. It's something I applaud."

She stared at him. That had been undeniably sincere. And his tone had been the polar opposite of her own: warm, gentle and understanding. It made her feel like a starched shirt on a humid day, suddenly wilted. She reached out blindly for one of the dining table chairs, then recoiled as she realized it would put her sitting right by that damned cart.

"I'm sorry," she said. "I just—" Her voice cracked.

"Hush. I know."

He took her arm then and led her out to the living room. She barely made it to the couch before her knees gave out. He nudged aside her stack of books so he could sit on the edge of the coffee table facing her. Again she felt chilled. And then she realized she was shivering. Actually shivering. In August.

"I can't... I don't know...what's wrong."

"What you're feeling now is the fade," Brett said gently. "Your adrenaline spiked, gave you the power to protect yourself. It hangs around for a while afterward, takes some time to clear your system. Makes you edgy even after the crisis is over. But when your mind and body accept that you're safe again, it fades, and then the crash hits."

"Sounds like you've been there before," she said before she thought, then groaned inwardly. Of course he had; he was a cop. She just hadn't expected him to be so understanding. So gentle. So kind.

So caring.

*Stop it! Stop reading things into him just being a good cop.*

She pressed her hands together and jammed them between her knees, trying to stop the shaking. Grabbing at the first thing that popped into her mind, which hadn't quite gotten the message it could slow down now, she asked, "Why were you here? In the neighborhood, I mean."

"Got a report on a possible suspect sighting."

Her eyes widened. "Tell me I don't have a serial killer roaming my street along with that…that…" She shook her head sharply.

"No. Not him."

She let out a relieved sigh. The thought of a murderer like Len Davison roaming freely was bad enough without thinking he was in her neighborhood. Then shook her head again, slowly this time. "I don't know what's happening to this town."

"People come to smaller places for lots of reasons. Some to get away from what they hate about big cities. Some because they think the people are nicer. And some think the pickings will be easier."

She wrapped her arms around herself again as the chill continued. "Well, I certainly proved that last one right, didn't I? Stupid me, fantasizing about a real future, wondering if I could handle a life with a very busy, dedicated doctor. Thinking I'd finally found what I was looking for."

He was silent for a long moment, long enough that she looked at him, almost afraid of what she'd see in his face, in his bright blue eyes. Sympathy, sure, she could handle that. But pity? Not so much. Him thinking she was a stupid fool? Even worse.

"Don't say it," she muttered.

"Say what?"

"Whatever you're thinking."

"Just wondering what, exactly, you were looking for."

Her mouth twisted. She hoped it looked cynical rather

than what it was, an effort to keep her emotions at bay. If she started crying on top of everything else, she'd never be able to face the man again. She could just imagine her trying to dodge him when he brought Ember into her office, making someone else collect the dog and take her back, so she never had to lay eyes on his tall, well-built, masculine self again. Never had to look into those bottomless blue eyes.

"Annalise?"

She gave a sharp shake of her head. "Looking for? Oh, not much. Just Mr. Right. Just true love. Just happy forever, like almost everybody else in my family seems to have found this year."

She could have sworn he gave the slightest, barely perceptible nod of his head. Understanding? Or because she'd confirmed what he already thought? Or did she just think he'd nodded because a strand of his hair had fallen forward over his forehead? She liked the way it did that. Just as she liked so much else.

And she should not be thinking about those things at all. Especially not now.

"They have been dropping like flies since I've been here," he said.

Is that how he saw people finding the loves of their lives? Dropping like flies? Now there was cynical. And she didn't like the way he'd said it, either. "Is that why you left Lansing? Run through the supply of casual hookups?" She nearly gasped at how completely nasty that had sounded. She didn't do that. "I'm sorry. That was very snarky of me."

He'd never even blinked. "Glad to hear it," he said neutrally.

She did blink. What was he saying? That he was glad

she now knew that was all he was interested in, romantically? Why would he care, unless he—

"It means you're reviving a little, after the shock. So maybe we can get to a few more questions."

Of course. He was the consummate cop; all he cared about was the case. This was not at all personal for him. She was the one who was off-kilter. Her mind making silly leaps into forbidden territory.

"Right," she muttered. Then, with an effort, she said as briskly as she could manage, "Ask away."

He began by asking questions she would have expected, what she and the nonexistent "Sam" had talked about in the beginning. And that he'd asked early on if she was related to the police Coltons.

"Did you save all your texts?"

"Yes," she admitted, wondering how silly that sounded, that she'd saved them thinking one day she and…Sam might read back over them and laugh at how their relationship had begun.

When he asked her, handing her the phone now encased in an evidence bag like her purse, she went through her messages. She found the first texts, the beginning of the… luring. The seduction.

The scam. Sam's scam. It rhymed. God, she was descending into lunacy.

She handed the phone back, knowing she had no choice, and that now she would get to sit here and watch this man, of all men, read through her miserable attempt at a love life.

"Well, that will make things interesting," Brett murmured.

"What?"

"That's what he said, when you eventually told him

you were related to some of 'those' Coltons. That it would make things interesting."

"So?"

"Kind of an odd thing to say."

"It was…new. I just thought he didn't know what else to say. You must know how some people react when they find out you're a cop or connected to the police somehow." She paused before asking, "Or do you only go out with people who already know?"

He never looked up from the screen. "Told you, I don't."

"So you're what, a monk on the side?"

That made him look up, and she couldn't deny she felt a jab of satisfaction. But he didn't answer. Which didn't surprise her, since she'd slipped into snark again. What was it about this guy that sent her off the rails so easily?

No, it wasn't him. It had to be what had happened tonight. She grabbed for some semblance of composure and asked, "Why was what he said odd?"

"Said a certain way, it could be a response to a challenge."

She frowned. "A challenge?"

"Like when you find out a suspect you didn't know was armed has a weapon. It makes things more interesting."

Annalise nearly gaped at him. "Interesting? It makes things interesting?" He merely raised his eyebrows at her. "I swear, men," she muttered.

"Guilty," he said, and looked back at the screen.

*You certainly are.*

She sank back into the couch cushions, wondering just how much more humiliation she would have to endure. Her brain was spinning now, and she closed her eyes. But then she saw his face, that nasty little man with his dart, and they snapped open again.

It was going to be a very, very long night.

# Chapter 7

She was, all things considered, doing fairly well, Brett thought. Obviously embarrassed. Maybe more embarrassed than anything, which he found a little odd, considering what Annalise might well have narrowly escaped. Of course, she was still processing that the guy she'd connected with on that app didn't really exist. And clearly the possibility had never even occurred to her. He understood. As well-known as the phenomenon was, as often as it happened, somehow it was always a shock when it happened to you.

He wasn't sure if the fact that apparently she was that innocent was reason to feel bad for her, or to be admired. That trusting nature had always boggled him. That she seemed to have it surprised him more than most. True, while she wasn't on the department, she worked with a lot of officers, and had a lot of cops or people who worked with them in her immediate family. And then of course there was Chief Colton, her cousin. You'd think she would have been more aware just listening to them talk.

Did it take effort to keep that kind of outlook? He didn't know; he'd never tried. He'd grown up with a man whose biggest lesson had been to expect the worst of people, because you'd rarely be disappointed. He'd also never experienced the kind of big family the Coltons had, more than a dozen of them here in Grave Gulch alone. Not to mention the others, closely and loosely connected across the country. He'd asked Troy, whenever he'd seen the name in the news somewhere, if that was another distant branch of his family. He'd done it jokingly, but then realized the answer was almost always yes. It had gotten so that any time he saw the name, he assumed the connection.

Annalise had lapsed into silence for now, while he made some notes and mentally organized the report he was going to have to write. Which was going to have to be damned near perfect, since it involved a Colton. He foresaw a long night ahead, in more ways than one.

Then he heard her suck in an audible breath. He looked up, saw her expression. And realized the possible endgame had finally hit her.

He grimaced inwardly; he should have thought more about what he was going to say when this inevitably happened. No one was *that* naive.

"What do you think he wanted?" she asked, her voice unsteady and quiet.

"No way to be sure, yet," he said, keeping his tone very level.

"Rape? Murder?"

"Annalise, there's no reason to go there yet."

"Yet. So either is a possibility."

*Or both.* The grim thought had been in his head ever since she'd mentioned the tranquilizer dart. And the thought of this woman, this kind, warm, dog-loving woman, as that kind of victim did more than unsettle him, it made him feel a chill inside he rarely felt anymore. He'd seen a lot, both in his prior job in Lansing and in the military before that. He'd seen horrible, bloody things he wished he could forget but knew he never would. He'd seen first hand and cleaned up the aftermath of a kind of cold-bloodedness that had forever changed his view of mankind. It was hard to find any kind of trust when you'd seen people butchered and children blown to pieces.

But the thought of Annalise, who hadn't lost that capacity to trust, suffering that kind of fate…

What if she hadn't had the nerve she'd had, to fight back, give herself a chance to escape? What if she hadn't and he'd been even just a minute later? What were the odds of the waiter even being here, on her street at this moment? Brett didn't know, didn't even want to think about it. It had happened the way it had, and she'd had the presence of mind and the nerve to do what she'd done. So in the end, stacked up against that, maybe her naivete didn't really matter.

She was staring down at her hands, fingers knotted together, in her lap. She was no longer shaking, but he suspected that was a conscious effort on her part.

"If you hadn't been here," she began shakily.

"Annalise, you saved yourself."

"He would have caught up with me. Stupid shoes. Impossible to run in."

He glanced at the heels she'd had on, kicked off when she'd sat down on the couch. Strappy, summery things that seemed indeed impossible to run in. Hell, to him they looked impossible to walk in. He didn't know how women did it.

But he knew why. "But sexy," he said, and regretted

it the instant the words were out. She gave him a startled look, and that alone told him he'd strayed into inappropriate. What was it about her that had him not just thinking dangerous things, but saying them?

Maybe it was that he rarely saw her out of her element. It was almost always at the training center, a repurposed old jail. She was the main trainer at the facility, the one Sergeant Kenwood said was the best, and the reason why had quickly become obvious once he'd seen her working not just with Ember but the other dogs, as well. The first time he'd seen her put the big sable German shepherd Bear through his paces, he'd been convinced.

At the training center, she was relaxed, confident and happy, working with the animals she clearly loved. Here and now, understandably, she was an entirely different person. Shaken, and probably scared now that she'd realized how this night could have ended.

He'd seen women in similar situations lots of times. His job was to deal with the crime, not the emotions. That's what counselors were for, and he carried around their business cards for just that reason.

So why did seeing Annalise so shaken, and knowing she'd had a narrow escape from what could have been horrific, have him feeling like he should do something, anything, to comfort her?

Finally he said the only positive thing he could think of. "They're almost done." He nodded toward the CSI techs who were starting to wheel out the delivery cart. She merely glanced and nodded. "Shall I call your family back?"

Her gaze shot to his face then. "No!" He blinked at the harsh exclamation. "No," she repeated, more calmly. "Absolutely not. It's embarrassing enough that you have to... know all this."

"I'm a cop, Annalise. I've seen worse. Much worse."

"I know that. That's not what I— Never mind," she said, cutting off whatever she'd been about to say.

Not what she meant? Then what did she mean? That it was embarrassing not that an officer in general knew what had happened, but that he, specifically did?

*Do not go there, Shea.*

For once he followed his own order. After all, it was obvious what she wanted, judging by what she thought she'd found in the nonexistent Dr. Sam Rivers. The texts had made it quite clear: long term, with an eye toward permanence. The kind of thing he had no interest in at all. He'd tried that once, a time or two, and it had ended in a debacle both times. That it was for completely different reasons both times had seemingly made it clear he was the problem, and so he'd sworn off.

When his phone rang he was almost relieved. Knowing the victim in any case made it more complicated, but this was really getting to him.

It was Ellie. "Excuse me," he said and got up to walk a few feet away. He didn't expect anything that would upset Annalise even more, but at this point he wasn't taking the chance.

He listened to Ellie's report, amazed as always at how much she managed to find out so quickly. And in this case she had a lot. And it put a different cast to this whole incident. He thanked her, then put his phone back in his pocket and walked back to once more sit opposite Annalise.

"It's…different than we thought," he said.

Her head came up. "Better or worse?"

"A little of both. He's very careful, but Ellie dug into the app, traced IP addresses and worked her way back to one. She tracked that one and ran a county-wide search and the provider—" He stopped, shaking his head. "Let's just call it magic, okay?"

To his surprise, Annalise smiled. "Okay. What did she find?"

"Bottom line, he's done this same thing before. At least twice here in the county, and those cases are still open. Ellie's spreading the net wider now."

She went still. "Was anyone hurt?"

"No. He apparently doesn't harm his victims, so you weren't in physical danger." He gave her a crooked smile. "I'd say you did more damage to him. His ears are probably still ringing, the way that lid clanged on his head."

That got him a smile in return. And more steadily now she said, "What else?"

He nodded. "This is going to sting a bit. His MO is to pretend to be a wealthy do-gooder. So far he's presented as an oil magnate, a big-shot lawyer, and in your case a dedicated doctor."

She winced, but said only, "Go ahead." She was definitely getting her feet under her again.

"He lures in his victim, which he's very, very good at, *hits all the right notes*, Ellie said. Then when the hook is set, he gets into his victim's home with his little dart, tranqs her then steals anything of value and portable."

She blinked, drew back slightly. "Wait…all this was to stage a robbery?"

"So it seems. At least, that's what happened in the other two cases we know about. You're the only one who's stopped him in the act."

Even as he said it his brow furrowed. *Stopped him in the act.* He didn't like the thought that had struck him as he'd heard his own words.

"What?" she asked, clearly seeing his change in expression. "Stopping him couldn't be a bad thing."

"Of course not. Is anything else missing, besides your purse?"

She looked as if she was having trouble processing this shift in perspective. "I... I don't—" Then, suddenly, she was on her feet. "Oh, no."

She ran over to the table beside the front door, where she'd said her purse had been. CSI had already dusted for prints there, so he followed but didn't try to stop her. Then she knelt down to search on the floor, clearly hoping something had simply fallen. But tonight she didn't have that kind of luck. When she straightened, there were tears glistening in her eyes.

He had to again resist the urge to comfort. "What?"

"Gran's bracelet. It was here on the table—I was going to wear it tonight."

"Bracelet? Valuable?"

"To a thief...yes, valuable. It was a diamond bracelet, worth quite a bit." She made a low, harsh sound, as if she were fighting breaking into sobs. After a moment she managed to say, with a clearly strained effort, "To me, it's priceless. My grandmother left it to me, specifically."

Somehow it was the attempt at staying calm that tipped him over the edge into doing something he never did: make a promise he couldn't be sure of keeping.

"I'll get it back for you, Annalise. I'll find this scumbag and get your grandmother's bracelet back."

"I..." She sucked in a breath. "Thank you. I hope you can."

Then with an effort that was visible she steadied herself. She reached out again, touched the table, then looked at her fingertip, dusty with fingerprint powder. Crime-scene investigation was by nature a messy process, and he remembered a victim back in the city who had bemoaned that the cleanup afterward was like going through the crime all over again.

"Let's get this cleaned up," he said suddenly. "You've got towels and cleaner of some kind?"

"I… In the pantry. But that's hardly your job."

"It shouldn't be yours, either. Let's just get it done."

She gave him an odd look then, one he couldn't interpret. But she went to the kitchen and pulled open a cabinet door. Then, armed with the cleaning materials, they tackled it.

"Floors last," was all she said.

He nodded. "Where everything we miss ends up."

She gave him a slight smile, probably the best she could manage at the moment. And more than many could.

It was sometime later, after he'd finished cleaning the dust off the chair the suspect had moved—he'd taken that task so she didn't have to go near it—and she had finished with the floor everywhere but there when she spoke again.

"What was it you thought of, before?" Brett asked. "When you said he'd never been stopped before."

He wished she hadn't remembered, didn't want her dwelling on it, but perhaps it was better she be prepared. She'd already proven she didn't dissolve into helplessness at a threat.

"It's just…there are some guys like that," Brett said, "when the scenario they've spent so much time on doesn't go the way it was supposed to, sometimes they can get caught up in trying to…fix it."

"Fix it?"

He held her gaze then. "Make sure it does go right."

She frowned. "How?"

He struggled with how to phrase it. He didn't want to scare her all over again, after the evening she'd had. But he couldn't think of any gentle way to say it, this real reason he'd wanted to stay.

And then he didn't have to. Because Annalise was far, far from stupid, and she got there herself. He saw the moment when it hit her by the way her eyes widened and her breath caught.

She stared at him as she put it into words.

"You think he might come back."

# Chapter 8

She should have realized.

Annalise stood there with a damp cleaning rag in her hand, feeling a fool all over again. This cleanup truly wasn't his job. And he hadn't stayed to do it out of the kindness of his heart. Or—she barely allowed the thought to form—because he was trying to help her, personally.

He was doing it because he thought that scrawny faker, that loser, was going to come back.

"You'll be all right," he said quickly. "There'll be units in the area, and I'll stay just in case."

Stay? Here? In her house, with her? She spent what seemed like a long, silent moment wondering what on earth was wrong with her. After what had happened tonight, how could this idea make her pulse jump? And it took her another moment to realize this had blasted the thought of that scummy little man coming back right out of her mind.

*Don't be an idiot all over again. You know it's not per-*

*sonal. None of it is, for him. It's Brett's job. You're a victim. He just wants to catch the guy.*

"Well, that would be a feather," she muttered.

"What?"

"In your cap. To catch the guy the same night he strikes."

He looked surprised, almost as if that hadn't actually been his first thought. "Would I like to put him away that fast? Sure, I would. But I want to be sure you stay safe."

He said it as if that was more important. She'd like to believe it was. But believing what she wanted to believe hadn't worked out so well. Not just tonight, with Sam-who-didn't-exist, but ever. And that put a bit of snap in her words.

"Afraid you'll have the big boss to answer to if you let her cousin get hurt?"

His gaze narrowed. And when he answered, his voice was chilly. "Thanks for the reminder."

She groaned inwardly. "I'm sorry. I shouldn't have said that."

"Don't be. I always need to remember."

She felt suddenly as chilled as his voice had been. That he had to deal with Coltons differently? Remember that she was a Colton? Was that why he'd never—

"Brett—"

"It's probably safe to let your dogs out now," he said, his tone as brisk now as it had been cool.

"Oh. Yes. I should. Should have thought…" She stumbled over the words. "About a lot of things," she finished lamely.

The dogs were delighted when she released them from their temporary captivity. They practically leaped into her arms. They, at least, didn't care what she said, as long as it wasn't in that "You're in trouble" voice. And when she spoke their names in that loving tone they squirmed with delight.

*If you ever used that tone on Brett, he'd squirm, all right. In discomfort.*

She had to stop this. He was popping into her head at the most awkward times and in inappropriate ways.

By the time they were back in the living room she thought she had herself under control. And she was determined to write off all these reeling thoughts to the adrenaline spike he'd talked about. Who could be expected to think normally under these conditions?

Now that things were calmer, Jack and Apple trotted over to where Ember, in the down position just inside the front door, was watching with great interest.

"Can she come off 'stay' now?" Annalise asked without looking at Brett, who was tidily gathering up all the cleaning supplies. She could have given the command herself, and as her trainer the dog probably would have responded, but that was a breach of protocol and the training itself; Ember was on duty and thus her handler was in charge.

He didn't answer her, but said, "Ember, at ease."

The Lab responded to the military command eagerly, quickly jumped to her feet and, tail wagging, greeted the two smaller dogs. Annalise did look then, saw Brett was watching the trio and said, "This is Jack, and the shaggy one is Apple."

"Mmm," he said, then suddenly looked at her. "Apple… and Jack?"

She gave him a half roll of her eyes and a sheepish smile. "They named them at the shelter. After someone's favorite cereal. The company that makes it does come from Michigan, after all."

The three dogs were busy getting acquainted, and Brett went back to watching, rather guardedly.

"They're good with other animals," she assured him. "Warier around people. Especially men."

"But not too afraid to come into the room with me."

He was so good with Ember Annalise couldn't imagine any dog being afraid of him, but that was her emotions talking. Again. As a trainer she knew that, just like with humans, a dog's fears could be almost instinctive, so deeply ingrained that logic couldn't even make a dent.

"No," she answered. "A good sign. I think they'll be fine, if you take it slow."

"Always my motto," he said.

Annalise's head snapped around. He still wasn't looking at her, was neatly putting away the stuff he'd collected. Obviously that agreement about taking it slow hadn't meant... anything.

Okay, she was in worse shape, mentally at least, than she'd thought. And having him in close quarters was going to be hazardous if she couldn't keep her mind in line. And if she kept letting her thoughts make it to her mouth before thinking them through, she was going to be facing a night of potential mortification. As if she hadn't had enough of that already.

Catfished.

God, she was such a fool.

She sank down on the couch again. "Do you really think he'll come back? After nearly being caught?" She hated the way she sounded, shaky still, but she couldn't seem to help it.

Brett didn't answer right away. He finished in the pantry—and why did the fact that he'd noticed where she got the stuff and put it back in the right place get to her?—and came back, pausing to stroke Ember's head and visibly notice how her two backed away from him. But he made no effort to reach out to them. She realized suddenly he was ignoring them with purpose, counting on innate curiosity to bring them around eventually. He couldn't have made a better choice for these two. And somehow that didn't surprise her.

He walked over and this time sat in the chair at a right angle to her seat on the couch, as if he'd decided she didn't need him quite so close this time. Or as if he didn't want to be quite so close.

And she hadn't realized—or at least admitted—that she'd been hoping he'd sit next to her on the couch until she realized it was disappointment she was feeling as he took the chair.

Chastising herself yet again for being a fool as big as Lake Michigan, she watched the two dogs move around the room, clearly engrossed in all the new scents left behind by the chaos.

"So what's their story?" he asked.

She knew he knew of her work fostering homeless dogs, getting them accustomed to living with people, so they were more likely to be permanently adopted. They'd talked about it when he'd met one of her prior fosters at the training center.

"They came in to the shelter together," she said, feeling an unexpected relief at the change in subject. "They'd obviously been together for a while."

Brett looked at the two, who had worked their way over to where Ember had been, still sniffing madly. Apple was smaller, his soft, longer coat in a black-and-white pattern that spoke of some spaniel in his ancestry, while Jack was a solid forty pounds of black-tipped brown mutt.

"Safe bet," Brett said neutrally. He shifted his gaze back to her. "How long have you had them?"

"About six weeks. I got them shortly after they came in. They'd obviously been on their own for a while—they were skinny, dirty and a little wild. Scared. We didn't want to put them up for adoption for fear some dog-fight promoter would come along and interpret their fear and nerves as aggression."

His mouth twisted in distaste when she mentioned dog fights. She found it hard to believe—and appalling—that such things still happened. Apparently so did he.

"Anyway," she went on, shifting her gaze back to the canine pair as they worked their way toward Brett, clearly curious, "another two weeks and they go back for reassessment, to see if they're ready to go into the adoption pool. They're obviously bonded, so we'll be trying to keep them together."

"They calmed down pretty fast after all the excitement. You've done a good job."

There was no reason for her to blush; she'd been told that before, and often. Yet here she was, staring down at the dogs because if she looked up she was afraid he'd look at her and see. But then she realized he was watching the dogs as well, and she knew he'd realized they'd decided he was their next thing to be investigated. He shifted one arm on the arm of the chair, letting his hand hang over the edge fingers extended but not moving or reaching.

"So who's the boss?" he asked.

She smiled at that. "Jack tries to be, and Apple lets him get away with it a lot of the time. But he's got limits, and no problem expressing them. And I think Jack is mostly bravado, because in stressful situations, like tonight, he lets Apple take the lead."

"Sounds like they've found a balance."

As he said it Apple reached out with his nose, stretching his neck so he was still at what he must consider a safe distance. He sniffed Brett's hand. Brett didn't move, not even the fingers the dog's nose was intent on. And she realized his knowledge of dogs wasn't limited to just Ember and her training and tactics. He understood them. Was as patient with these two as he was with the Lab.

On the thought, Ember, who had been lying down now near Brett's feet, rose to a sit.

"Hey, Ember girl, don't get territorial now," he murmured softly, soothingly to his partner. "You've had it easy compared to these two. You've never been homeless or gone hungry. Besides, you're on guard duty."

He reached out with his other hand to scratch Ember's ears. The big dog, leaner and more muscular than a typical family pet, leaned into it with a blissful sigh. And that, apparently, was enough for Apple. He nudged that motionless hand with his nose, almost insistently. Brett did the same with him, scratching behind Apple's floppy ears. The dog wiggled a little. Which made Jack crowd in to get his share.

Annalise sat there staring as he charmed three dogs at once, two of whom he'd never met before tonight, and who an hour ago had been nearly hysterical, and a few weeks ago downright snarly.

And she drew in a very deep breath as she admitted, way down deep, that the animals weren't the only ones being charmed.

# Chapter 9

Annalise had relaxed, finally. Talking about the dogs had done it, as he'd hoped. They were her refuge, as Ember was his.

Brett looked into the two pairs of dark brown eyes staring up at him, and kept talking softly, mostly nonsense, as he stroked and scratched. When, finally, both sets of those eyes went half-closed, he knew he had them. For now, anyway. He admired her patience to take this on, again and again, because he knew enough about rescued and scared creatures to know that he might have to go through it all over again next time.

*Next time?*

He'd thought that like it was a given there would be a next time, here, alone with them.

With Annalise.

*Nope. Not happening. She's a Colton, and that is a pool of problems you do not want to dive into.*

No, his job was to get her through tonight, while Ellie and others hunted down what details they could find on their catfisher. Then his job would be to find him.

If he hadn't come back here first.

Yes, staying tonight was definitely the right plan. And it would be fine. He was just feeling…protective. Understandable—she was Ember's trainer, so they had a connection. And speaking of Ember, she was being remarkably patient, while he paid attention to two other dogs. True, he'd given her the watch command, which told her she was on duty, but still.

He'd have to make it up to her later, with a fetch session. Maybe he could last until she tired out this time, instead of the other way around. Although that was unlikely. More than once he'd had a vision of his older self, gimping around with an unworkable right shoulder, victim of endless hours of throwing a tennis ball far enough to keep Ember happy.

He looked up to find her watching him. Intently. No, watching her dogs, he immediately thought, his mind skittering away from that flicker he'd seen in her blue-gray eyes. It had been watchfulness, care for her animals, that's all. An assessment of how her fosters were doing with a stranger. Didn't he already know how much she loved dogs? That was all that had been, not a snap of connection.

Casting about for something to say, he blurted, "How did you end up training dogs?"

She smiled, so maybe it wasn't so stupid after all. "They always responded to me, and I loved them, but I never thought about making a career out of it until my mother suggested it. I was working in an office, but volunteering with a rescue group. She told me she'd never seen me happier than when I was working with the dogs, and that I should go for it."

"Nice. That she saw it and said it." His own mother hadn't cared what he did, as long as he stayed out of any trouble that would embarrass her. He'd overheard her once saying she wished she'd never had him, And it didn't take a math genius to realize his parents' wedding had come months after he'd been conceived.

He supposed that was the answer to why they were the way they were. What he knew for sure was that he'd spent years trying to please them, before he'd realized he couldn't, no matter what he did. So he never expected much from family. Which was probably why the Coltons seemed so…overwhelming.

"She's the best," Annalise said. "And she knows a little something about going after what you love."

He didn't know her mother, Leanne Palmer Colton, except by sight. Troy had told him about how his father had met her sometime after his own mother had been tragically murdered when Troy had been a child. Geoff Colton had apparently been hesitant, not only because of his first wife's awful death, but because she was much younger than he was. But Leanne had fallen hard for the restaurateur, had known what she wanted.

*Leanne has been pretty much the only mother I've known. And she raised Desiree and I as if we were hers as much as Annalise and Grace, and Palmer. Heart of gold, that woman.* Troy's words echoed in his head as he looked at Annalise, who bore a distinct resemblance to her mother. Did she on the inside as well?

"You mean she wanted your father?" he asked.

She nodded. Then sighed, audibly. "Theirs is a true love story."

He managed not to snort his disbelief in the idea that such a thing existed. Attraction, yes, he'd go for that. Or even a long-term connection. But true love, the kind that had made her eyes grow warm and her mouth go soft? Not a chance.

*And you'd better stop thinking words like that. Warm. Soft. You're losing focus again.*

"So that's what you're looking for?"

She blinked. "What?"

He realized belatedly that that could have sounded as if he were asking her for…personal reasons. He scrambled to recover. "The app. Is that what you were hoping to find there?"

She grimaced then. "You don't need to remind me how foolish that was."

"Wasn't trying to."

This time the sigh was even more audible. And yet different. How could she get differing emotions into a simple exhale of breath? Wistfulness when talking about her parents, and now…disgust? At him, for asking? Or herself?

"I," she pronounced firmly, "am never dating again."

"Ever?" he asked, very carefully.

"Ever. I'm clearly too stupid to—"

"Stop it. You're not stupid. These guys are good. Really good."

"Right." She gave him a sideways look. "I'll bet you never would have been taken in."

He started to say he wouldn't have been on the app at all, since he wasn't looking. But some belated sense of caution stopped him. He searched for something else to say. The words were out before he realized they were probably worse. "I believed a woman who said she loved me once. Worst mistake of my life."

She looked at him straight on this time. "That's why you don't date?"

"I'm not the issue," he said, determined to divert this right now.

"But just because a couple of women burned you, you shouldn't give up on love altogether."

"You have to believe in love before you can give up on it."

She stared at him. "But you have to believe in it, or at least that it exists. Otherwise life is pointless. And if you cut yourself off because of one bad experience, you'll never find the real thing." He said nothing, just looked at her. And after a moment she started again. "You can't really want to stay alone forever. Once burned, twice shy is one thing, but once burned, forever shy is something else altogether."

He kept looking at her, biting the inside of his lip to keep from smiling. A stifled "Mmm" was all he could allow himself.

"What?" she demanded.

She was irritated now. Good. That meant she wasn't scared. "Just thinking you might want to listen to yourself."

"What?" Her tone was puzzled this time.

"You're the one who said you were never dating again."

"And you said you don't date."

"Not exactly. I said I'm not looking."

Her cheeks flushed. "Oh. I'm sorry. I didn't realize you were…with someone."

Where had that come from? Did she really think the only reason someone wouldn't be in a dating frenzy was because they were in a relationship?

"I'm not." He only wondered after he'd said it why he'd felt compelled to clarify that with her. "I meant I'm not looking…for what you're looking for." *I'm not sure it even exists.* "But since you clearly are, you'll have to take your own advice."

She looked thoughtful, as if she was going over what she'd said in her mind. And then she gave him a wry, almost embarrassed smile. "I guess I did kind of contradict myself there."

"Kind of," he agreed.

She let out a long breath. Then, with a wry grimace, she said, "I'll probably try again. Maybe in a year or two. Or ten."

"Ten? So, when you're thirty?"

He got her third "What?" and this time it was startled. "Just how young do you think I am?"

"Don't all women want to be thought younger?"

"Not when it means you think I'm a…kid, practically."

*Oh, believe me, I don't think of you as a kid, in any way.*

"Not a kid. Young, maybe."

"You mean naive," she accused. This time he couldn't stop his slight smile. And it gave him away. Her expression cleared, to be replaced with realization. "You did this on purpose, didn't you? All of this. To get my mind off what happened."

"People think more clearly when they're not scared," he said.

"How about when they're angry?" She glared at him. Or rather, tried to. The slight twitch at one corner of her mouth—damn, that mouth—gave her away in turn. And after a moment, she actually laughed.

"Okay, it worked," she said, and this time the breath she took looked deep and relaxing.

Brett wondered if she had any idea how amazing it was that she was able to even smile, let alone laugh, after the night she'd had. Annalise Colton had resilience, among a multitude of other qualities. And it struck him that he should have realized that earlier, when despite the night's events, she'd still preached to him about true love. Or the real thing, as she'd called it.

She still believed in it.

He wasn't sure he ever had.

## Chapter 10

She should have known.

Annalise chastised herself silently for her oversight. Brett hadn't gotten where he was, coming from Lansing with a stellar reputation, already establishing himself here in Grave Gulch, and—possibly most important—earning the clearly limitless adoration of a very smart dog, without knowing what he was doing. And clearly he knew how to calm a rattled victim.

*Victim.*

God, she hated the word. She'd rather be the injured party, even a casualty, but victim implied a helplessness she loathed. She wasn't helpless. Naive? Foolish? Stupid? Maybe.

*Stop it. You're not stupid.*

His words probably shouldn't have soothed her as much as they had. She was afraid it was because they had come from him. His opinion of her mattered. And telling herself it was only because he was a colleague of sorts, that she had to work with him, wasn't working too well.

She tried to focus on Apple and Jack, who had climbed up to join her on the couch. Ember had settled at Brett's feet, but her head was up, her ears active as she listened and sorted whatever she was hearing so far into the non-threatening category.

Annalise didn't get it. She worked with other cops, consulted with a couple of other departments who wanted a dog fine-tuned in her areas of expertise, even flirted with a handsome K-9 handler who had, sounding sweetly regretful, told her he was engaged.

But none of them made her feel the way this man did. The man who had her thinking about him even as she was getting ready for what was supposed to be the best date of her life and had instead turned into a disaster. What that said about her, she wasn't sure, but—

"—say it's going to break ninety tomorrow."

She snapped out of her reverie. She refused to ask *What?* yet again, so instead she said, "It is?"

He nodded. "Maybe you should take the day off. Head for the beach."

"I can't," she said, almost automatically. "I have three sessions scheduled in the morning."

"Reschedule. Go get some sand in your shoes."

Her mouth quirked. "If only it only got in your shoes."

In an instant, tension snapped between them, as if they were both thinking of all the different places beach sand could get, under varying circumstances. And she found herself wondering if he'd ever had sex on the beach somewhere. Probably. The guy obviously could have his choice of companions for the activity.

But he'd said he wasn't with anyone. And he wasn't

looking. Had the women in his past really soured him that much?

And there she was again, wondering, speculating.

"Not a beach lover?" he asked, his voice maybe just a shade too even.

"Oh, I am." She smiled. "Funny isn't it, how things are different depending on where you're from? I went to school with a girl from California, and to her the only real beach was at the ocean. For us, the Great Lakes are our ocean."

He smiled back at that. "I worked with a guy who was startled we had sand dunes. He thought the same thing."

A memory struck, made her smile. "We went to Leelanau State Park one year, when I was a kid. I rolled all the way down the Sleeping Bear Dunes. Talk about sand!" She had herself in hand enough to look at him now. "Have you ever been there?"

He shook his head. "I went for Silver Lake," he said.

She studied him for a moment. Then said teasingly, "Let me guess. The off-road-vehicle section?"

In keeping with all her reactions to him it seemed, the smile he gave her then warmed her more than it should have. "Guilty." He shrugged. "Hey, it's the only place east of the Mississippi you can ride sand dunes."

"I didn't realize. I can see the appeal, but seeing little kids out on those dirt bikes is worrying."

"I wasn't a little kid at the time. My family didn't go in for things like that."

"Beach trips?"

"Family trips."

"Oh." Somehow that seemed very sad to her. "I'm sorry. They were great fun."

"My father never—"

He stopped suddenly, and she wondered what he'd been

going to say. Wondered if there was anything to do with this man that she didn't wonder about.

"My dad worked hard," she said. "The Grill has been his life since he started there as a busboy. But he always made sure he was a hundred percent there for us on those trips, you know? Of course Mom would have chewed him out if he hadn't. But he ran down the dunes right beside us."

His head tilted slightly. "Your father worked at the Grave Gulch Grill as a busboy?"

She nodded. "When he was eighteen. And now he owns it. I'm incredibly proud of him."

"You should be. That's quite an accomplishment."

"What does your father do?"

"Now? No idea."

She blinked. "What?"

"We're not in touch much. Last time I talked to him, he was unemployed."

"When was that?"

He looked as if he was thinking. She couldn't imagine having to think so hard to remember when the last time you talked to your father was.

"Don't remember exactly," he finally said. "Couple of years ago."

She made a mental note to call hers and thank him for being a real father. And, since this clearly wasn't an easy subject for Brett, she quickly changed it. "So what do you do, in your time off?"

He glanced down at the dog arrayed on his feet. "Throw tennis balls?" he suggested.

She laughed. "She's such a sweetie. She'll work her heart out for you, so she deserves her play time."

"She is, she does and she does."

"Do you ever wish you'd gone with a 'bite-and-hold' dog?" From her own experience she knew working with dogs used mainly for scent work was quite different than the archetypal police K-9 people first think of. Bear, Grave Gulch's big sable German shepherd, was an entirely different type of dog, the kind who usually got the glory—and deserved it. But so did the quiet ones like Ember, whose nose had literally saved lives.

"If I ever did, she cured me."

*Like your ex cured you of the desire to date?*

There was a long, silent moment while Annalise reassured herself that she hadn't said it out loud. He didn't react, so she knew she hadn't. She had to get a handle on her errant thoughts. Thoughts like *Hey, since we're both not dating, maybe we should not date together.*

This was getting to be too much. Although she couldn't deny there was a certain appeal to hanging out with a guy who wasn't interested and therefore it didn't matter what she said, did or looked like. And with Brett, she somehow knew that last, what she looked like, would indeed be the last on his list, if he had a checklist of qualities he was looking for. Except he wasn't looking.

She needed to derail this train of thought in a hurry. She grabbed at the only thing she could think of powerful enough to distract her.

"Do you really think he'll come back?"

To his credit—among the many things to his credit—he didn't dissemble. "I don't know if he'll be back tonight, but I'd bet money he will be back, in some way, at some point."

"Why, now that I know he's a fake, wouldn't he just cut his losses?"

"His plan worked for him at least twice. Given how polished he is at it, probably more than that, elsewhere. He's going to be angry that it didn't work this time."

Well, maybe she would have preferred a little dissembling. "Great. So not only will he be back, but he'll be mad?"

"If he is, he'll have a surprise waiting now."

*And what happens if he comes back tomorrow night? Or the night after?* It sounded pitiful even in her mind. But worse was the thought of being here alone when that…that *thing* was out there.

And it wasn't like Brett could stay here until the guy was caught.

She sucked in a quick breath, fighting down the feelings that idea stirred in her. She was still off-balance after what had happened, that was all. She simply wasn't thinking straight.

"I'll get him, Annalise," he said. "And we'll get your bracelet back, too."

She nodded, thinking it safer than trying to speak. And in that moment of silence, a wave of exhaustion swept over her. She should just stay silent. That was the best plan.

Because too often her mouth outran her brain around this man.

# Chapter 11

Brett saw the moment when the crash hit. He'd known it was coming, it had to, it was how things worked. The fight-or-flight response was effective, built-in…and draining, once safety was achieved. The aftereffects of an adrenaline spike were something he was all too familiar with. She'd lasted longer than he would have expected.

"You should try and get some rest, if you're going to work tomorrow," he said, trying to make his tone casual.

He could see the effort she had to make to even respond in a similar tone. "I could say the same to you."

"I'm good for a while yet. I'll sleep a little later."

She sighed, and sat silently for a moment. Then she perked up slightly before asking, "Are you into comfort food?"

He blinked. "That depends," he said carefully. Growing up in his house, that had usually consisted of his mother's attempts at colcannon, the Irish mashed-potato-and-cabbage classic. She'd insisted on kale, which he hated, instead of cabbage, had never quite gotten the hang of the pickled cream and refused to just buy buttermilk. He'd only found out how good it could be when he'd one day had it made by an expert, and the difference was astounding. Her soda bread had been good, though, and a big chunk of it still warm from the oven would indeed be on his list of comfort foods, if he had one.

Somehow he doubted Annalise was thinking of either of those.

"Dream Bakes."

"Oh." Okay, anything from the popular bakery downtown qualified as comfort food, he was sure.

She smiled at his reaction. "My brother Palmer is engaged to the owner. It means I get him dropping off leftovers a lot."

He remembered his earlier thought. "Troy mentioned how they were tangled up in that murder case last month."

She nodded, with a sad expression. "Soledad's best friend. They have custody of the baby now." A smile flashed then. "And Palmer's taking to fatherhood. He had a rough start in life himself, so it's wonderful to see."

"Some people have the knack." *And some don't.*

And he didn't think he mistook the rather wistful look that flashed in her eyes for a moment. She really did want the whole thing, kids and all. Just talking about her brother's new family had seemingly given her a second wind. Judging by the way she was with the dogs, she'd be good at parenting. He hoped she got what she wanted someday. With someone.

He cut off that train of thought before it could stray down a siding that would be utterly pointless.

"So what's their idea of comfort food?"

"Today the options are an excellent cherry pie, made

from fresh Michigan cherries, or—" her expression slid into a grin "—a wickedly decadent salted-caramel Irish whiskey cake." He blinked at that. Tried to imagine the taste. Failed utterly. Annalise laughed. "All righty then," she said.

And with a final pat for the two foster dogs, she got up and headed for the kitchen, clearly reenergized. Didn't the woman realize most other people would be broken down weeping or curled up in bed in a fetal position, at this point?

He gave himself a mental slap; the last thing he needed to be doing was thinking about Annalise in bed in any position.

The cake was the most amazing thing he'd ever tasted. He hadn't thought much about the whole salted-caramel frenzy—his notions of food were mostly as fuel, with the exception of a good, rare steak or a quality shepherd's pie—but this made him think he could be convinced. *Decadent* had to be the right word.

"I'll need to be running an extra five miles to offload that," he said as he finished the last bite and resisted scraping the plate clean with his fork.

"Isn't it deliciously evil?" she agreed. She'd taken a smaller slice, but had finished it, as well. "I don't even want to know the calorie count. It's too good to worry about."

"Not like you have to worry about it," he said, unable to stop himself from giving her trim shape a once-over. The instant he realized he was doing it, he forced his gaze back to his empty plate.

"Hah," she said. "I'll be starving for two days to make up for this."

She gathered up the plates and forks. "I can do that," he said.

"I know you could. And probably would. But frankly, I need to…do things."

He understood that. And allowed himself another glimpse as she bent to put the plates and utensils in the dishwasher. As she straightened again, his thoughts slipped the leash once more. She really did have the sweetest—

"There's a police car across the street." She was staring out the kitchen window.

"And there will be, off and on. It won't be 24/7, but they'll be around when they can, for a while at least."

She turned to look at him. "They're…guarding me?"

*You're a Colton. The chief's a Colton. What did you expect?*

"Not guarding, exactly. If someone's got a report to do, or has downtime between calls, they'll spend it there. And Ember and I will make a few rounds, in case you hear us outside."

She looked as if she couldn't decide if she was glad about this or not. "But…won't that scare him off?"

He stared at her. "That's what you're worried about?"

"I thought you wanted to catch him."

"I want you safe more."

Only when her eyes widened did he realize how that had sounded. Not the words so much, because that was in fact his priority, but the way they'd sounded. As if something happening to her, as if her being hurt or worse, would hit him in a very down-deep way. Not just as a failure of the department and of he himself as a cop, but as…an immeasurable loss. To him. Personally.

He had to move, to stop looking at her. At the way she was looking at him. He got up, figuring he'd do a check of all the windows, although she'd told him they were secured because she'd been going to leave. For her date. The date she'd been going on in her search for true love.

The part of him that snorted inwardly at the idea sparred briefly with the part of him that secretly admired her faith in it. Or envied it. But then apparently she'd grown up with good examples of it, whereas he…hadn't. He'd often wondered why they'd even stayed together, since the most loving emotion he'd ever seen them share was a sort of armed neutrality.

He'd just checked the west-side window when a slight gleam from a shelf beside it caught his eye. He looked, saw a small shiny rock, rounded, smooth, and showing small roughly hexagonal markings.

"My Petoskey stone," she said as she came up behind him. Close behind him. He kept his gaze on the rock.

"I've never seen one like that." He knew the stones were a combination of rock and fossilized coral, moved and deposited by glaciers. He thought they were unique to Michigan, maybe even to the lower part of the state.

"I found it when I was a kid, and Dad polished it up for me."

Such a simple thing, yet he couldn't imagine his father doing it. For that matter he couldn't image the wealthy, successful Geoff Colton doing it. But from what she'd said, he hadn't always been that way. Brett had an innate respect for a self-made man and it seemed that's what her father was.

That, and a man who would do something so simple just to make his little girl happy. The little girl who had not only hung on to the keepsake, but placed it somewhere where she could see it all the time. What must that have been like, to have parents like that? Is that what it took to turn out someone as sharp and dedicated as Troy, as talented as his sister Desiree, to take a troubled kid like Palmer and turn him around and to produce a woman like Annalise, so full of compassion, so—

He cut himself off before he launched on a list of all

the things Annalise was. "You really should try and get some rest," he said abruptly. "This second wind isn't going to last."

"Voice of experience?"

"Yes."

He guessed it was a sign that he was right that she didn't really resist. She got a blanket and pillow from a cabinet in the hall and put them on the couch without comment.

"Good night," she said as she turned to head down the hall. He muttered something, he wasn't even sure what, as he fought off imaginings of what her bedroom might look like.

"Annalise?"

She spun around, a look of…anticipation on her face that rattled him enough that it took him a moment to remember what he'd been going to tell her. "Keep your door open." Her eyes widened. "So I can hear anything that happens," he said quickly.

She blinked. "Oh. Okay."

What had she thought, that he wanted her to leave her bedroom door open…for him?

He stared after her as she walked down the hall. This was irrational; he felt as off-balance as if he'd been the one who had the traumatic night. He'd never personally known a victim before the crime occurred before, but that didn't seem like enough to explain his reaction. He was feeling too drawn, too protective, and that she was Ember's trainer didn't seem enough to explain it.

He turned on his heel and methodically went about getting himself settled. He appreciated that she'd thought of the pillow and blanket, but he had no intention of actually sleeping, not like that anyway. The chair closest to the outside wall would do, with a window open enough for him—and Ember—to hear anything suspicious. He could doze a bit, just enough to keep going. An hour or two would do. Sidearm on the table beside the chair, within instant reach, leave the shoes on in case he had to run, and he was good.

Later, he went on one of those external perimeter checks he'd mentioned to her. Then, a unit pulled up and parked near where the one she'd seen earlier had been. Since Ember had signaled nothing new, he headed that way. The woman in uniform was alert and aware enough that she either saw or sensed him coming from a good distance away. Then she spotted Ember, and Brett saw her snap the safety strap that held her weapon in the holster, indicating she'd been ready to draw if she had to.

"Officer Fulton," he said, reminded once again of why he'd come here; in Lansing it could have been a cop who'd been on the force for years and he might never have spoken with them before. But here, in less than a year, he'd already interacted with everybody on the force at one point or another.

"Detective," she said. "All calm?"

He nodded. "He may be done for the night."

"But not for good?"

"I don't think so." Brett felt his mouth quirk. "But what do I know?"

"More than most, from what I've heard." She said it as if it was as true and real as the lake just to the west, and he felt a burst of satisfaction. Before he had to formulate a response she asked, "How's she doing?"

"Amazingly well," he admitted. "She was worried that marked units hanging around meant we wouldn't catch the guy."

Fulton smiled. "Well, she's made of tough stuff. So's the family, or the boss would have buckled long ago under all this pressure."

He couldn't deny that. The protests were getting louder

and rowdier. Chief Colton had withstood it all so far, but he didn't know how much longer she could hold on. "It's getting uglier," he said.

"Yeah." She glanced toward the tidy little house. "You're staying, I hear?"

Well, that hadn't taken long, for that to get around. "Yeah. Just in case."

The officer's gaze shifted to Ember. "Have to keep your dog's trainer safe, huh?"

"Yeah." *Your dog's trainer.* That's what she was, and he'd best remember that.

As he went back to the house, Officer Fulton's words echoed in his head.

He was already an outsider in this seemingly Colton-dominated enclave. He wasn't about to make it worse by getting involved with one of their own.

No matter how much he might want to.

## Chapter 12

Annalise stared into the darkness, hoping that forcing herself to keep her eyes open would perversely trigger the overwhelming urge to sleep. It was her last resort; she'd been lying here for two hours, unable to find a way to turn off, or at least slow down, her whirling thoughts.

And the fact that a few minutes ago Brett had come to her open doorway and lingered a moment didn't help.

She'd heard the faint creak of a floorboard and felt a spike of that adrenaline rush before she realized it was him. That realization caused a spike of an entirely different kind until she heard him walk away and realized he'd only been checking on her.

*What did you expect? That he'd climb into bed with you?*

She rolled over and buried her face in her pillow, wondering why these wild thoughts kept careening into her mind. What kind of woman was she, to have been so very excited about her date tonight—never mind that it had all been a scam—yet almost simultaneously so attracted to this man who had no interest at all in her that way? Or in anything like the kind of relationship she was looking for?

*I'm not looking for what you're looking for.*

He meant it. She didn't doubt that. And she knew she should consider it fair warning. A warning some men would never bother to give. Why had he? She felt her cheeks heat at the thought that maybe he knew, how she reacted to him. Maybe she'd betrayed it somehow. That would be embarrassing. They'd always gotten on well in the joint training sessions with Ember, but her focus had been on the smart, willing dog, not on him.

Well, not any more than usual. Qualified, capable K-9 officers with a record like his weren't thick on the ground, and he'd proven that rep well-earned in their first exercises together. That he was quietly competent and apparently unaware of his own looks were big points in his favor, in her book.

She'd assumed at first he was married, because how could he not be? He didn't wear a ring, but some men didn't. Then Troy had told her a week later he wasn't and had never been.

*You have to believe in love before you can give up on it.*

She sighed into the darkness. That just might be the saddest thing she'd ever heard. Yet he didn't seem sad to her. Or bitter. Just…closed off. Except with Ember. That alone told Annalise that he wasn't completely closed off.

But that didn't mean she should be lying here thinking about him.

And about what she would have done if he had climbed into bed with her.

"I can drive myself—"

"I know you can," Brett said patiently to Annalise the

next morning, "but I have to drop Ember off anyway." He didn't mention that he also didn't want her taking off to go get lunch or something. He wanted her under observation at all times, and he'd already called Sergeant Kenwood to let him know to keep an eye on her; the man might be retired from active duty, but his instincts were as sharp as ever.

"But I'll need my car to get home."

"I'll pick you up when I come get her," he said, with a scratch of the Lab's soft ears. "After I talk to the two other women this jerk targeted."

"I want to take Apple and Jack," she said. "I don't want to leave them alone. They were scared, too."

And that was Annalise Colton in a nutshell, he thought. "Fine. There's room. And Ember won't mind."

And so he ended up with a carload of three dogs and the woman adored by them all.

*Including you?*

He yanked his mind off that fruitless path. He drove, trying to concentrate on mentally organizing his day.

As he dropped her, the two foster dogs and Ember off at the training center, he didn't mention that his first stop was going to be the chief's office. He also didn't mention the early morning text from said chief that had precipitated that visit. The boss was concerned about her cousin, which was only natural. His family might not be close, but he understood—envied?—those who were.

And that was also part of why working here was turning out to be much more complicated than he'd expected. If he'd studied the roster and seen how many times the Colton name popped up, it might have sent up a red flag. But he hadn't. So now here he was, dodging Coltons at every turn.

As he walked down the hallway to the chief's office, he remembered the first time he'd made this trek. The day of his final interview for this job. He'd been impressed with Chief Colton when she'd met with him personally to ask him to take the position, because they both needed and wanted people like him on the job. And when she'd promised he could slide right into an available K-9 position because he already had the knowledge, it had been the lure that had had him agreeing.

Her office hadn't changed since he'd been here, and yet it felt different. He could only imagine what it must be like to be the holder of this position, with the Bowe case ongoing, and the integrity of one of the most crucial parts of the department under such intense scrutiny. He knew many in the mobs outside had made up their minds already, some before any, let alone all of the evidence was in, but he supposed that was to be expected given that it was evidence itself that had been brought into question in a very public way.

If it was starting to have the air of a bunker, it was only to be expected.

Chief Colton rose the moment he opened the door to her office after her aide had cleared him through. The tall, fit redhead—they'd joked about that in that interview, that she was all for hiring more redheads—did look a bit more harried than she had during his final interview. But something else had changed with her, something it took him a moment to put his finger on. He finally realized that under all the tension, both the kind that naturally came with the job and that caused by a serial killer on the loose, not to mention the whole tainted-evidence scandal, she was…not happy, but not as stressed as she had been.

That things must be going well at home was his first thought. He knew she and the owner of the Grave Gulch Hotel, Antonio Ruiz, had connected during the whole fiasco at Mary Suzuki's wedding, when Desiree's little boy had been grabbed as leverage to get Grave Gulch PD to reopen an old case. And they'd fallen in love and gotten engaged; Troy had mentioned they would likely be seeing a wedding as soon as things resolved and Melissa and Antonio both wanted a family.

*Just like her cousin. She wants the whole thing, love, family and probably the damn white picket fence, too.*

He shook it off and proceeded to assure the chief that her cousin was fine.

"She actually dealt with it very well, considering she had no idea he doesn't generally injure his victims."

"I'm just glad you were there," Melissa said, and it was clearly heartfelt.

"She would have been okay anyway, I think. She used what was at hand and got away from him, before I was close enough to help."

"And after?"

He shrugged. "The crash was a little rough, but she recovered quickly. Much more quickly than I expected."

"You stayed with her?"

He hesitated a moment. "I did, with my dog, just to be sure," he finally said. "And any units in the area who had downtime or reports to write in the field, did it on her block."

"Thank you," she said, and again there was no questioning the true feeling behind it. "You're sure it's the same guy from those two other cases in the county?"

"Fairly. MO's the same. Tailors the profile to their tastes, initiates the contact, can't or won't video chat, cancels out on the first in-person meet for some dramatic reason, it's all there. I'll know more after I interview the other two victims."

"And you're headed there now?"

He nodded. "I just dropped An—Ms. Colton off at the

training center. Sergeant Kenwood knows what happened and will keep a close eye on her." He decided not to mention that he'd be going back to pick her up this afternoon. He was avoiding thinking about it himself, because he didn't want to think about dropping her at home and then leaving her there. Alone. But he'd deal with that later.

Something had shifted in the chief's eyes—bluer than Annalise's blue-gray, he noted—when he changed to the more formal *Ms. Colton* midsentence. But all she said was, "I'd like you to take—"

She didn't finish because a tone came from the cell phone on her desk, the sound enhanced by the vibration of the device. She glanced down at it, frowned, tapped the screen and called up a messaging app. Brett would have left while she handled whatever this was if she hadn't begun an order before the interruption. Because that's what an "I'd like you to" was when it came from the occupant of this office.

Barely a second after the message appeared, Chief Colton stiffened, staring. And under her breath muttered something he decided quickly he was probably glad not to be able to hear. She stared at the screen a moment longer, then looked up at him.

"It's Bowe," she said.

## Chapter 13

Brett stared at her. "Randall Bowe just texted you?"

She nodded. "It says he wants to make a deal."

For a long, wire-taut moment neither of them said anything more. He could almost feel her mind racing. Then she gestured him over to her and gave him a look that was almost apologetic.

"I'm sorry, but with the current state of things, I might need a witness to this conversation."

He understood what she was saying. The department had been under the microscope for months now, and she had to tread very carefully. He would not want to be in her shoes. He remembered talking to the chief in Lansing shortly after he'd started as a cop, and how the man had assumed everyone aspired to his position. Brett had laughed, saying he should get his feet under him in the job first. But in less than six months of watching what the man had to deal with, his answer was *no way*. He couldn't imagine a job he'd want less. His former partner had joked that that was why he should get the gig, because he didn't want it.

She held out the phone and he read the message. Let's make a deal. Cute. He noted the number it had come from. "Not his known cell number, I presume." The chief nodded, still staring at the screen. "Your provider back up your texts so Ellie can get the data?" She nodded again.

"I think for the moment we have to go on the assumption this is really him."

He nodded in turn. "Agreed."

She looked up at him then. "Troy tells me you're deep into finding Bowe."

"I want him, yes."

"Then you've studied him?"

"Read every case file."

Her eyebrows rose. "That's a lot of cases."

"Tell me about it."

"Did you find out anything?"

"He's good. Very good." He grimaced. "And he knows it."

"My take, as well. So…do we want to take Bowe down a peg or stroke his ego to lure him in?" He thought she was just thinking out loud, but then realized she was looking at him, waiting. She'd been asking him his opinion on how to proceed with the case? "Troy told me he sometimes feels like when we earn your trust, we'll be on our way to earning back the trust of those protesters."

He blinked at the seeming non sequitur. But then had the thought maybe it wasn't a non sequitur at all. "Troy said that?"

"He did. He thinks a lot of you. And he's a good judge."

He had no idea what to say to that, so went back to her original question. "My gut says it's too early to try and get in his face. Bowe needs to think he's going to get what he wants, because of course this is his plan, and he's the best."

"Belief in his own infallibility," she said.

"Yes. And if we try to play him now, he's liable to decide he needs to prove to us just how in control of this he is. And I don't like thinking about what he might come up with to try and do that."

"Agreed. So no telling him he's in no position to deal."

"Because sadly, he is."

She let out a long breath, and then tapped out a short reply.

What are you offering?

Nothing came back. They waited. Still nothing. "Did I take too long?" she finally asked aloud.

"I'm betting we'll wait almost exactly as long as we made him wait."

She drew back slightly. "You think he timed it?"

"One way or another. If I'm right, he'll answer…right… about…now."

The chime went off a split second after he said the last word. The chief gave him a wide smile. "Points to you, Detective."

Everything you want to know.

The chief sighed. Brett raised a brow at her. "I really, really want to be a smart ass back at him, I'm so angry," she said. "But I know you're right. Not yet."

The chief typed, then sent, I'm listening.

First, don't bother trying to trace this phone—it'll be dead the instant we're done.

Still listening.

I'll give you all the cases I had my fun with.

The price?

You find my brother.

The chief's brow furrowed. "His brother," she murmured.

"We've been looking for him for months, just for an interview," Brett said, frowning. "Troy even had me check with a contact of mine from the marshal's office, to see if he was in witness protection, but there was nothing."

We've been looking. No luck.

Look harder. If you want that info. When you find him, set up a call. I have a burner phone just waiting.

Puzzled, Brett said, "Bowe's wife said she doesn't know Baldwin's location. They've been estranged for years."

"I wonder why he wants to talk to him now?"

Brett shrugged. "Ask him."

She typed it out. Why? You haven't spoken in years.

I have a score to settle with dear Baldwin.

"A score to settle?" the chief asked. "After all this time?"

"He's obviously not rational to begin with," Brett answered. "Who knows what idea he's got in his head about his brother."

"And he's on edge anyway," she agreed. She let out an

audible breath. Brett could only imagine the pressure she must be under. Yet she was handling it well. He wondered if any of that composure came out of the newfound love in her life. Then he laughed inwardly at himself. *When the hell did you become a romantic, Shea?*

He pushed away an image of Annalise, cuddled up with her dogs. That was the last thing he needed to distract him right now, when they had a major suspect reaching out, and he was standing here with Annalise's cousin, who also happened to be his boss.

I'm waiting, dear chief. Is it a deal?

"Impatient," Brett said.

"I suppose it's too much to wish he's on edge enough to make a mistake," the chief mused aloud.

We'll keep looking, she sent. And find him ASAP.

After a moment Bowe answered with an emoji of a skull with burning eyes.

"Well that's charming," the chief said sourly.

You'd better, he sent then.

Three minutes ticked by and the screen remained unchanged. They looked at each other, and Brett knew they were thinking the same thing.

Bowe was gone.

And the phone he'd called from was probably already in pieces somewhere.

# Chapter 14

"Well," the chief said as she dropped her phone back on her desk, "that was…interesting."

"It was."

She turned to look at him. "I'm glad you were here when that happened." His brows rose in question. She grimaced, and a touch of bitterness came into her voice as she explained, "These days having a non-Colton witness seems crucial."

He'd never thought about it from that angle before all this had happened, that having half your family on or working with the department could have a serious downside. And she looked tense enough he decided that the comment about him being a non-Colton hadn't been a jab.

And then she was all business, the command-and-control side of her jumping to the fore. "I'll call Troy in and give him this info. You need to get back to this catfish case."

He'd never really left Annalise's case, merely been distracted for the moment. But at her words it came rushing back. He did need to continue with the active investigation. Not only to clear the case and catch the guy, and to get back Annalise's precious bracelet, but so he could put her out of his mind again, thinking of her only when Ember had a training session.

*Yeah, right. Just put her right out of your mind. No problem. You do it all the time with cases, once they're over.*

Over. Done with. No need to ever see her again, except at the training center. That's what he wanted. Wasn't it? Wasn't that—

"—take someone along with you to these interviews, if you don't mind."

He snapped back to reality. Ran the words back through his mind, including the last ones, which hadn't been in the tone of a question. No, that had been the chief speaking, and it was an order despite the polite wording.

"I... Sure." Not much else he could say, really.

"She's a rookie, so we're trying to get her as much varied experience as we can. And watching a veteran like you tackle a case like this could teach her a lot."

As she walked past him to the door—which he noted because he'd known a supervisor or five who would be above it, instead using the intercom to order someone else to do it, wanting that sense of being a superior—a touch of trepidation hit him. *She. A rookie.*

He groaned inwardly when the newcomer appeared in the doorway. He'd been right. Grace Colton.

Normally he wouldn't mind at all having a rookie tag along; it only helped him later if the beat cops had an idea what he did and how he did it. He tried to shake off the feeling, but it was difficult as he stood there with the two Coltons.

Did it have to be Annalise's sister?

*Of course it did.*

And if he didn't get moving, Troy would probably show up for the news on Bowe's contact. Then he could be in the middle of a freaking Colton family reunion.

"Let's get moving," he said gruffly.

She looked a little startled, probably at his tone, of maybe the fact that he hadn't even said hello, but he was feeling a bit surrounded at the moment. Absurd, given there were only two of them, but then they were Coltons and that was, as always, different. He'd heard that Grace was smart and capable, from people he respected, so that's what he needed to focus on. Not her last name.

Somewhat to his surprise her first question when they got into his unit wasn't about her sister. Instead, she glanced in the back of the SUV and then asked, "Where's your dog?"

"Training."

"Oh. Annalise didn't mention she had Ember today."

Belatedly it hit him. She didn't need to ask about her sister, because she'd probably already talked to her. This was different territory for him, these close family ties.

A memory of the look on Annalise's face when he'd said he had no idea what his father was doing these days, and that he hadn't talked to him in a couple of years, shot through his mind. She'd been truly shocked. He took it as a matter of course. Maybe that's why they made him nervous, all these Coltons. It was just nerves, wasn't it?

He pondered that as he drove—leaving out the back way to avoid the cluster of protesters out front; they seemed to have a schedule set up so there were always a few around—hoping his edginess around anyone named Colton stemmed only from sheer numbers and the close ties, and not out of some subconscious feeling that they were guilty of everything those people with the signs and placards were claiming.

He couldn't believe it. He'd swear an oath that Troy wasn't; the man was one of the best cops he'd ever worked with. For that matter, none of the Coltons seemed the type to him. He'd seen enough of them now to recognize the genuineness of their family bond, and he was honest enough to admit his unease at being surrounded by them was in large part due to his own lack of those same bonds with his own family. It was simply foreign to him.

Yet he felt a secret small bit of relief that Annalise wasn't as closely connected to the department as the others, and not likely to get sucked into whatever happened in the end.

No, she had her own troubles. And that's what he needed to be focused on right now.

"—for being there for my sister last night."

Yet again he snapped out of a reverie. Daydreaming something he was normally prone to, but since last night he couldn't seem to stop. He glanced at the woman in the passenger seat.

"Lucky coincidence," he said.

"But she told me this morning that you stayed, took care of her. Thank you for that. She was so shaken."

He shrugged. Tried not to read anything into that *took care of her.* Tried not to remember those long hours when he'd wanted more than that. And waited until he could speak evenly to say, "That's to be expected. And she recovered pretty quickly. Handled it well, overall."

She dropped the subject then, not saying another word about her sister. He should be grateful, he supposed. And would have been if he hadn't suspected it was because he wasn't a member of the club.

Instead she focused on the interviews ahead, asking him what he would do, how he would handle them, what he would ask. Good, intelligent questions. She had potential, he thought.

They spent the rest of the drive—north to a neighboring hamlet for this first one—talking about the forthcoming interviews. While he drove she read him what information they had on the first woman who'd been catfished by this man, including the actual crime report. He liked to know as much as he could about a victim before talking with them, because it helped guide his approach.

"She's owned Lively Gifts—that's their last name, Lively—for three years. It was the family business, started by her mother ten years ago."

"She inherited it when her mother died, right?"

"Yes."

"Kids?"

She drew back slightly. "Does that matter?"

"Might. Some parents, thinking you might have put your kids at risk is the worst part of what happened."

With his peripheral vision he saw her study him for a moment. Finally she said, "Some parents?"

He shrugged. A gesture that had become quite useful when dealing with this family who seemed to have invaded his life. "Some wouldn't care. Or even think about it."

"My mother," she said flatly, "would have wanted him dead."

She said it with flat confidence, and he wondered what it must have been like, to have grown up with that kind of feeling, that kind of certainty of a parent's love. He'd mostly felt he was a nuisance they'd be glad to be rid of, if he survived to eighteen.

And her mother was Annalise's. And the woman who had raised her to believe in true love. The real thing. Whatever. The thing that had her searching for it, which had gotten her into this mess.

Elizabeth Lively was small, with dark shoulder-length hair and medium brown eyes. He paused outside, looking through the window. She was a quick mover; he watched her flit around the store, straightening a display on the middle row, speaking briefly to a customer looking at a little ceramic thing like those some people apparently liked to dust, tidying a card rack over near the register, then walking behind the counter to fiddle with something underneath.

"Think she's nervous?" Grace asked from beside him.

"Or looking to restore order. Her incident was the most recent prior to Annalise. She might still be dealing."

"I'm not sure you ever stop dealing with something like this," she said, surprising him. "After you've been fooled like that."

He soon discovered Elizabeth Lively was, above all else, embarrassed as she recounted the tale of her "heartfelt" connection—she'd thought—with a man who had the same passion for art that she had. She'd planned to meet at a drawing class in a local park. And how he had had to cancel last minute, but had—so sweetly, she'd thought—arranged for the teacher of that class to come to her home and give her a personal lesson.

"He gave me a lesson, all right," she said bitterly. "Nothing like waking up in the ER—thank goodness my sister came over and found me—and finding out you've been drugged and everything of value you own stolen."

And she turned bright red when shown the sketch of Annalise's catfish, and nodded before she closed her eyes in obvious humiliation.

"That's him," she said.

He tried to tell her what he'd told Annalise. "Don't feel

so bad. The guy is very good, very smooth, very practiced at this."

"While I'm too stupid to live. I give up. I'm never dating again."

Exactly what Annalise had said. "That would just please him," he said. "Don't let him win."

The woman gave him a thoughtful look, then said quietly, "Thank you. That was nice of you to say." Nice? Maybe. He didn't know. Because he had no idea what had made him say it all in the first place. "But for now I'm just going to focus on making this the best and most popular gift shop in the county."

"You go, girl," Grace said with a wide smile.

Elizabeth smiled back. "I intend to."

"That *was* nice of you to say," Grace said when they were back in the car.

He shrugged. Again.

They headed the opposite direction this time, drove through Grave Gulch to the south, to a small shopping center just outside the city limits. This time the goal was a small hair salon, not a place where he would feel in the least comfortable.

"You look like you're about to get off a plane in Afghanistan or something," Grace said teasingly.

He gave her a sharp look. "Trust me," he said coolly, "this is nothing like that."

She looked sufficiently abashed and stayed quiet as they went in. He had no idea what happened in these places, but guessed what he could smell was some kind of hair dye or treatment. Someone in the back was apparently getting a manicure, from what little he knew about that process.

A woman approached them, and he recognized Natasha Tracy from the file photo. Tall, curvy, with long hair that was about ten different shades of blond that somehow all seemed to blend.

"Wow," Grace said, sounding as if it was almost involuntary. "Whoever does your hair, I want them."

Natasha looked startled, then smiled. And seemed to relax a little, so Brett gave Grace an approving nod. "My partner does it. She's here on weekends, if you want to make an appointment. I'm Natasha." Her gaze shifted to Brett, lingered. "Let me guess. Detective Shea?"

He nodded. But looked at Grace and whispered, "All yours."

Grace's eyes widened but she recovered quickly and asked if there was someplace they could talk. The woman led them to the small room at the back of the salon, where there was a table just big enough for the two chairs around it. When Brett told them to take the seats, Ms. Tracy sighed.

"A real gentleman. Unlike the imposter I got duped by."

Grace worked the encounter carefully, slowly, taking her time and asking good questions even as she exhibited full compassion for the victim's roiled emotions. Clearly she'd separated her personal connection; she was a cop now, not the latest victim's sister.

*Annalise's sister.*

The story that came out was very similar to the others. A carefully crafted luring, a slow build and a final cancellation with an excuse and an impressive action to make up for it—in this case a delivery from Dream Bakes, a sampler of luscious treats and a pitcher of their famous cherry lemonade. Then the dart, oblivion, and waking to the aftermath.

And when the sketch came out again, she winced visibly.

"Yes, that's him. God, I am so stupid. That's what I get

for trusting him. For trusting anyone," she ended, rather vehemently. "Never again. I'm done, with all of it."

A string of thoughts tumbled through Brett's mind. Elizabeth Lively, running the family business; this woman had started her own, clearly neither weak nor foolish people. And Annalise, warm, caring and confident in her work and her love for the dogs she trained. This was more than just a scam to steal; it was an undermining of faith and hope, and it turned his stomach.

"Stop blaming yourself," he found himself saying. "None of this is on you. He's a scumbag, a weak, pathetic excuse for a man who has to trick people because he's incapable of doing anything worthwhile. Don't let him steal that…light from you." He faltered a little at the end, wondering where the hell all that had come from. Both women were staring at him. He ended it awkwardly, retreating to what he'd said before. "I'm just saying don't let him win. There are plenty of good guys out there."

Ms. Tracy's expression changed then. And the smile she gave him made him feel even more awkward. "Obviously," she said, looking him up and down. "Question is, are you single?"

"I…uh…" *Well that's articulate, Shea.* With the feeling he'd just walked himself into a mine field, because after what she'd been through a quick rebuff could be a harsh blow, he scrambled for a tactful answer. "Thanks. And if I was in the market, I'd…be interested." He tried a smile. "But I'm not the only good guy around. Might want to pass on the dating app thing though."

She didn't seem to take offense, only grimaced and said, "I deleted it the instant I got my phone back."

They were back in his unit when Grace said, "That was a good thing you did. Again."

He shrugged, not knowing what to say since he had no

idea what had brought on the outburst. "You did well with her. Just the right balance."

"Thank you." Grace sighed. "She looked cool and calm on the outside, but she's still hurting."

"Yeah. She's had her foundation rocked."

"Just like the woman at the gift shop. And my sister."

"Yes."

There was a moment of silence in the car before Grace added quietly, "No wonder Annalise felt safe with you."

He had no idea what to say to that, so he said nothing, just drove. And thought. About the twisted mentality of a man who made his way in life by duping innocent women. He thought of everything he'd learned over the years about men like that, characteristics, how they thought, the kinds of things they did and where they went. He was building a picture in his mind, a picture that he hoped would lead him down the right path.

*You're going down, catfish.*

It was both promise and vow, to himself and the victims. Especially Annalise.

## *Chapter 15*

Back at the station, Brett made a call and found out the person he wanted to see, the psychologist they sometimes consulted, wasn't due back for another hour, so instead of going inside he dropped Grace off and headed over to the training center. He arrived just as Annalise was finishing her session with Ember in the big arena. He could tell that by the praise she was lavishing on the delighted Lab. Even as he watched she dropped down to her knees, not caring about the dirt, not when it came to stroking and hugging and petting the dog, who looked utterly ecstatic.

*Like you wouldn't be if she was doing that to you?*

A blast of heat rocketed through him as the image formed in his mind, and he was glad he'd stayed in the car, because he had no doubts his thoughts would be reflected in his face. Not to mention another body part she seemed able to wake up simply by existing.

He had the sudden thought that the dog would be delighted to have Annalise around all the time. And a fantasy of them all together rose in his mind as fully formed as if he'd been thinking about it every day.

But he hadn't been. Had he?

And then Ember, ever alert even at this distance, whirled around, ears up and nose in the air. He heard her let out a happy bark and she broke away and headed for him at a run. Annalise stood, but made no move to call her back. Instead she followed—at a much slower pace— and reached them after Brett had had a chance to properly greet the loyal animal.

"She did well. We're really pushing the envelope on older scents and complicated ones. And I worked a bit more with her on air scenting," she added, referring to the knack of tracking airborne odors as well as those on the ground. "I think she's really getting it."

"She's the best."

"I would not argue that," Annalise said with a smile.

He hesitated, but decided it was part of his job and asked, "How are you doing?"

"All right." Her effort at a smile was almost believable. "You told Sergeant Kenwood to keep an eye on me, didn't you?"

It wasn't really a question, so he only shrugged and said, "He was already here."

"But not usually hovering the way he did today."

"You needed to feel safe."

"Yes. I did. I wasn't complaining." She gave him a sideways look and a small smile that sent his insides tumbling as his earlier thoughts had.

He had to get out of here. Get away from her. She did too many things to him. He was too drawn to her, and the pull was getting harder to resist. He'd managed to keep it at bay before, but somehow last night, holding her, seeing her scared, vulnerable and self-condemning, had crumbled the walls he hid behind around her.

He hated that she felt any part of what had happened was her fault. It had been bad enough with the two other victims today, but with her it was magnified, amplified… personal. And wound him up until he wanted to find this catfish and pound him into the ground.

"I need to get to the station and tie up some things. You get off at five, right?" At her nod he went on. "I'll be back to pick you up then."

He didn't wait for her to acknowledge, not when what he really wanted to do was grab her and hold her until she was her bright, happy self again. He turned on his heel and headed back to his vehicle, Ember at his side.

*Ember, the only female you should be thinking about sharing a house—and a life—with.*

Well, that had been a little abrupt.

"Goodbye to you, too," Annalise muttered as she watched him go without even giving her a hint about how the interviews had gone. Then she felt bad. She should cut him some slack; he was obviously focused on the case. And that's what she wanted, right? She wanted that guy found and put away for what he'd done. Preferably for a very, very long time.

Yet some small part of her, a tiny voice she tried to smother, was saying something quite different. It was saying what she really wanted was more of last night's time with Brett—specifically that time when he'd simply held her until all the stress, all the worry, all the humiliation had seemed to leech out of her. When she'd abandoned her efforts at being strong, and let the reaction take hold and work its way through, as he'd said it would whether she fought it or not.

He'd been so kind, so gentle…and yet she'd never felt as if it was because he thought her weak.

*You're the one who fought back, with the only weapon you had at hand. That's not something I laugh at. It's something I applaud.*

The words echoed in her mind, in the same obviously sincere tone in which he'd said them. He'd meant it. While she'd been thinking the worst of herself, he'd been thinking the best. And he had the experience to know, didn't he? He must have seen people in bad situations countless times, seen how they reacted, what they did or didn't do. So surely—

Her phone cut off her thoughts with the tone she had assigned to family. It was the theme of an old movie her father had so loved they had all ended up seeing it countless times growing up.

She pulled it out and glanced at the screen. Grace. She automatically reached to swipe up to answer, then froze.

Grace. Who had just spent the entire morning with Brett.

She had to fortify herself with the knowledge her little sister wasn't a gossip about family. But she could chatter when nervous, and Annalise already knew she had been nervous about the chance to go on an investigation with the quietly effective and efficient detective. So it was a moment before she could make herself complete the swiping motion.

"How'd the interviews go?" she asked, before Grace could ask how she was; she didn't want to go through that again.

"Great! I learned so much. Br—Detective Shea even let me do the second one myself."

"Congratulations," Annalise said. "That's his kind of high praise."

"I know. I was so excited he trusted me, but I had to hide it. Wouldn't do to show I was thrilled in front of a victim." She caught herself. "Except I just did, didn't I?"

Annalise laughed, for the most part because she was relieved that *victim* hadn't been the first thing in her sister's mind when it came to her. She let Grace go on with what she could reveal—which wasn't much, even though Annalise was a victim herself, since it was an ongoing investigation—the bottom line of which was both women had positively identified Desiree's sketch as the man who had shown up at their door after a canceled date.

Annalise didn't know if this news made her feel better, knowing that she wasn't alone in her foolishness, or worse because after working with the police for this long, she should have been the one to realize something was off with… Sam-who-doesn't-exist.

"But you know what impressed me the most?" Grace asked. "About him, I mean?"

Annalise was almost afraid to ask. Her sister sounded a bit awed, and she wasn't sure she liked that. "I assume you don't mean his big blue eyes," she said dryly.

"No," Grace said, in that teasing tone she'd heard from the time her sister had been old enough to talk. "That's your department." *What's that supposed to mean?* "But both women, they're smart, they run businesses, but they still felt like you did, like they'd been stupid and would never trust anyone again, and never, ever date again."

Annalise was wondering where Grace was heading with this. True, it made her feel…something, not comfort really, but more a sense of a burden shared, to know others felt the same.

"Anyway," Grace went on, "Brett was great with the first woman, but he really stepped up with the second, told her not to feel that way, not to let him steal that light from her, because that would mean this guy had won."

"He…said that?"

"Yes. And he reminded her there were plenty of good guys out there. Of course then she tried to flirt with him, but—"

"She flirted with Brett?" Okay, that had come out a little sharp.

"He wasn't having any of it, but he was very kind about it. Just said he wasn't on the market, but there were lots of other good guys out there."

*At least he's consistent.* "He told me that, too, that he wasn't…looking."

"Oh." Grace sounded disappointed. "I was hoping it was because of you."

"What?"

"That he wasn't looking because you and he—"

"Don't be silly!" That had come out even more sharply. And she could just picture the expression on her little sister's face. The one she always wore when attacking a puzzle of any kind.

And Annalise was fairly sure she'd just given her a very big clue.

Brett had been about to text the chief the interview results when he remembered she probably didn't have her phone, that Ellie was probably going through it with her deep-reaching, fine-byte comb. He changed direction and headed for the tech whiz's desk instead, Ember at his heels. The dog was used to coming in here, because Brett always brought her inside if he was going to be a while. She was popular among the troops, and especially liked to visit the records section, where the clerks cooed over her and gave her treats from the jar they had hidden in a drawer.

Ellie's domain was one the rest of the department regarded with wary awe. Brett was reasonably competent with tech, but even he treated it—and her—with the respect she'd earned by being able to find things it would take him five times as long to find, or things he never would have found at all.

"I matched the photos of the guy on Annalise's phone," Ellie greeted him without preamble. He liked that, too, that she didn't require a lot of niceties, not when she was hot on a trail. "They're from a stock photo site. The real model does everything from fitness shoots to—surprise, surprise—medical stuff, complete with the stereotypical stethoscope around his neck."

"Watermarked?"

She nodded. "Wouldn't be that hard to mask that, if you had some basic skills. Do you think he'd actually buy the pics to use?"

Brett shrugged. "No idea. You'd think he wouldn't want to leave a trail, but I can't say he didn't. He might think he's clever enough to hide it."

"Don't they all think they are?" Ellie said wryly.

"Point taken," Brett agreed. "Give me the numbers on the images you matched and I'll look into getting a warrant for their records on who's purchased those particular shots."

Ellie nodded and moved on in her usual, rapid-fire manner. "I think I have at least three other cases, maybe four. I'm comparing the texts now and finding definite similarities."

"Where?"

"None here in Grave Gulch," she said, "but all in the county, and within the last year."

"I'll need copies of their reports," he began. "I—"

"Already in the works."

Brett turned quickly, recognizing Melissa's voice from behind him. He nodded to her. "Chief." She smiled back. It was a better smile these days, no doubt thanks to her fiancé.

"Thank you for taking Grace with you," she said.

"She did a good job taking lead on the second interview. Built a rapport with the victim right away."

The smile widened, but only for a moment before she turned serious again. "And they both made a positive ID on the sketch?"

"Positively. No hesitation, it was him."

He gave her what other details they had, although he guessed Grace had probably given her a full report already. And that she listened intently to his told him she valued all input. That mattered to him and was one of the reasons he didn't bail on this Colton-dominated department. That and the fact that if he did, it could be used against the GGPD by the media and the mob, and he wasn't about to throw gas on that fire.

"What's your next step?"

He liked that, too, that she made it clear he was to proceed as he saw fit, not as she ordered. Again he remembered his final interview with her before he'd taken the job, when she'd said, *I try to hire the best, then let them do their best.* That had been a deciding factor, although he hadn't told her that. Mainly because he'd known he wouldn't find out for a while if that was a real, guiding philosophy, or just talk.

"A talk with Dr. Masters," he said.

Somewhat to his surprise, he'd ended up liking the department's consulting forensic psychologist, Dr. Matthew Masters. They didn't use him often, but he'd been very helpful when they had.

"Good idea," the chief agreed. "And he is back from court—I just saw him outside his office."

Although he was only fifty, Dr. Matthew Masters looked like everyone's ideal of the sweet old grandfather. Or maybe Santa Claus, Brett thought as the man opened the office door to his knock, with his silver hair and a tidy little beard, roundish face and a wide, genuine-seeming smile.

"Been expecting you," he said, ushering him inside. "I saw the report on poor Ms. Colton this morning. She trains your pup, doesn't she?" he asked as he bent to pet the dog's head. Brett liked that the man had no problem with Ember's presence; in fact they had once had a discussion about therapy animals, in which the man was a firm believer. "Once you've seen someone so desperate they've attempted suicide respond to the simple presence of a loving dog, you'll never dismiss it again," he'd said.

"Yes," Brett answered, "she does train Ember. She's brilliant with her."

Dr. Masters didn't go to his desk but took a seat in one of the chairs opposite it, and gestured Brett to the other. As he sat, Brett wondered if there was some reason for that, some messaging that he wasn't looking at him as a patient or something like that. Then he wondered why he was wondering that, and if everybody who dealt with a shrink in some form or another had similar thoughts every time.

And if his wandering thoughts were more of his strenuous efforts to stop thinking about Annalise, he didn't admit it even to himself.

## Chapter 16

"How's Annalise doing with this?" Dr. Masters asked.

"Rattled. Uncertain," Brett answered. *And no longer really trusting herself or anyone else.*

"To be expected."

Brett nodded. "But she did great during the incident," he felt compelled to add.

"Clobbered him with a plate cover, I believe the report said."

Brett found himself smiling as he nodded again. "She did. Bought herself enough time to get away."

"Good for her."

"Yes." He only hoped she would eventually get that, how rare it was that she had the presence of mind and the nerve to do anything but freeze in horror, as most people would when confronted with such a situation.

Even as he thought it, Dr. Masters verbalized a similar thought. "That should help her accept, later, when she has more perspective. She'll see she wasn't a helpless victim."

"She—they all feel—like fools." He had to stop doing that. Annalise wasn't the only crime victim here, even if she was the one he thought about most. And that wasn't right.

"Also to be expected. It will take time for them to realize he's at fault, not them." Dr. Masters leaned back in the chair and steepled his fingers. "What's your take on him?"

Brett had an answer ready, since it had been the only thing able to keep his thoughts off paths he should not follow. And he'd spent a long time studying Desiree's sketch, as if it was a pathway into this predator's mind. He'd studied the narrow, rather pointy face, thought about the size and lack of body mass of the man he'd seen running; if he didn't know, Brett would have thought him a kid. And he couldn't help thinking that all played into this, that his size was part of what had made this con artist into what he was.

"I think this is a case where the suspect wouldn't be able to do what he does without the internet and mobile technology, and the ability to fake. His appearance would sink him if he tried to scam anyone in person."

"We're such a shallow society," the doctor said, and Brett couldn't tell if he was being dramatic or serious with the pronouncement. "But he does look a bit…shady."

"Yes," Brett agreed. Personally, he thought the man looked like a ferret, but that wasn't something he was about to say. "You're the expert, not me, so correct me if I've gone wrong. My guess is he resents that people see him that way and has worked that up into a 'the world owes me' mindset. And that he chooses women to victimize because he feels they in particular owe him, because they've likely ignored him or turned him away. He probably doesn't feel guilty at all, because he doesn't think of his victims at all, only himself."

Dr. Masters raised his eyebrows. "Been reading up?"

"A little. I like to know what I'm dealing with." But Brett well knew he didn't have the training and experience the psychologist had. And he'd seen him testify in court, and knew he made no idle arguments and could back them up if questioned. "But I'm not assuming I'm right," he added, out of respect for the man's position and title.

"I think you probably are, for the most part. His approach and method are the classic catfish. Showing up himself is a blip, but I don't know how serious."

"How will being interrupted and almost caught affect him?"

"A very good question I'm afraid I can't answer without further knowledge of him."

"Would the history of his interactions on the dating app help?"

"It would."

"I'll see that you get them." He'd need them himself anyway, because he'd had an idea.

Dr. Masters pondered for a moment. "In a way," he said finally, "Ms. Colton is fortunate."

Brett didn't think the man meant simply that she hadn't been physically hurt. "To have had the nerve to fight back?" he asked.

Dr. Masters smiled. "Yes, that, most definitely. But I meant the fact that this was clearly a catfish with the intent of theft, not solely a social one."

Brett wondered when the law would catch up with tech and make such impersonations and scams prosecutable. Considering the relative speed—or lack thereof—of both, he wasn't optimistic. But in this case, at least, the catfish had violated laws already on the books. He nodded then. "So it's a crime, and she has recourse."

"And you on her side," the man said.

Brett started to speak then stopped himself, certain Dr.

Masters hadn't meant that the way he had first taken it, with a far-too-personal interpretation. "We can pursue it, yes."

"But there's also another aspect. Most people find such an elaborate scam for the purpose of stealing more…understandable than those who do it merely because they can, or like to toy cruelly with other people, or require the attention they believe they aren't getting any other way."

Brett hadn't thought of it in that way, but it made sense. One was simple, a crime he could understand. The other was more twisted, malevolent in a way he understood only logically even as it made his stomach churn and sparked the kind of outrage he rarely felt. In part, he suspected, because he was helpless even as a cop to do anything about it.

"Not a crime," he muttered.

"Yes," Dr. Masters said, his tone echoing some of Brett's own feelings, "but with victims nevertheless."

Victims who would perhaps never be the same. Like Elizabeth Lively and Natasha Tracy. And Annalise.

"Will she—" He caught himself and changed his words. "Will they ever be able to trust again?"

If Dr. Masters caught the break and change, he didn't say so, for which Brett was thankful. "Trust? To some extent, yes. As wholeheartedly or as easily as they once did? Not for a long time, if ever. At the least, they will have a sense of wariness they did not have before." He smiled then. "And perhaps, as painful as the lesson is, that's not a bad thing."

As he and Ember headed back out to the unit he pondered that. If it would help keep her safe, he supposed it was true the lesson might be worth it. Even if it was painful to think of Annalise's normally sunny nature curbed by mistrust, that was a lot better than a couple of alternatives he could think of. There was a lot less evil to deal with here in this small town—even if a big chunk of it had been under their own roof apparently, in the person of Randall Bowe—but that didn't mean it didn't exist.

So in that way, yes, she had been lucky. This fake suitor had been after money, property, not herself. It truly could have been much, much worse. In ways that made his stomach churn far more than the simpler crime did.

In ways he was having more and more trouble denying were personal.


Annalise settled Apple and Jack in the cushy bed beside her desk, at this point in their progress fairly satisfied they would stay there until she was finished. They were quiet and seemingly happy—they'd had a busy day, and she'd been able to work with them a lot between her other clients.

She made her final notation on the training session with Bear the German shepherd. She smiled as she did so, because she had just finished writing up Ember's session, and the differences between the two dogs were quite evident. In large part it was the intrinsic differences in the two breeds, and she spent some time musing about that as she often did, that the shepherds were bred to protect and control, the Labs to retrieve, and how that played into their skills in police work and the military. Bear was an absolute terror to criminals—there was a reason cops were required to give a suspect the chance to surrender before unleashing him—and skilled in tracking, but he didn't have the nose Ember did. Ember was not an apprehension dog, but could find just about anything under conditions most would think impossible.

But Annalise always said the biggest factor was their hearts, and the need and drive to please their pack leader. Their beloved human. That she had no doubts about.

As she went to close the files she saw again the photo of

the black Lab. And as if sparked by the picture the memories of last night flooded her again. She supposed the fact that her thoughts of the catfish, the images of the skinny little man who had stolen not just her grandmother's bracelet but big chunks of her trust and self-esteem, were quickly pushed aside by warmer memories, of Brett Shea's efficient investigating, his quiet understanding, his warm compassion, was a sign of progress.

The memories of his arms around her, and what that had made her feel, were something else altogether.

"Stupid," she said aloud. "That's the word for it, stupid."

"Who you calling stupid?" Sergeant Kenwood's voice from the doorway was full of clearly mock belligerence.

Annalise looked up and smiled. "Not you, ever."

The man smiled, his teasing expression turning to one of understanding. "Don't call yourself that, either," he said. "Those slimy guys are cunning in a way good, honest people never see coming."

She managed a smile, touched that the sometimes gruff veteran had made the effort at comfort.

He turned to go, but then looked back over his shoulder. "Oh, and your ride home just pulled in."

Brett. He was here. Early. Her pulse leaped, and she could only hope nothing of her inner reaction showed on the outside. Judging by the sudden narrowing of Sergeant Kenwood's gaze, she doubted she had that much luck.

## Chapter 17

Focus.

That was his problem, Brett decided as he sat in his unit after turning the engine off. He needed to keep his focus on the case, the crime, the suspect, as he normally did. His ability to exclude distraction had been a large part of his success as a detective, and it was irritating that he was having trouble at the moment doing what usually came easily.

It was beyond irritating that he knew perfectly well the distraction he couldn't seem to exclude on this case had a name, beautiful blue-gray eyes, a mane of silky blond hair and curves that made his fingers curl. It was downright frustrating, and in more ways than one. He hadn't wrestled with the urges of his body this much in years.

*She's a coworker. Something you swore off the day you got the badge.*

Except she wasn't, really. Not in the sense that they were on the job together. She was a few steps back. Which actually worked well sometimes—she had enough knowledge from her work with the department K-9s to understand what he did, but she wasn't directly involved in it. Several of his fellow cops in Lansing had ended up marrying emergency-room nurses or physicians, because they understood the high-stakes, high-tension life that came with their jobs.

So, scratch that reasoning.

He sat there, tapping his fingers on the steering wheel. He glanced at the clock in the dash. Four fifty-four. *Six minutes to get your head together, Shea.*

*She's Ember's trainer. You don't want to mess that up.*

Right. As if she'd ever let anything affect how she felt about the sweet Lab. Not Annalise. Her love for the dog, for all the dogs, both the ones she worked with and the ones she fostered, was heartfelt and pure, and nothing would ever change it. He knew that as surely as he knew his eyes were blue.

And the fact that that acknowledgment of this embedded aspect of her made him wonder if her love for a man, if she ever gave it, would be the same, only tangled him up more.

He let out a disgusted breath. He wasn't having much luck here. He watched the clock roll over to four fifty-eight. If he got out now, he'd hit the office right at five, as promised.

But he'd still be in this quandary.

In desperation he fell back on the only thing he had left. *She's a Colton.*

And yet hadn't every Colton he'd dealt with so far, from the chief down to rookie Grace, been completely accepting of him? Hadn't he found them all competent and then some, each in their own job? Yes, they were under fire right now, and maybe that was part of the reason they seemed to be such a solid unit; they'd had to pull together. Which was more than his own family would have done, or ever had done.

Or was it really only the idea that there were so many of them, and that they were a family—and a family so unlike his own—that had made him feel the outsider? And was that feeling not their problem, but his?

He didn't know anymore.

With a sharp movement he yanked the door handle and got out, willing his body to calm down. On impulse he also let Ember out, thinking the dog would be a good buffer. He could always focus on her, no matter who else was around. She seemed a bit puzzled to be back at the training center, but she trotted along amiably.

*Coward. Hiding behind a dog.*

Brett sighed inwardly, getting with the distinct feeling he was losing it as he walked toward the building.

And toward the woman who was the cause of it all.

She had worried for nothing.

Annalise sighed inwardly as she fastened the seat belt in his car. She'd gotten herself all worked up in expectation of Brett's arrival, her pulse kicking up at the thought of seeing him again, of him taking her home. She'd even been trying to decide if she dared ask him to stay for a while. She'd offer to fix dinner for them, just as a thank-you, of course, for his kindness the night before. Nothing more than that, of course. It wasn't like she would ask him to spend the night. Again.

But her imagination had run riot with that scenario, and what might happen, and she'd ended up in a tangle of emotions ranging from keen anticipation to self-condemnation, because just last night she'd been committed to starting a relationship with another man. And yet had spent a great deal of that night thinking about Brett Shea instead of the man she'd planned to be with. And she didn't like the way that made her feel.

That that man didn't and never had existed didn't change that. All it did was prove that she was a fool. But Brett had never made her feel that way, had in fact gone a long way toward easing that uncomfortable assessment of herself.

At least, the Brett who had been with her last night had. The one who was here now was a different creature altogether. The one who was here now was brisk to the point of brusque, businesslike and utterly impersonal. There was not a trace of the connection she'd felt last night. Not even the connection she usually felt when they worked with Ember. It was as if he'd put a wall up between them.

*Can you blame him?*

It wasn't personal, she tried to tell herself. He was simply being what he was, a professional. He'd helped her through last night, but now that was over. Maybe he did that with every victim he dealt with, helped them.

*Spent the night with them?*

Well, it wasn't like he'd really spent the night with her; he'd merely spent it under her roof. To keep her safe. But why? She doubted he did that with every victim. Was it simply because he knew her? Because she was Ember's trainer?

Or…because she was a Colton?

That thought gave her pause. Had he only gone out of his way because she was related to his boss? Was it that simple? She didn't want to think so, but it was something she couldn't be sure didn't factor in.

God, being a Colton was so darn complicated sometimes.

The silence in the unit as they headed toward her house began to seem like a physical thing. It wore on her, dug at her, until she finally blurted out, "Grace told me how good you were with those other victims."

He glanced at her, his expression unreadable. "She talked to you about the interviews?"

"Not about the case. She never would," she said hastily. She breathed again when his gaze went back to the road ahead. "She just told me how...supportive you were to them. Telling them it wasn't their fault." She bit the inside of her lip but the next words came out anyway. "Like you were with me."

There was a pause, so brief it could have been a search for words or merely a registering the vehicle approaching on the left at the intersection, before he said in that same businesslike tone he'd greeted her with back at the training center, "All in a day's work."

That stung as if it had been a slap. Which told her how far out of line she'd gotten. She was obviously only that: part of a day's work. He was making it clear where she stood, what she was to him.

And what she wasn't.

As they turned into her driveway she reached for the seat belt so she could be ready to get out—and get away—the moment they stopped.

"Hold on," Brett said. Startled, she glanced at him. He wasn't looking at her, but obviously he'd seen or sensed her move. "Just wait a minute."

He'd put down his window and was studying the house. Her pulse kicked up for an entirely different reason than it usually did around him. "Is there something—"

She stopped when he held up a hand. He was listening intently. All she could hear was the occasional slight snap of the engine cooling. Finally he put the window back up and looked at her.

"What?" she asked, unable to hold it back any longer. "Did you see something? Hear something?"

"No." He said it flatly, and his brow was furrowed in a way that didn't fit the denial. In a way that seemed familiar to her.

"Then what?" she asked.

"I don't know. Just…never mind. Let's go."

She gathered up her dogs from where they'd ridden in the back with Ember, gave the Lab a goodbye pat and headed for the house. Her dogs squirmed as if eager to make their usual circuit of the little yard when they came back from anywhere, so she let them loose once they were safely inside the fence.

She and Brett were nearly to the door when it hit her what had seemed familiar to her about his expression. It was the same look she'd seen on Troy's face when he'd been trying to explain the gut feeling he sometimes got on a case to Grace, back when she'd been considering joining the department.

*I can't explain it. It's just a feeling. Sometimes it's that I'm missing something. Or that there's something wrong I can't see. Sometimes it's that I'm going down a wrong path. But it's strongest when I'm on the right track.*

*Something wrong I can't see…*

The words were still ringing in her mind when, after she'd unlocked it, Brett pushed the front door open. They stepped inside.

All seemed quiet, calm. The living room, which faced west, was getting the full force of the summer evening sun. It looked pleasant and peaceful, and she liked the way the sun caught and gleamed through the blue glass bottles she'd arranged on the window ledge.

She breathed more easily. Brett was walking around, checking all the windows. Annalise headed toward the kitchen and dining room, already thinking about what she could fix for dinner that he might like, if he would stay if she asked, if she could even work up the nerve to do it. She'd made extra spaghetti sauce the last time she'd fixed it, and there was a tub of it in the freezer. Or there was the—

She was two steps into the dining and kitchen space when she stopped dead. A shriek rose in her throat, and she couldn't stop it.

Because there, there in nearly the exact spot as before, was a near duplicate of the delivery cart from last night.

He was back.

# Chapter 18

"Don't move." Brett snapped out the order. Annalise didn't seem to hear and took a step toward the cart. He grabbed her and pulled her back. "Don't," he repeated. He felt the shivers going through her and, unable to stop himself he pulled her against him.

She was sucking in quick, shaky breaths, and he hated the sound of it. Hated the thought that she was being terrorized in her own home. He wanted to get her out of here, take her someplace where she would feel safe again. Where she would be able to simply smile again, coo over her lucky dogs, use that amazing connection she had to push Ember to even greater success.

He wanted it more than he wanted to get this guy, and that realization sent up not just a red flag but a warning signal as loud as a klaxon. He never, ever put the personal side ahead of the job, not on an active case. At least, he never had before. And that thought sent up another warning; he had no business even thinking about a personal side here.

Still, he kept one arm around her as he pulled out his phone and called it in, all the while staring at the food cart. The same pristine white tablecloth, but that's where the similarities ended. This time the table held, most noticeably, a large bouquet of white roses in a gold vase. The platters under the covers appeared to be gold, as well. Stepping up the game? Announcing she was a valuable target he wasn't about to give up on?

"Two," he murmured as he finished the call and put the phone away. There were two platters on the table this time. He didn't like the implications of that, which were that somehow the catfish knew he'd stayed here last night, after the first abortive attempt.

He pulled out the key ring that held the fob for the unit and pressed the button combination that would open the back hatch. Ember would be here in seconds. Annalise murmured something against his chest, where her face was pressed against him. It was unbelievable, that in the middle of all this all he could think in that moment was how much he liked holding her like this. And that realization snapped him back to the job at hand.

"Annalise," he said firmly, "Ember has to do a search. I need you to wait in the unit while she—"

"No!" Her head came up sharply, and he heard her quick intake of breath. "I can't. I need to get my dogs. What if he's still outside? I should have thought of that first, before I let them loose in the yard—what if he was still there and he hurt them? I—"

"I'll get them," he promised, hoping she was wrong, because he wouldn't put it past the guy to take the animals out however he could. But how like her that this was her first thought, her main worry.

"But—"

"Annalise, please." As he heard Ember's sharp bark

from the front porch, he went for a temporary stall. "Just stay here—right here, don't move an inch—while I let her in. We have to let her do her job."

As he knew it would, putting the focus on the dog settled her. He went to the front door and let the eager animal in. He walked Ember over to the cart, saw the quiver that went through her as her nose filled with the remembered scent. For Brett, that was as good as a sworn statement that it was the ferret again. Not that he'd had any doubts.

"Find," he ordered.

The dog practically snapped to attention and began to hunt. The animal was so well trained, she went right past the person who had helped make her that keen searcher without a glance; she was working now, and that was all she was focused on.

Brett let her do it, only moving when the steady black Lab moved from the cart to the kitchen. He guessed her goal by the time she'd gone the first three feet: the back door. Clearly the guy had come in that way this time. Vehicle in the alley, and through the back gate no doubt. Which would explain why he hadn't been seen—back door, no dogs home to raise a ruckus. Brett knew that the watch over her house wouldn't have been as intense since Annalise was safely at work, and the guy probably waited for his moment, when whoever had been watching was sent on another call.

He looked back at Annalise, who was standing in place, watching. "You locked it, right?"

"Yes. Of course."

*For all the good it does.* He looked at the door with the window in the upper half. Within easy reach of the doorknob and the lock. If he had his way, that kind of door would never be installed anywhere. "Ember, hold." The dog stopped instantly, although obviously not happy about it. But if what Brett suspected was true, he didn't want her over there yet.

Ember sat, practically vibrating, staring at the back door, clearly wanting to go on. Brett reached into his pocket and pulled out a glove; he didn't want to mess up any prints that might be salvageable. He walked over, his gaze on the floor just inside the door. There was no sign of the broken glass he'd feared having Ember step on. So did they have a lock picker on their hands? That took some skill, and his gut was saying *not this guy*. He relied on his scam to get him inside.

He nudged aside the blind that covered the window. Not a lock picker. He'd been right. A tidy, nearly perfect circle was cut out of the glass at the bottom corner of the window, near the knob. It was just big enough for a hand, and clearly done with a glass cutter.

A chorus of barks and yaps came from outside as Jack and Apple charged up onto the small back porch. He wasn't worried about contamination there; neither the CSI nor Ember would mistake the dogs' trails for their suspect's. But he did want them contained when the troops arrived.

"Annalise, can you come over here and get the dogs, without touching anything else?"

"Of course."

"And try to keep them from running around and messing up any evidence inside."

"I can put them in their crates," she suggested. "We crate train our fosters, for the feeling of safety it gives them."

"Great," he said.

She did it quickly and efficiently, and he guessed she was glad to have them to focus on instead of what she'd come home to. He could hardly blame her for that. He wondered if she realized yet all the implications of the catfish's return.

He opened the door, and almost immediately spotted the glint from the intact circle of glass lying on the ground a foot away. He let Ember out, gave her the command to track. The dog sniffed at the glass, but then followed the exact path he'd expected, straight to the back gate that led out to the alley behind the house. He followed her, careful to take a route to one side of the path she'd followed; he couldn't see any footprints, but he didn't want to take the chance.

When he got there he opened the gate and looked, holding Ember back for a moment. It was empty except for a dirty brown sedan that looked as if it hadn't moved since last summer, parked several houses down. He sent Ember through, and after some intent snuffling around about six feet north of the gate she sat, giving the signal the scent ended here.

So now they knew where he'd likely been parked.

He had to, as always after a fruitless search, convince Ember not finding the quarry was not her fault; the dog seemed to take any unsuccessful search as a personal affront. They'd have to do a door-to-door to see if anyone had seen the vehicle—maybe the same van—or the "delivery."

Or the ferret.

He went back, and found Annalise standing next to the cart. Staring at the array. "I can't tell you how much I hate that he was in my house, again."

"I know," he said quietly.

He heard the sound of at least two vehicles out front. The cavalry had arrived. But he wanted a look before they moved in and took over. He reached out with his gloved hand and lifted the lid over the closest platter. And went still.

On the rather ornate china plate lay a scrawny rat, very dead. Tented over the body was a note card, bearing a word in large block letters.

COP.

Annalise moved. He tried to stop her, but she got her head turned around enough to see. For a moment she just stared, her eyes wide with shock. He tightened his arm around her, hating once more that she was going through this. But then the shocked expression faded and he saw her gaze shift to the second platter.

"Let me look. You don't need to see…whatever's there."

Her chin came up, and she straightened. Pulled back. He let go of her, with a reluctance he didn't want to acknowledge even to himself.

"Yes, I do." She said it with surprising firmness. "This is my life he's screwing with, Brett. He's scared me into near panic twice now. He's not going to do it a third time."

He looked at her, at the determined expression on her face. And couldn't help but smile. "I think the phrase, according to Grace anyway, is *You go, girl.* Not sure a guy can say that though."

"You can," she said quietly. "To me, anyway."

He wasn't sure how to take that, so instead he turned back to the task at hand. He could hear voices outside now, close, so he moved quickly, lifting the second lid.

By comparison, what was on the platter was lovely. An elaborately decorated chocolate heart. But the note was more ominous, not just promise but threat, in the sort of way that made him think of old-time villains cackling.

*Soon enough, my sweet. I'll be coming for you.*

And with that gut-level cop instinct that he didn't need Dr. Masters to confirm, he knew this had just shifted to an entirely new level. He'd wondered how the catfish would react to being found out in the act, to having one of his victims see through him and fight back.

Now he knew.

And Annalise was in danger of more than just smashed expectations.

# Chapter 19

"Grab what you need for a few days. You're coming back to my place."

"What?" Annalise knew she was probably not reacting normally after everything that had happened, but she was not used to feeling totally blank after hearing such a simple statement.

"You can't stay here," Brett said flatly. He wasn't looking at her, instead watching the CSIs work.

"I…don't want to, but…"

"It's after eight. Too late to go hunting down someplace else for you to go. It's the easiest thing to do."

She focused on his first words. She'd never realized before how long a thorough crime-scene investigation really took, especially when there was more evidence. She knew a couple of uniformed officers were going door-to-door talking to her neighbors, on the chance one of them might have been both home and looking into the alley when the guy had been here. It didn't seem likely to her, but she'd overheard enough tales of pure luck in investigations that she didn't discount it entirely.

But the rest of what he'd said hammered at her. Easiest? There was absolutely nothing easy about the thought of…going home with him.

He finally looked at her. His expression was unreadable to her, and his tone a little too neutral for her comfort when he said, "Unless you want to call Grace, or Troy or maybe the chief?"

She shuddered inwardly. They would descend on her, loving but smothering. They'd hover, and worry, and they already had enough to worry about. Especially Melissa.

Besides, she didn't like the way he'd said that. As if he'd forgotten but then suddenly remembered she was a Colton. And it made a difference to him.

"No," she said hastily. "No, I don't. It'll be bad enough when they find out. But the dogs. I—"

"There's plenty of room. Ember will enjoy having them there to play, once she knows she's off duty."

"What about you?" The words were out before she could stop them.

She thought she saw something flicker in his gaze before he turned it back to the investigators again. "I'll be able to focus on what I need to, once you're safely out of here," he said, back to that very neutral tone again.

Well, that was…businesslike enough. Clearly he wasn't feeling any of the internal tumult she was. But then, his house hadn't been broken into. Twice, essentially, once by subterfuge, once by flat-out burglary.

She wasn't sure she'd consciously made the decision, but she found herself in her bedroom dragging out the backpack she used for hikes through the forest. She began gathering necessities.

Necessities. Which for a hike in the woods would be quite different than a night spent at Brett's.

A shiver went through her, and this time it was not of the horrified, my-life-has-been-invaded kind. No, this was entirely different, and if she had to put a name to it, it would be…anticipation. And no amount of telling herself it wasn't like that could completely quash the sensation. And in the end for her clothes she went for her bigger bag and tried not to call herself a fool as she added her favorite perfume. Just in case.

*In case of what? He's overwhelmed by your charms?*

She grimaced at her own foolishness. And that got her through to zipping up the bag and going back to the living room, where he was talking to the last CSI to pack up. He turned to look at her, nodded at the sight of the bag, but said only, "Do you want to take the dog's crates? Are they nervous in a new place?"

She liked—maybe too much—that he'd even thought of that. "It wouldn't hurt," she said. And so she, Apple and Jack, their crates and Ember were all loaded into his K-9 unit. He got in, connected his phone to the in-vehicle system and started the engine.

He didn't speak as he drove, and she decided it would be wisest not to force a conversation. They were at the intersection with Grave Gulch Boulevard when there was the chime of an incoming call. She instinctively glanced at the screen and saw Ellie Bloomberg's name. He tapped a button.

"Ellie?"

"Brett, I just heard. Is Annalise okay?"

"We arrived after the fact. She's with me, and you're on the car system."

"Annalise, I'm so sorry! You've had a horrible couple of days."

"I'm fine. But thank you," Annalise said.

"Brett will get this guy," Ellie promised. "He's the best."

Annalise glanced at the man behind the wheel, just in time to see one corner of his mouth quirk. But all he said was, "Did you have something for me?"

"Oh, yeah. I just wanted to let you know that I did a little hunting in the outlying areas, outside town. And over near the gift shop you were at, I found a burglary report from a veterinarian's office."

"The dart!" Annalise almost yelped it.

"Exactly," Ellie said. "Usually it's drugs, but this time their entire stock of tranquilizer darts was all that was taken."

"I'll need the report," Brett said.

"Already on its way. Take care of Annalise, Brett."

"I intend to," he said, and Annalise couldn't read anything into his tone. *As well you shouldn't.*

It wasn't until the call had ended and they were through downtown that it occurred to her that the tech whiz assumed she and Brett would be physically together for him to take care of her.

She had just decided she was reading too much into Ellie's no doubt casual words—she must have meant the instruction in the "she's one of us" sense that the entire GGPD seemed to have, even for those who, like her, were on the periphery—when they turned away from the lake on a residential street that looked quiet and peaceful, shaded from the summer sun by large trees. The houses were large family-sized, and angled for, she guessed, a glimpse of the water. They went on until the houses got smaller but the lots much bigger, then made a turn onto a short cul-de-sac.

He drove to the end, to the last house on the right. It was set far back from the road, a cottage-style one story with a single garage attached, small but well-kept, painted a medium blue with crisp white trim. He pulled off the road into the long driveway. This time of year there was still plenty of light even well after nine o'clock, and she caught a glimpse of the area behind the house.

"Wow," she said. "Judging by the fence, you weren't kidding—you've got a lot of room."

"The lot is nearly two acres."

"Lots of upkeep."

He glanced at her. "I've surrendered about half of it. Not enough time, and Ember likes romping through the tall grass."

She managed a smile, the first real one since they'd walked back into her worsening nightmare. "I'll bet she does."

They pulled into the garage. It, like the outside of the house, was tidy, with a workbench along one wall, a few tools, including an intimidating-looking chain saw. He opened the hatch to release Ember, who hopped out easily and trotted toward the door into the house. Brett glanced at Annalise, and she shook her head.

"They can stay in the car a few minutes, until I bring the crates in for them."

He merely nodded and closed the hatch again. The two smaller dogs weren't happy but didn't fuss. They truly had come a long way in the weeks she'd had them.

The inner door opened into what appeared to be a combination mud/laundry room. A laundry room he apparently used, because there was a basket with a few items of clothing—including a blue shirt she recognized—on the floor beside the washer.

She followed him into the next room, an open space with a kitchen area along the closest wall, an island with stools and on the end of the counter what looked to have been set up as a charging station for various devices. Next to that on the counter was an odd-looking box with what looked like a fingerprint reader.

Ember walked over to a raised set of bowls near a door that clearly led out to the back—and had a doggie door big enough for her in it, although it appeared currently latched—drank some water, nosed at the dry food, then ambled off into the large living area beyond. Annalise could see there was a hallway on the far side she supposed led to whatever bedrooms there were. Including his. In the back, with all that open space behind it. Quiet. Private. Very private.

Her mind skittered away from the thought of his bedroom and she focused on the room they were in. She didn't know what she'd expected. Denied to herself that she'd spent as much time as she had wondering what his home would look like. Trying to imagine what would suit a man like Brett Shea.

What suited him apparently were cool colors, mostly the blue and green of the lake and trees, a sectional couch that looked infinitely rearrangable, with a side table on the far end that held another of those odd boxes, and a stack of books. Actual books. That seemed significant somehow. And they apparently weren't for show, because behind the table was a torchère-style lamp with a reading light attached.

There was a flat-screen TV on the wall opposite the couch, but while big enough it wasn't huge. In front of the end table and against the wall was a dog bed, adorned with some toys and a half-finished chew that Ember picked up before she plopped on the bed and went to work on it. That made her smile; Ember was obviously not relegated to a kennel or crate when at home. Not that she would have expected that. No, Brett loved his furry partner.

*Ember's the only girl in my life.*

"Welcome to Chez Shea," he rhymed, tossing his keys down next to the charging station in what was obviously a familiar habit.

She laughed. Actually laughed. Which after tonight on top of last night was no small miracle. And when she did, Brett smiled back.

"Now that was a nice sound," he said.

"It felt good," she admitted. "Thank you."

"For a silly rhyme?"

"For bothering."

He shrugged. "Just an old joke."

She wondered how many times he'd used it. And on who. *Ember's the only girl in my life.* The words ran through her mind again.

She doubted that meant he never…indulged. And a guy who looked like him would surely have no trouble finding a casual hookup when he wanted one. Had there been a parade of women through this place? Somehow she doubted that, but at the moment she had so little faith in her own judgment she didn't trust her assessments on anything with fewer than four legs.

*Especially that damned catfish.*

# *Chapter 20*

Once they were all settled in, Brett found himself wondering why he'd thought this a good idea. He didn't mind the two dog crates taking up a chunk of the kitchen, didn't mind their nonstop racing around, and he even enjoyed watching what they were doing now, Ember playing hostess as the two smaller dogs explored the expansive space out back.

No, he didn't mind the dogs at all. It was Annalise who was getting under his skin. Not because of anything she was doing, because she was exquisitely polite, the perfect guest, looking for things to do and arrange so that she and the dogs had as little impact on his home as possible, clearing everything she did with him first.

But then, the impact on his home wasn't the issue. It was her impact on him.

He'd reacted from the gut, wanting her in a safe place where he could protect her if necessary. He'd thought they'd come here, he would settle in to work while she did…something. Anything. And she was trying to fit into that image, even without knowing it.

No, he was the problem. He was the one who stood stock still watching her, trying to ignore how…right it felt to have her in his home. He'd never brought a woman here. In fact, except for an unexpected, one-night encounter with a blatantly sexy brunette who was just passing through, he'd pretty much ignored that aspect of his life since he'd gotten to Grave Gulch.

That had to be it. It had just been too long. This constant ache was just pent-up need, that was all. And that was not something he could or would slake with Annalise Colton, even if she was willing. But she wouldn't be, not for what he needed. Because she was looking for more.

Because even after the betrayal of this stinking catfish, she still believed in love.

*You shouldn't give up on love altogether.*

*You have to believe in love before you can give up on it.*

*But you have to believe in it, or at least that it exists. Otherwise life is pointless.*

The remembered exchange echoed in his mind, and it was warning enough for him to tamp down his response to her. A little, anyway.

"They're having such fun," she exclaimed suddenly, snapping him out of this frantic reverie. "They've never been able to run free like this. They pulled them out of a hoarding situation where they were never outside a cage." She sighed. "It's so wonderful to see them like this."

He dared to glance at her, now that he had himself under control. Sort of. She was watching the three animals bounding through Ember's beloved tall grass.

"Just don't let them out on their own. Once they figure it out we'll have to keep the doggie door latched if we or

Ember aren't with them. There's at least one coyote in the neighborhood, and they're just small enough to be tempting." Her eyes widened, and he hastened to reassure her. "With Ember they'll be fine. She and that wild one have reached a respectful accord."

At his words her expression changed, and she smiled. "I love the way you put that."

He couldn't say why her words pleased him so much, but they did.

It wasn't until they called the dogs back—with Ember carefully making sure her new companions were coming, too—that a slight growl from his belly reminded him he'd usually have had dinner by now. And he hadn't even thought about feeding her. Them. He usually went for something simple like grilling a steak, or frozen meals, or takeout, but that was when it was only him.

"Let me get her fed," he said, "and then we can figure out dinner for us."

"I'm not really hungry," she said.

"Not surprising. But you need the fuel, especially now." He tried a slight smile. "And so do I, frankly."

She let out an audible breath. "Of course."

"Afraid I'm not really prepared. We can scrounge or order in."

She grimaced. "As long as it doesn't come on a fancy cart."

He couldn't help it; he chuckled. She gave him a slightly startled look and then, to his surprise, she was laughing. Again. And again it was one of the most wonderful sounds he'd ever heard.

"How about in a box? Paola's delivers. Or if you'd prefer to avoid delivery people altogether, we can go get it." He badly wanted to get to work on that idea he'd had earlier, but right now food—whether she wanted it or not—

was paramount. Besides, he could work and eat pizza at the same time.

"I love their Hawaiian pizza, sacrilegious though it may be to some," she said, still smiling.

He gave a very exaggerated sigh. "I suppose, under the circumstances, I can allow that. We can do it half and half."

She laughed yet again, and he let the sound of it wash over him and allowed himself a little satisfaction that he'd made it happen. "I'll be okay. With delivery, I mean. As long as you go to the door."

"I will." He gave a mock eye roll. "And the delivery kid knows me, a bit too well."

Another sweet laugh, this time with a grin that had him thinking he'd even eat her silly Hawaiian pizza to keep it on her face.

They were waiting on the delivery when a text notification sounded on his phone. A very particular one, that had him going for it quickly.

Annalise? the chief asked. She must have gotten her phone back already. Ellie would move fast, not only because the text she'd gotten when he'd been in her office was from Bowe, but because it was the chief. Or maybe she just got a new message.

Safe. With me for the moment, he sent back.

For the night?

Well, this had sure turned into a minefield in a freaking hurry. He considered his words as he'd once considered his next step in one of those minefields. And ended up answering without really answering.

She needed to be out of there.

Yes. Thank you for seeing to her. Status report in the morning, please. **That, he noted, was not a request.**

Affirmative. I have an idea.

Share?

I want to set up a profile on that dating app. See if I can lure him.

Good idea. Annalise can help, since she'll know what makes him bite.

I can give her access?

Fine. Ellie's already been compiling info from the other profiles he interacted with, for commonalities, to see if we can head off other victims.

That info might help. I'll contact her.

Hang on... **He waited a moment, then read,** She'll be sending it to you.

And again he noted the chief didn't hold herself above such basic tasks. Not if it would help get the job done. He sent back a response.

Thx.

Give Annalise my love.

Brett tried to ignore the ideas and images that routine phrase brought on. It was harder to ignore the rush of heat that flooded him. Heat he couldn't write off simply to it being an August evening.

They both signed off—thankfully—and Brett put down the phone. He tried to think of words again, wondered why it was so darned hard with Annalise, and finally just said "Your cousin sends her love."

"My cousin the chief?"

He nodded. "Her main reason for texting was she wanted to know how you were." She was staring at him now, and oddly, her expression seemed amused. "What?" he finally asked.

"Your notification tone for her is *'Hail to the Chief'*?"

"I...yes." He shrugged, and knew his expression was a little sheepish. Hers was definitely amused. "What can I say—I like a little warning."

"Does she know this?"

"By now? Probably. I'm sure it's gone off in front of one Colton or another at some point."

The amusement faded. "So you assume that a Colton told her? Which one do you think it was who ratted you out? Troy? Desiree? Grace? Maybe Jillian, she's got nothing else on her mind right now."

Brett felt a jab of remorse. When she put it like that, named the names, he realized he wouldn't really suspect any of them of doing such a small thing. Troy would never betray him like that, Desiree would just find it funny, Grace was too mindful of her rookie status and he'd never spent much time around Jillian.

"Sorry," he muttered. He ran a hand over his face, feeling a little weary. The stubble on his jaw didn't help, but shaving had fallen by the wayside a bit lately. As had haircuts—he shoved back an errant strand that was tickling his forehead. "I don't..." He stopped, but the thought that he owed her at least an explanation prodded him. "My family's not like yours. Connected. Protective."

Her brow furrowed in that thoughtful way. "To me, that's what family is."

She sounded so puzzled it made him say something he rarely talked about. "My parents kicked my sister and me out when we were eighteen, saying their job was done and it was up to us now."

Her eyes widened then, in something that looked a bit like horror. "Just…kicked you out?"

He nodded. "Her first, then me. She's six years older, so we lost contact after she left."

"Desiree's seven years older than me, and we'd never…"

"Like I said, connected."

She was gaping at him now. "No wonder you don't get us. We're totally outside your life experience."

He grimaced. "A rather shrink-y way to put it, but yes."

"I'm sorry. I can't imagine growing up that way. We've had our problems and we don't all always get along, but when the chips are down…"

"The Coltons pull together," he finished for her.

"Yes." The look she gave him then was very different, and he couldn't put a name to it. "And that's why you always assume we'll pull together, even if it's against you?"

*Sad.* That was the word for her expression. She was sad, sorry that he felt that way. And something tickled at the edge of his mind, something important, but at the moment, with her looking right at him, he couldn't put his finger on it.

"That doesn't matter, not right now," he said briskly. "What does is catching this guy. So I need to get to work."

She blinked. "A little late, isn't it?"

"In more ways than one," he muttered. Because he

wanted this guy, wanted him bad. And he told himself firmly he would feel just as strongly even if Annalise hadn't been one of the victims.

He even almost believed it.

# Chapter 21

Annalise looked around the room Brett clearly used mostly as an office. He'd said the house had only the two bedrooms, that he seriously considered using the master as his office because it was bigger, and he only slept in the other.

*Only slept?* She firmly directed her mind out of the gutter it leaped into at that, and said merely, "What was the deciding factor?"

He gave her a half shrug. "There wasn't really enough room for Ember to sprawl out in here."

Annalise's heart melted a little. He said it as if it were a given decision, and anyone would make it that way. When in truth she knew too many who wouldn't even consider that.

"Do you mind if I stay? I'll be quiet, promise."

He looked at her for a moment, and she wondered if he was trying to think of a tactful way to say no. But in the end he just shrugged and said, "Make yourself at home."

She knew it was just a saying, but it still sent her pulse racing a little.

He sat down at the L-shaped desk in the corner. It was clearly well used, and likely often, judging by the size of the monitor hooked up to the laptop, the array of notes on the desk and pinned to a corkboard on the wall and notebooks on the shelves above. Ember had followed them in, and promptly hopped up on the small sofa on the opposite wall. Her two furry ones were sound asleep in their open crates, where they'd gone to den up happily, exhausted after their explorations outside. She really needed to look into a place with land like this.

She sat down next to Ember, who shifted a bit to look at her, then plopped her chin on Annalise's leg. That made her smile, and she began to stroke the dog's head and soft, silken ears.

It felt cozy here in this smaller room, as he sat reading an email and she snuggled with the sweet, willing Lab. It felt comfortable.

It felt right.

And she wasn't having much luck keeping thoughts like that out of her head.

She saw him nodding to himself as he read. He picked up a pen and made some handwritten notes as he went. And then tapped the end of the pen on the notepad a few times before swiveling halfway around in the office chair.

"You want to help?" he asked.

"Of course," she said, not really caring what he meant, specifically. "With what?"

"I need to set up a profile on that dating app."

She blinked. "You do?"

"You can walk me through it, since you've done it before."

"I…of course," she repeated, feeling a little rattled. "But why?"

"Ellie put together a list of commonalities across all the profiles our catfish interacted with. I'm going to set one up with as many of them as I think I can without him getting suspicious."

She stared at him. "You're going to use the app to… lure him?"

He nodded. "The chief recommended I do it. I want to get that started while we're waiting for the info on who bought the photos from the stock site. Although I doubt he used his real name there, either."

She fought down the hideous embarrassment she felt every time she thought about mooning over those pictures. "Do you think he actually did buy them, and not just lift them from their website?"

"Ellie does. She said she couldn't see any trace of the watermark being removed or fudged from the profile images."

The embarrassment won out when she belatedly realized just how many people were going to know about her folly by the time this was over.

"Annalise?" he asked with a slight frown, and she realized she'd been sitting there silently for a bit too long.

"Sorry," she said sourly. "Just realizing how far my humiliation has and will spread."

He tossed down the pen. Turned around the rest of the way on the chair, leaned forward to rest his elbows on his knees, so he was at eye level with her. "You're neither the first, nor will you be the last, to get fooled. And no one thinks any the less of you because of it."

"I wish I could believe that."

His gaze shifted to the floor for a moment, and she heard him let out a breath. Then he looked back at her face.

"Some of us don't even have the excuse of being fooled by a perfectly manufactured online profile. Some of us get fooled with the real person right there in front of us."

Her breath stopped in her throat. What he'd said that first night rang in her head. *I believed a woman who said she loved me once. Worst mistake of my life.*

She stared at the steady, dedicated man before her. She knew what it felt like to care—and worry—about someone in law enforcement. She'd often wondered how anyone who fell in love with a cop stood it. But that wondering had suddenly become much more personal. And specific.

And finally she said the only truth she could think of at the moment. "She was the fool, not you."

He drew back slightly. But he didn't look away. In fact, he was looking at her so intently she felt as if she guessed a suspect must feel under that piercing, utterly focused gaze.

Then, so low she was fairly sure it wasn't aimed at her, he muttered "Not going there," and straightened up again.

Annalise had only a moment to wonder if that had meant he wanted to go "there" but wouldn't. Or if he simply was trying to keep this professional because that's what he was, a professional.

Or if he simply didn't want to go there with her.

Okay, so bringing her into his home was one of his stupider moves. It was done, and he couldn't change it now. Brett gave himself an inward shake.

*Focus. It's what you're good at, right? What you're known for?*

The image of a long-ago day with his very first training officer shot through his mind. A day when he'd walked right past a crucial bit of evidence in pursuit of another bit of evidence. That evening's debriefing had been a rough one.

*You've got great focus, Shea. But you're going to have to learn that sometimes focus becomes tunnel vision.*

Well, he could use a little tunnel vision just now. Then maybe he could concentrate on this case instead of...the victim. *This* victim.

*She was the fool, not you.*

She'd said it so softly, looking right at him, and it had been a tremendous effort not to read more into it than was there. She'd just meant what he'd meant, that it hadn't been his fault. She was just being kind, supportive. Trying to pay him back a little, he supposed.

This was getting...muddy. He usually had no trouble thinking big picture, and he would usually be determined to take this guy down for the sake of all of the victims. But this time his usually disciplined mind seemed to have stubbornly decided this one, this woman, was who he was doing it for. As if he had some personal stake in this. As if he wanted to do it just for her, because...because...

Because what? Because she was, in a way, a colleague? Because she was so good with Ember? Because she was in many ways an innocent, who'd been taken advantage of? Because she'd looked at him with tears in those big eyes? Because he wanted to see her smile again, see those dimples flash?

Or was it because—he might as well admit it—he had the hots for her? But then, what man wouldn't? What man could look into those eyes and not want to jump?

He swore silently. He sounded like some hormonal teenager with a crush. He hadn't spent so much time in useless mental meanderings since high school.

"Let's get this set up," he said, not quite gruffly, as he turned back to the computer. "Just the basics now. I want to see what's involved in setting up a profile. Ellie's working on some details and photos, then I can actually start setting it up."

They began, and more than once when an app question popped up that seemed very personal and private to him, he glanced at her and asked, "People really answer all these…questions? Share all this, with people they've never even met?" At her expression he added hastily, "I'm not accusing, just asking."

Still, it was a moment before she answered. "You don't have to answer everything, to set up your profile. But I answered most of it. It seemed the best way to find a good match." She sighed audibly, and he knew she was about to say something self-condemning again, so he held up a hand.

"Don't. Try and make this…clinical. Not personal." *Good advice, Shea. Take it yourself.*

"Right."

"Walk me through the ones you did answer." Something had just occurred to him. "I want to compare it to the other profiles he interacted with."

"Why?"

"In case that's a factor in his choices."

"Oh." He knew she was thinking, not just reacting now. "You mean…if he went for those who answered most or all?" Her mouth quirked wryly. "The oversharers, so to speak?"

He nodded. "They might seem, to him anyway, more…" He stopped himself, but she supplied the exact word he'd almost used.

"Desperate?" Her tone was dry, but better than the pained, hurt tone that stabbed at him.

"Yes," he agreed. Then, more thinking out loud than anything, added, "He's not used to your kind of plain honesty and openness. He isn't himself, so he doesn't look for it or expect it in others."

Her expression changed again. He'd always been, by necessity, fairly decent at reading people. He'd had to be, growing up with his parents. But since then it had always been business, part of the job. Looking for reactions, for tells, that would lead him down the right path in an investigation. This was different. Everything with this case—with her—was different.

When she spoke, there was a change in her voice, as well. "Was that a veiled compliment, Detective Shea? Or was it a warning, not to be that way?"

He couldn't hold her gaze, and that was a rarity. He turned back to the form on the screen and said merely, "Yes." Even as he thought how much he would hate to see her close herself off, and no longer be the honest and sweetly open woman he'd known.

And that might be the biggest reason to take this scum down. He had no right to do that. Not to anyone.

Especially not to Annalise.

# Chapter 22

"Now what?" Annalise asked when—between bites of the pizza that had arrived, neatly divided between her pineapple-adorned Hawaiian and his more traditional sausage and cheese—he'd finally seen all the queries on the profile questionnaire.

"We already know he doesn't go for just one physical type. Because that's not what he's after. He's looking for a certain…mental state."

"Desperation again?" she asked, making sure she sounded more sour than hurt.

"More like…hopeful. I think—and this is just gut instinct on my part—he likes destroying that."

Something in his expression when he said it made Annalise feel, unexpectedly, almost sorry for this twisted human being when Brett caught up with him. And Brett would.

She looked at the array of information they'd compiled.

"So we answer the ones everybody he interacted with answered?" They'd found nine questions every victim or potential victim had answered. Including her.

Brett nodded. "In a similar way. Then we'll go through and see if we can find anything in the other answers each one gave that might have steered him to them. With an eye out for any strong answers."

"Strong?"

"Like not just *I don't like olives* but *I hate them*. Not just *I prefer classical music* but *I hate everything else*."

Her brow furrowed. "But…wouldn't that maybe scare him off? Strong feelings like that?"

He gave her an approving smile. "Exactly. That's why I want to see if those correlate with profiles he interacted with but didn't pursue."

Feeling absurdly pleased at his words and tone, she went back to going through the profiles. But the feeling faded as the similarities she saw gradually got through to her.

They all loved animals.

They all liked spending time at the lake.

They all worked hard, hoping for a better future.

They all hoped for a lasting relationship.

Hope. Exactly what Brett had said. He liked to destroy hope.

She didn't know how long they'd been working on it when she heard Brett say, very quietly.

"I've got the gist of it now. Take a break."

"But you want to get this done fast, right?"

"Yes, but once it's done, it's going to take time for him to bite, if he's going to. He's going to be warier now. There'll be enough for you to do if he does bite."

She wrested her mind out of the rut it had slipped into, going through the profiles. "There will?"

"I'm reasonably sure I suck at sounding like a woman,

even on an app." To her shock, she laughed, at both his words and his wry smile.

"I would imagine so," she said.

"So that's when I'll need help. Why don't you get some rest?"

*While you keep working, because that's the kind of guy you are?*

She smothered a sigh. "I'm not tired," she said. "Just…"

"Just what?"

She gestured at the profiles they'd been poring over, in essence taking an answer here and an answer there to build an image they hoped the catfish wouldn't be able to resist, even after his narrow escape.

"They're all so…so…familiar." She couldn't seem to help the forlorn note that crept into her voice. "They sound like me."

It was a moment before he said softly, "You mean, like kind, giving, caring people you'd be lucky to have in your life? Yeah, they do."

She stared at him. Probably gaping again. And for a moment that seemed to spin out forever, yet at the same time seemed far too short, he held her gaze. And when he turned back to his laptop, she felt stunningly bereft.

*Kind, giving, caring… He meant it in a friend way. Not in an attractive, sexy, I'm-going-to-die-if-I-don't-kiss-this-person kind of way.*

Not the way she felt about him.

The truth hit her with a thud she felt must have been audible. But he didn't react, so it must have been just in her mind.

*And that's where it needs to stay. Haven't you made a big enough fool out of yourself?*

"I'm going to go check on the kids," she said, giving Ember a final pat and getting to her feet.

Only when his head came around sharply did she realize that her usual, affectionate term for her two fosters could be taken in a very different way under different circumstances. And she couldn't get out of that suddenly far too small room fast enough.

*Kids. Talking about kids in front of the guy you just finally admitted to yourself you're totally hot for. Could you be more stupid?*

She answered her own internal question with a stern reminder of just how stupid she could be. Stupid enough to fall for a guy who didn't even exist, to think he was finally *the* one, just a couple of days ago.

And now she'd switched to poor Brett, who not only was in essence a coworker, but who didn't trust her because of her name.

*That's carrying rebounding a bit far, isn't it?*

That thought seemed to steady her. She saw Jack and Apple were restless, signaling a trip outside was required. She was about to let them out into the spacious backyard when she remembered the coyote. So told them to sit and stay—they'd progressed to where they were good for a couple of minutes—and headed back to the office.

"The dogs need to go out," she said without preamble. "Will the coyote be around?"

Brett, intent on something on screen now, barely glanced at her. "Take Ember," he said. The Lab's head came up. "Go," he told her. "Watchdog."

Without hesitation the dog scrambled off the couch and trotted over to Annalise. "Thank you," she said, and left it for Brett to decide if that was aimed at him or the dog.

Ember clearly understood and took her duty seriously, just as Annalise would have expected. She ushered the two smaller dogs as if she'd been born to herd instead of retrieve, and as Annalise watched, Ember made sure neither of them strayed too far from the other. It would be a foolish coyote to take her on when she was in guardian mode.

Motion-sensing floodlights had come on the moment the dogs had left the small back deck, illuminating a large portion of the space. When the canine trio started to near the demarcation between light and night—she'd been surprised to see by the clock on the microwave that it was nearly eleven—she tensed a little, but as if Ember understood this was the limit in this mode, she nudged them back. She truly was a remarkable dog.

But then, her handler—and clearly her chosen master—was a remarkable guy.

When they got back inside and the dogs were once more settled, she followed Ember back to the office, where Brett was still focused on the screen before him. For a moment she thought he wasn't even aware, until he spoke without looking around.

"Go okay?"

"Fine. Yes. She was the perfect shepherd." Brett's head turned then. "In the literal sense, not the breed sense," she added hastily.

"Don't tell me—tell her," he said, nodding at Ember. "She's the one you insulted."

"I didn't mean—" She stopped when she saw the corner of his mouth twitch. "Cute," she said wryly.

There was the briefest hesitation, just long enough to register, before he said, "Thanks." And turned back to his work before she could even react.

She'd meant, of course, his joke. But he'd reacted as if she'd meant it as a personal compliment. As if she'd been saying he was cute. Which he was, of course. Along with a host of other things. None of which she was about to say.

In fact, it would probably be best right now to say nothing at all. That way she couldn't get in trouble. Any more trouble, anyway.

She resumed her seat on the couch, watching as he wrote what appeared to be an email. Ember hopped up beside her and settled in. It was a long email, and several minutes passed before he finally sent it. Then he stood up out of the chair and stretched.

Annalise yanked her gaze away when she realized how avidly she was watching the way he moved, the way his shoulders flexed and his back arched as he raised his arms over his head, fingers interlaced as he stretched. The man was really put together, no getting around it. But she focused on petting Ember, lest he catch her gaping at him yet again.

"You're spoiling her," he said when he relaxed and turned to face her.

"A little spoiling won't hurt her," she said, without looking up at him. "Besides, it's me, not the boss."

"You're her boss, too."

"Not like you are." There was no missing that after a few minutes of observing them together. She did look at him then. "She'd die to protect you, you know."

"I know. That's why it's part of my job to be sure she's never put in that position."

She wasn't sure why that answer made her tear up, but she couldn't deny the moisture gathering in her eyes. Before he could see—she hoped—she grasped at something else to say. "Was that email about the case?"

He nodded. "To Ellie. She's going to set our fictitious woman up as a teacher. She'll contact somebody at the school district to plant records and photos. Then she's going to do a search for an empty house and get with the county to dummy up records on it in our teacher's name."

"That's a lot of work."

"Knowing Ellie, she'll have it done by lunch tomorrow. Which is good, because I want it in place for the weekend."

"You think he'll bite that soon?"

"No. I'm guessing it'll take a while. But I want the bait in place ASAP."

She nodded; that made sense. At this point she welcomed doing anything, as long as it was something. That it made sense was gravy.

"It's late—you need to get some rest after all you've been through."

She knew she was tired. She could feel a crash hovering. More making sense, she thought rather inanely.

But then he knocked all sense out of her.

"My bed will be better for you."

*Yes. Oh, yes, it would.* Her mind practically shouted the words. But all she managed to say out loud was a faint, "What?"

"Come on. We'll move your stuff in there."

"I…" She couldn't say another word because he'd stolen her breath away. The images racing through her mind were tempting, vivid and impossibly hot. From visualizing him naked to imagining what it would feel like to have his hands on her, everywhere, and to be able to touch him in turn, they swamped her. And suddenly tired was the last thing she was feeling.

Belatedly he seemed to realize where her mind had gone. For a moment an answering heat seemed to flare in those blue eyes, but she knew she had to be mistaken, because gently—too gently, as if he was trying not to embarrass her for her silly thoughts—he said, "I'll crash on the couch. I've still got some things to do, but you need to get some sleep."

Her suddenly busy mind wanted to read something into even those innocent words.

Something like, if he went with her, they wouldn't be sleeping.

# Chapter 23

Brett realized he'd been staring at the computer screen without really seeing anything, for…well, for way too long. But then, he hadn't been running on all cylinders since that moment he'd seen that flash of searing, tempting heat in Annalise's eyes when he'd told her to use his bed. As if she'd thought he'd meant to join her. As if he'd meant for her to use him, too.

*Use him.*

And the instant those words formed in his mind he almost lost it, thinking of all the ways he'd want that to happen. Thinking of Annalise touching him, stroking him, kissing him…riding him. He tossed down the pen he'd been tapping against the desk, shook his head in silent disgust.

He spent a few minutes in denial. Telling himself that this wasn't a sudden case of unexpected lust for someone he knew, worked with, had known for months. It was simply his usual feeling of concern for a victim, and it had somehow gotten distorted by the fact that he knew her, worked with her. And that Ember liked her, trusted her. He had a lot of faith in the dog's judgment, and maybe that was coloring his feelings.

It had nothing to do with his suddenly awakened libido. It had just been too long since he'd indulged. It was only natural that being in close quarters with a beautiful woman would cause...something.

But this? This overwhelming sense of longing, wanting, need? This aching for something he'd never had, had never quite believed in?

*You shouldn't give up on love altogether...you have to believe in it, or at least that it exists. Otherwise life is pointless.*

His life wasn't pointless. Far from it. He had a calling, something he was good at, something worthwhile. Something that kept the roof from falling in on the innocent, or found them justice when it did. He'd always been proud of his work and had convinced himself—or so he'd thought—that that was enough, all he needed from life. It was more than a lot of people got, after all. So why was he thinking like this? Why did he have to keep fighting his mind heading down pathways he didn't want—didn't dare—take?

Maybe it was simpler. Maybe it was the whole family thing. He'd never known the kind of closeness the Coltons had, where even if you were on the outs on the inside, if a threat came from outside, they all stood together. Maybe he was just...envious. He could admit that much.

Of course, that didn't explain why he was sitting here, overheating at the thought of Annalise in his bed.

*I should have told her to lock the damned door.*

No, an invitation from her would shatter every defense he had, and that was a position he was not used to being in.

It was a good thing that invitation would never come.

He rubbed at eyes that had had about enough of staring at a computer screen. He'd set up everything he could think of to lure this jerk in. It had been a fine line to walk, getting enough of his temptations in, but not so many he got suspicious. He'd carefully constructed a persona, a rather quiet, shy schoolteacher who found using the dating app awkward, but was somewhat new to the area and didn't have a lot of friends yet. That had been Annalise's idea, and he thought it a good one.

Especially after he'd tried messing with a Colton.

*Something you might do well to remember yourself, Shea.*

He'd had the idea to add another kind of lure and sent off another email to Ellie asking if she could find a photo of their "bait" wearing an expensive-looking piece of jewelry. Not as the focus of the shot, like an advertisement, but just visible—he was certain the slimeball wouldn't miss something like that. And as he thought again of Annalise's precious bracelet, from her grandmother, the determination to get it back for her rose in him again.

Once that email was gone, he leaned back in the chair he'd been sitting in for far too long. He could do no more until he got the details from Ellie, that she had the cover employment records and location setup. Then they would take it live, and wait. Not that he would stop hunting, this was just a baited hook, a lure his quarry might or might not take. It didn't mean he'd stop looking in other ways. No, he wanted this guy, wanted to toss him in a cell personally, and he'd do whatever that took.

He went quietly down the hall, resolutely not looking at the closed door to his bedroom. He let Ember out, after checking on Apple and Jack, who seemed content in their little dens. Why they hadn't demanded to be snuggled up in bed with Annalise he didn't know.

*Just because that's where you'd rather be…*

He swore under his breath at himself. Gave himself a severe self-lecture ending with a rather fierce order to his unruly mind to knock it off.

Ember gave him a puzzled look when he hit the couch, grabbing one of the throw pillows and shoving it under his head.

"We're here for now," he told the dog. "Settle."

With a low, quiet whuff that sounded like the canine equivalent of *If you say so*, she went over to her bed, circled once and plopped.

It was going to be a long night.

Annalise drew in yet another deep, savoring breath. How could something be so unsettling and comforting at the same time? Yet here she was, wearing her comfortable shorts and T-shirt as pajamas—she wouldn't have dared bring the sexy nightgown she'd bought on a stupid whim, with visions of a certain nonexistent doctor in her mind— catching the faint lingering piney scent on the pillow that told her this was the one he used, and trying not to think about what it would be like if he'd joined her.

*Not like you're sleeping, anyway.*

She smothered a sigh and rolled over onto her other side. There was more than enough room, given it was a king-size bed. Something he probably needed, given his height. And thinking about that, and that while tall and lean he was also as well-muscled as any good hunting dog she'd ever seen, made her thoughts about him joining her linger, and when she finally slid into sleep it was restless. Not simply because she was in a strange place, but because her revved-up brain kept spinning out heated dreams in which Brett actually had joined her. Dreams of them sharing his bed, and each other, in all the ways two people could share.

When she opened her eyes, gritty and resistant, the room was faintly lighter, telling her the early summertime dawn was approaching. Somewhere between five-thirty and six o'clock, she guessed, not wanting to reach for her phone to confirm the time. Too early to get up and start making noise—Brett hadn't left his office until well after midnight. She'd still been wide awake, wrestling with tangled emotions, when she'd at last heard him walking quietly down the hall.

She tried to go back to sleep, but she'd gotten just enough, and had made the mistake of letting her brain click on. Her thoughts were already humming, and the possibility of more sleep retreated quickly. A night of racy dreams, followed by awakening to the reality of her life at the moment, was a dichotomy that shattered any lingering sleepiness.

She didn't know how long she had been lying there contemplating her pitiful situation when she heard the sound of running water, and realized he was up. And the sound triggered a sudden need for the bathroom, so she quickly decided she should do it while she knew he was already awake. She sat up, rubbed at eyes that would like more rest if only the mind would cooperate, then swung her legs over the side of the bed. She yawned as she stood up. Glimpsed herself in the dresser mirror and realized her body would betray her in an instant; her nipples were still rigidly tight from her dreams, and poked at the cloth of the T-shirt.

Feeling her cheeks heat, she grabbed at the blouse she'd been wearing yesterday and threw it on over the too-thin T-shirt. Then she cautiously opened the door and, hearing nothing for a moment and thinking he must be done, she tiptoed down the hall toward the bathroom door.

The bathroom door that opened just as she got there. And suddenly she was face to chest with Brett. Face to bare, broad, delightfully sculpted chest. And abs. And navel, with the slight trail of hair leading downward. And jeans that were only half-zipped and riding low, leaving far too much naked to her hungry eyes.

His voice was low, rough, and sexy as hell as he rumbled, "See anything you like?"

*Yes. Oh, yes...*

She felt her hand twitch and fought the urge to reach up and touch him, run her fingers over that smooth skin. When she found herself wondering if his nipples were sensitive she had to curl her fingers so that her nails dug into her palm to stop herself from finding out.

She tried for some calm, some cool, some semblance of not being stupid. "I've always thought you were...nicely put together."

His mouth quirked. "I seem to remember you saying that about a dog once."

"Probably," she admitted. "I admire beauty, wherever it is."

He snorted. "Beauty? Hardly. I'm just a hardheaded Irishman."

He wasn't kidding, Annalise realized. He didn't know how beautiful he was. To her, anyway. "Luckily," she said quietly, "you don't get to decide what I think is beautiful."

He looked disconcerted then, and she lost her battle with the need to touch. She lifted a hand, extended just her index finger where it was directly in her line of sight and realized with a sharp little prod of need that she didn't want to just touch, she wanted to see her hands on him. She'd never felt anything like that before, and it made it suddenly hard to breathe. And when she did touch, the feel of him, of solid, powerful muscle, of hot, sleek skin, breathing became impossible.

Only the fact that his abs visibly tightened at her touch, as if he were feeling the same way, kept her from pulling back in embarrassed shock. Who was this woman she became with him?

And then Brett's fingers were around her wrist, gently but firmly. "You need to stop." Heat flooded her cheeks. Humiliation, a too familiar sensation of late, began to build inside her. And then he dashed that too by adding, "You need to stop because I don't want to."

The heat that flooded her then was of an entirely different kind. And when she lifted her gaze to meet his, she saw the same kind of heat reflected there, as if he, too, was fighting a very primal urge.

When he pulled back and edged past her, headed back out to the couch where he'd spent the night so she could spend restless hours in his bed, Annalise stood there, wondering if she could or would ever move from this spot.

It had been an innocent, maybe flirting at most, encounter by some standards. And yet she'd felt more in these brief moments than she'd ever felt in her life.

And she'd done it herself. She'd been the first to reach out, to touch.

An odd idea struck her, about all the guys she'd dated, about her sisters teasing her about her penchant for bad boys before she'd sworn them off, asking her why she went for them. Was it this? Was it that simple, that with the "bad boys" she never had to make the first move? This was an aspect of her vow to give them up for nice guys she hadn't thought of before. But then, she'd never really wanted to make the first move. Until now. With Brett. But that need to touch him, to watch herself touch him, had been overwhelming, irresistible.

*You need to stop because I don't want to.* And if she hadn't stopped? Would he have...given in?

When she could finally move again she darted into the bathroom and closed the door. It shouldn't be that stunning a realization, but it was.

With Brett, she would have to make the first move. And knowing her stubborn Irishman, maybe the second and third, too.

And she didn't even realize until she was staring at her tired eyes in the mirror that she'd thought of him as hers.

# *Chapter 24*

Brett threw his pen down in disgust. He'd been staring unseeingly at the computer screen for so long the screen saver had popped up. And if asked what had been on the screen before that, he wouldn't have been able to answer. He was truly losing it.

He rubbed at his eyes. He'd tried going back to sleep after they'd…collided outside the bathroom, but had failed utterly. His body seemed to have a mind of its own and was fixated on that moment when he'd felt her touch on his skin, and his mind couldn't seem to find the strength to divert from the memory. Or the sudden, fierce craving for more of the same.

Much more.

He'd slept on that couch before, usually inadvertently, falling asleep while reading or watching something that hadn't held his attention, so it wasn't that it was too uncomfortable to sleep on. No, the reason for his restless and nearly sleepless night was now just down the hall. In the shower, God help him. Hence his staring at the screen unseeingly. Because his mind was full of images of Annalise, naked, with lucky, lucky water sluicing over her body, finding and sliding over every sweet curve, every delightful inch of her.

And all while his body was still aching, even a couple of hours later, from his own swift, fierce response the instant she'd touched him.

*I admire beauty, wherever it is.*

He'd been called many things in his life. Rugged, he'd been told. Masculine, which hopefully was a given, although he'd had the feeling they might mean it in a different way. Even, now and then, sexy. And a few less complimentary things on occasion. But beautiful? Never.

*Luckily, you don't get to decide what I think is beautiful.*

He let out a low groan. Tried to recite to himself all the reasons this would be wrong. She was a colleague.

She was Ember's trainer. If it went sour, what about Ember?

She was a Colton.

She was looking for forever.

And he was not a forever guy. He'd grown up with parents who'd stayed together, but with all the fighting it seemed to him it was in spite of each other, not because of each other. He wasn't even sure the latter existed. At the same time he looked at Troy and Evangeline, or even the chief and her fiancé, and he'd swear they were together for life. So was it he just didn't believe it was possible for him? Because of what he'd grown up with?

But that made no sense either. Troy had had to deal with much worse, a loving mother who had died in the ugliest of ways, murdered during a home invasion, when he'd been a toddler. It was, Brett knew, the reason Troy and probably all of the GGPD Coltons had gone into police work; the case had never been solved, the murderer never caught. Sometimes he thought the reason Troy in particular was so dogged, dedicated and determined was to bring as much justice to the world as he could, to make up for what they hadn't been able to do for his mother.

But Troy wasn't letting the past tragedy hold him back. He was going for it, for the big prize, with Evangeline. Full out, no holds barred.

*Maybe that's it. Troy is just braver than I am. Give me a bomb to disarm any day.*

Brett froze at his own thought. No wonder he never spent much time in this kind of introspection, if this was the kind of thing he came up with. Give him a bomb? He'd never been happier to walk away from anything than he had dealing with every kind of explosive device a human mind could devise. And some of those minds so twisted it had left him with nightmares for a long time? Was he really thinking *that* was preferable to taking the kind of risk Troy was taking, with his heart?

"Is that Big Sable?"

It was all he could do not to jump when her voice came from mere steps behind him. As it was he jerked around sharply. Half-afraid she'd be standing there wrapped in a towel from her shower or something. Thankfully for his grip on sanity, she'd dressed. Not so good for that grip was that she was in a pair of jeans that were tight enough to tempt, and a plain blue T-shirt that had found every damp spot to cling to. Her hair was pulled up into some kind of knot atop her head, but loose tendrils fell around her face, and his fingers curled against the need to reach out and brush them back. And stroke her cheek in the process.

He gave himself an inward shake and said, a bit too sharply, "What?"

She nodded toward the desk. "The picture. On Lake Michigan."

He was so surprised he'd been caught off guard by her appearance so close behind him without him being aware—something he was not used to at all—that it took him a moment to realize she meant the computer. He glanced at it and saw the screen saver image was indeed the Big Sable Point lighthouse. It was a beautiful shot, of the sun just touching the waters of the lake, casting a golden glow over the water, the sandy beach, and the grassy, rolling land behind it. He liked lighthouses, so that was why he'd picked the series of images for the slideshow.

"Yes. Yes, it is."

She came in then, and he noticed her feet were bare. Small, delicate looking feet, arched and tempting.

Feet? When the hell had he developed a thing for feet?

"I love that place. We went there a couple of times when I was a kid." She smiled at an apparent memory. "I always remember Desiree and Troy arguing about it."

He blinked. "Them arguing makes you smile?"

"Because it was funny. You have to pay to climb the tower, and they were arguing because Desiree called it a donation since that's what the sign said, but Troy said it can't be a donation if they make you pay it. Dad just laughed at them both and said, *Welcome to real life, kids.*"

"I'm inclined to agree with Troy on that one," Brett said.

Annalise smiled, and Brett felt a bit of wistful—and silly—wondering what it must have been like to be in a family that did things like that, together. A family with a father who laughed so easily.

"What did you do on weekends when you were a kid? On vacations?"

"Nothing."

Something in his tone must have registered, because

she was immediately apologetic. "I'm sorry. I shouldn't have assumed every family is as lucky as mine, to be able to afford to—"

"My family could have afforded it fine. My parents just didn't want to spend any more time with us than they had to." She stared at him, looking stunned. And he wasn't sure why that made him go on. "They didn't want to spend any more time with each other than they had to."

"Then why on earth did they stay married?"

He shrugged. "Hell if I know. Maybe they didn't want to have to learn how to fight with someone new."

"I…can't imagine. My parents disagree sometimes, but never for long. They love each other too much."

"So you've said."

"No wonder you looked like you didn't believe it."

He was on the edge of saying something even stupider, like *I believe it for some, but not for me.* There was no question he sucked at mornings after, and now he knew he sucked at them even when nothing had happened.

*Nothing? That's what you call going into overdrive with one simple touch?*

He was saved from further fumbling by her changing the subject.

"Do you need to get into the station? I don't have a client until noon, but I can always catch up on other things at the training center."

*Say yes. Anything to get some distance between you.*

But when he answered, it was with a shake of his head. "No rush. I'm waiting for Ellie to get the backing records set up, then I'll go live with the profile."

"And then we wait," she said, a bit glumly.

"That's a big part of what we do, sad to say." He tried for a smile. "It's not all action and excitement."

"And that," she said, in an entirely different tone, "is fine with me. I don't want you to—anyone to get hurt."

He didn't miss the midsentence change. Tried not to read anything into it. Was aware—and annoyed—that it was an effort. An effort he wasn't used to having to make.

He stood up abruptly. "I hope you like eggs for breakfast. That and bread for toast is about all I've got. Maybe some bacon, I think."

A supply run would be required. His brain leaped ahead to logistics. Make her make a list of what she wanted and leave her here, locked up in the house just in case? Alone, with no protection? He could leave Ember with her, knowing the dog would do what she could, but if the catfish had escalated to weaponry, even the dog couldn't stop him.

So take her with him? On something as…domestic as a grocery-shopping trip? How much that unexpectedly appealed rattled him. But from a safety standpoint, he'd be happier if she was with him, where he could take action if something happened. Leaving her here and going himself, he'd spend the whole time worrying. Not that he really thought the catfish would find her at his place, but he couldn't declare it impossible, and that was a risk he wasn't willing to take. Not with Annalise.

It was just his normal cop instinct, right? That gut feeling he'd learned to trust, just as he'd been able to spot booby traps overseas? He would have felt the same way about any victim of such a crime in his care. Wouldn't he? It wasn't—

"Will you let me fix breakfast? It's the least I can do."

He snapped out of his reverie, something he seemed to slip into around her far too often. He normally wasn't given to such constant introspection, and he didn't like it.

"Sure," he said, not quite sourly. "I need to go shave anyway."

Her gaze flicked to his chin, and he wondered if she was thinking, *About time.* He certainly was. But then her gaze met his again, and all he could think was how her eyes looked more blue than gray this morning, and he wondered if it was the blue shirt. If the reflected color of the cloth was what made them look like the lake on a sunny day. Or if they just somehow changed hue on their own, and how. Or—

"How do you like them?"

*They're beautiful.*

He sucked in a sharp breath. He hadn't said that out loud, had he? And then, belatedly—as he seemed to be reacting far too often around her—he realized she'd meant eggs, not her eyes.

"I…sunny-side up is fine," he said hastily.

He was surprised he didn't cut his throat while shaving, he was so…distracted. So distracted he shouldn't be trusted with anything as sharp as a razor. He'd already nicked his jawline. At least it hadn't bled much.

He had to steel himself to head back out to the kitchen. And when he did, he ended up pausing at the end of the hallway anyway.

She was singing.

Well, humming and singing, a light, lilting thing he didn't recognize. And she had a lovely voice, the kind that sort of brushed over you and made you smile. He stood there listening to the airy tune for a moment—okay, longer than a moment—and only when the smell of bacon make his stomach growl so loudly he was sure she must hear it did he move into the room.

"Just in time," she said with a smile. As if her life hadn't been upended completely, as if she didn't have a scummy catfish after her, one he was afraid might have taken her escape very personally. And if that had shifted this from theft to a more personal thing, as the latest offering had indicated, she could be in some serious danger.

She slid a plate across the counter toward him. He sat down on the stool in front of it as she turned to pour a cup of the fresh coffee she'd apparently also made. He doubted it was as strong as his usual brew, but he wasn't about to say anything about something he hadn't had to make himself.

Then he looked down at the plate. Stared. Then lifted his gaze to her.

"Seriously?" he asked.

She looked back over her shoulder at him. "Why not? We could use some cheer."

He looked back at the arrangement of two sunny-side up eggs—perfectly done, he noticed—and the strips of bacon, all arranged in the undeniable shape of a happy face. And he couldn't help it; he laughed.

"And that," Annalise said with obvious satisfaction, "was worth the effort."

## Chapter 25

This was, Annalise thought, a far, far more pleasant morning than she would have expected. Not simply because she was away from the scene of the crime—although she hated thinking of her home that way, she couldn't deny that at the moment that's what it was—but because Brett seemed willing to pretend that moment in the hallway in the predawn hour hadn't happened.

He sat over his empty plate and sipped at his coffee, saying nothing, as he had throughout the meal.

*He is probably too embarrassed to bring it up. You should never have touched him.*

Even thinking about it brought on a wave of remembered heat that rippled through her from head to toe, with a few interesting stops along the way. And once more she wondered what was wrong with her. How could she have gone so quickly from thinking she might have found "the one" in her nonexistent doctor, to lusting over—because she could no longer deny that was exactly what she was doing—Brett Shea?

Yes, it was true she'd always found him attractive, and that she loved the way he worked with Ember, and how much he obviously cared for the dog and thought of her welfare before his own. But why had it only now burst into something more? Circumstances, like her being terrified and angry and ashamed all at once? Proximity? Or, as she'd thought earlier, a fickleness she'd never recognized in herself before?

Or—her breath caught as another thought struck her—had it simply been that it had taken this illusion-shattering situation for her to wake up to what had been in front of her all along?

"This is a bit strong for you, isn't it?"

She snapped back to reality in an instant. Realized he was gesturing with the coffee mug. "Oh. Yes." She pulled herself together; not for the world did she want to betray what she'd been thinking just now. "I noticed that you always hit Sergeant Kenwood's coffeepot when you come into the training center, and I know his brew can melt spoons."

"That it can," he agreed, with that crooked smile she'd always liked, but that now made her pulse kick up. "What about you, how are you drinking it?"

She tried to return the smile. "I stole a lot of milk," she admitted. "Which I'll replace, of course."

He gave a one-shouldered shrug that was familiar to her too; it was what people got who tried to thank him, for just about anything. "Help yourself," he said. "Although we'll need a shopping trip soon, to stock up. I was kind of down to the bare bones anyway."

She'd started to smile again, better this time, when the full sense of what he was implying hit her. Stock up? Just how long was he assuming she'd be staying here? With him? Until...when? The catfish was caught? That could take weeks. Months even.

Or maybe they'd never catch him, then what?

She opened her mouth to ask, couldn't think of a single way to phrase it that wouldn't embarrass her further, and closed it again. Thankfully he was focused on draining the last of his coffee and didn't see her. And then his phone, on the counter beside him, sounded. He looked, and his entire demeanor changed.

"Ellie," he said without looking up. "She's got a location in place."

"Already?"

He did look at her then and nodded. "I asked her to put a rush on it." He grimaced slightly. "What can I say—I'm impatient. I want this guy."

*And to be rid of your houseguest? One who tries to... fondle you in the dark?*

"I'll clean up," she said as he started to gather up his dishes, her voice a little tight. "So you can get on this." She reached out to take his plate as she added a bit more vehemently, "I want this guy caught, too."

He reached out and put a hand over hers. She froze, staring down at his fingers, curled around hers, imbuing warmth and steadiness. "I'll get him, Annalise. I swear it."

"I know you will." Her voice was at least steadier now. As if he'd somehow given her some of his strength through that touch.

And then he was all business, glancing at his watch. "Let me go through what she set up, plug the details into the profile. Then you can look it over and...feminize it."

She somehow found the composure to smile at that. "Make it sound girly, you mean?"

"Sort of," he answered, sounding a bit uncomfortable.

"You know, put the emphasis on… I don't know, the garden instead of the tool shed. The flowers, not having to mow the grass."

To her own surprise, Annalise found herself smiling, then grinning at him. "Sexist much?"

There had never been a trace of that from him, so it was supposed to utterly be a joke. But his expression shifted and he said quietly, "I try not to be. But I think he is. The worst kind."

Her smile faded. The seriousness of what she was dealing with flooded back. "Excellent point," she said. "I'll be in as soon as I finish here."

Brett opened the email and smiled. Ellie had, as usual, done a stellar job. She'd not only found an empty house that had been rehabbed and not yet put on the market, but the renovator had some loose connection to the Coltons and had been willing to cooperate. He'd even offered to stage the place to make it look more real, since he was going to do it anyway.

He studied the photos she'd sent of the location, then opened his map program to look at the aerial view. A quiet-looking neighborhood, with only a couple of vehicles parked on the street. A switch to the street view showed neat, tidy houses, well-kept and homey.

He went back to the aerial view, zoomed in on the house Ellie had found. He noted what looked like a doghouse next door, and a children's play set in the backyard on the other side. That would help with details for the profile; dog barking on one side, kids yelling on the other. Nothing like complaining about your neighbors to make you seem real…

He signed into the department system remotely and began a stat check on the surrounding area, looking for any reports on file about anything someone living in that house would be aware of. While he was waiting for the results he would go back to the photos, note things like colors of the walls and the way the walkway to the front door bent around that big tree, the one he thought was a red oak.

Just as he sent the query, Annalise came in.

"Is that the house?" He nodded. And tensed despite himself when she leaned in to look. She was so close, and he could smell that sweet, rich, flowery kind of scent. He'd never cared much about women's perfume before, but this stuff practically made his fingers itch to—

*Not going there.*

"It's actually very nice," she said.

"It was just remodeled, but not on the market yet." He gave her a sideways look. "The flipper knows your uncle, so he was willing to help out."

"Oh." She drew back slightly, looking at him. "Another Colton connection, huh?" she asked, in a tone suggesting she knew what his reaction had been.

"Hard to avoid around here." He thought he'd said it neutrally, but apparently not neutrally enough.

"I can't help that. Any more than you can help your family being…not so connected. And if it makes you feel any better, we're not that close to my uncle Frank. Aunt Verity keeps trying to pull us all together."

"Verity?"

"She's Jillian's mom."

"Oh. That's got to be rough."

"Yes. She's always wished we were all closer." She let out a sad-sounding sigh. "I suppose she wants us to be close because she misses Richard so much, even after all these years."

"Richard?"

"Her kids' dad. He was killed when Jillian was only three."

"Sorry," he muttered, not knowing what else to say to her. So instead he went on with the matter at hand. "Once I go over the location check and pick out some details, you can go through that, too."

"And feminize it?"

He shot her a sideways glance, but she didn't seem to be jabbing at him. "Yes. All of the profile."

"You mean that our fictional target likes rom-com movies and roses and such."

"Yeah. And some other things from the list we have of commonalities."

"Okay." She gave him a look then he couldn't put a name to. But said, lightly, "But just for the record? Personally I prefer action flicks."

He blinked. "What?"

"I love watching the stunts and trying to figure out how they did them."

He couldn't help it, he laughed. "You didn't say that in your profile."

"I didn't answer that one. The same taste in movies isn't a criterion I think is all that important." Then she sighed. "But then, look where my choices got me."

"Get over it," he advised briskly. "Now, how about we go restock my pitiful kitchen?"

That seemed to perk her up. And as it turned out, he didn't mind at all; her enthusiasm over a task he usually found boring at best, annoying the rest of the time was… entertaining. Once he'd picked up his version of staples—coffee, more eggs and bacon, milk, bread and a couple of steaks and some chicken—he spent the rest of the expedition trying to figure out what her plans were for the collection she put together.

"Do you like lasagna?" she asked.

"Is there a human alive who doesn't?"

She grinned. Damn, that looked good on her. "While we're on Italian, what about a frittata?"

"I'm not even sure what that is."

"It's got eggs, veggies and lots of cheese. Any deal breaker there?"

He found himself smiling at the way she put it. "No."

"How about pancakes for breakfast?"

"Yes. But you don't have to—"

"I know. I want to." She wanted to…what? Cook? Or was it specifically cook for him? She went on cheerily. "I get the feeling you stick pretty much to grill-and-eat meals?"

"Interspersed with frozen packages of stuff," he said dryly.

"We'll fix that," she said.

"We?" He ignored that he liked the sound of that.

"Well, I will."

"Isn't that a bit sexist, the woman doing the cooking?" he asked, his tone ultrainnocent.

She turned to face him then, a carton of a dozen eggs in her hand. "Not if she likes to do it. It's the assumption she'll do it just because she's the woman that's—" She stopped abruptly, and he knew she'd gotten it. "You're using my own joke on me," she accused. She sounded as if she was trying for anger, but coming closer to laughter.

"What gave me away?"

"Oh, maybe that little twitch at the corner of your mouth?"

She said that with a smile, and he was glad enough that she wasn't really upset, that he managed not to focus— too much—on the admission that she'd been looking at his mouth. Especially given what raced through his mind when he looked at hers.

The rest of the expedition was…nice. An absurd word to use, in his mind, for something as mundane and usually annoying for him as grocery shopping. But it was. And when in the checkout line the woman behind them in line, who was buying a stack of the frozen dinners he had an even bigger stack of in his freezer, looked at the lasagna makings and said to the checker with a smile and an exaggerated sigh, "I want to have dinner at *their* house," he couldn't help grinning at her.

*Their house.*

It was only the woman's joke that had made him react that way. Not that phrase.

When they arrived back at the house they were greeted by the canine trio: Ember happily, going to Brett first, then Annalise. Jack and Apple went to Annalise first, much more frenzied, as if they still weren't sure she'd come back to them. But he got a greeting too, and it was nearly as bouncy. As if they'd accepted him into their lives, or at least trusted he wouldn't hurt them. He counted that as a win, even as he told himself the fact that her dogs liked him didn't really mean anything.

As they were putting away the supplies his phone sounded a work email notification. He checked, saw it was from Ellie and labeled *photos*.

"We've got our bait," he told Annalise, and headed for the office.

"That was fast," she said as she followed him down the hall.

"Ellie's got the bit in her teeth. I found out she used that dating app, before she met her boyfriend, Mick. I think she's taking this a bit personally, thinking it could have been her."

He walked into the office. Sat down, trying not to notice Annalise standing right behind him. He booted up the laptop and called up the email from Ellie. As usual, it was short and to the point.

*I was going to do it myself, but got an insistent volunteer. And if our suspect wants voice contact, she can do that, too. I think these pics are perfect. She went by the house location and the park up the street and took the selfies, and we just went to lunch together and took the rest. Note the necklace!*

Brett's brow furrowed. It hadn't occurred to him that Ellie might use a real person for the bait photos. But instead it was someone she knew? He opened the first image file. Blinked as Annalise cried out.

"Grace! No!"

# Chapter 26

"No," Annalise said firmly. "No, Grace."

"Anna—"

Annalise's grip on the phone tightened as she paced the small office. "I don't want you to do this."

"It's already done. It'll be fine, sis."

"But what if—"

"There's no way he could know who I am or find me. And if we end up talking live, he won't recognize my voice, either."

"You're not going to talk to him!"

"Only if it comes to that. That's Brett's call."

"But if he figures out you're a Colton—"

"He'll have no idea. I erased all my social media accounts recently, so I'm just an anonymous face, and as far as he knows Miss Brittany Hale, schoolteacher." She heard her little sister laugh. "I haven't cracked my big case and gotten my picture in the news yet."

"Grace—"

"Hey, you haven't even mentioned that gorgeous necklace! Isn't it outrageous?"

She had, of course, noticed the jewelry in the shot showing Grace in formal wear. She thought it was the dress her sister had worn to Mary Suzuki's wedding back in January. But Annalise knew she hadn't been wearing the elegant—and expensive looking—diamond necklace that sparkled at her throat in the image on that day. And she knew her little sister didn't own a piece like that. That extravagant.

"You didn't steal it, did you?" she asked dryly.

Grace laughed. "Actually, it is stolen. We borrowed it out of the evidence room. With permission, of course. It was about to be released back to the store it was taken from anyway. But the owner of the store liked the idea of using it to help catch another jewelry thief."

"Don't think I didn't notice that you're changing the subject."

"Not changing, that subject is closed."

Her tone was flat, uncompromising and final. Annalise blinked. When had her little sister become so...resolute? Having grown up with Grace, she wasn't fooled by her waiflike appearance, and it took some toughness to get through the police academy, but this was new.

"I'm a cop now, sister mine," Grace said quietly. "This is what I do." Then, briskly, she went on. "And I called Madison."

Annalise blinked. "Our cousin, Madison?" What on earth did she have to do with—

"She's going to send some pictures of her student's drawings she's saved over the years, to add to the whole teacher vibe. Oops, gotta run, my TO's waiting. Later!"

And that quickly she was listening to silence. Her mouth

quirked. "Well," she muttered, "don't keep your training officer waiting."

"I know her TO," Brett said as she handed him back his phone. "I wouldn't keep him waiting either."

Her gaze shot to his face. He looked utterly serious. "Oh."

"She'll be fine, Annalise. Grace may be a rookie, but she's got good instincts." He smiled. "That idea about the kid's drawings was great, given we're setting up our bait as an elementary school teacher."

They spent the next couple of hours doing just that, setting up the bait. Fleshing out details, adding in the photos, each one of which gave Annalise a qualm. It was one thing to accept that her strong, capable big brother Troy was a cop, another thing altogether to think of her little sister that way. What that said about herself, Annalise wasn't sure. Maybe she was the one who was sexist. Or maybe just overprotective, as Grace had always said she was.

*I love my sister, and I worry about her. That's all it is.*

It took her a few minutes to process this development. And only when she accepted that she couldn't do a darn thing about it was she able to focus on the task at hand.

She studied the photos of the house, found a couple of things to mention in the profile. Brett chose what seemed most likely to have attracted the catfish to the other profiles he'd interacted with and added them in, reworded or tweaked to be different yet similar, with Annalise adding the female spin he'd asked for. It took a surprisingly long time. Much longer than she had ever spent entering her real profile.

*Which may explain a lot about the disaster that turned into.*

Finally they retreated from the office, both weary of staring at the facade they were building. Brett put on a fresh pot of coffee while Annalise got down mugs. She was trying hard to put her head in that place, where their imaginary woman would be. But her mind kept straying into wondering if the catfish had done the same, put this much effort into building the imaginary Dr. Sam Rivers.

"I wonder if he tried to put himself into an imagined mindset, like this. Or did he concentrate on what would be the best lure for the victim he was hunting for?"

She only realized she'd been musing out loud when Brett looked up from watching the coffee drip and said, "You mean did he just build his trap and wait for whoever's attention he caught, or study profiles and build his fake one from there specifically to draw them in? I don't know. I suspect the latter. Or a combination of both. He's obviously been at this a while, so I'm guessing he's developed a system."

Clearly, he'd been thinking about that, too. She put the two mugs down next to the coffee maker, then stood there looking at him. She looked at the set of his jaw and the glint in his blue eyes; she realized how down-to-the-bone determined he was to catch this guy. He was going to take down this catfish no matter what it took.

Or what risks he had to take.

Her breath caught, and it must have been audible because his gaze narrowed suddenly. And her thoughts must have shown in her face because he asked, with some concern, "What?"

"I… I just…be careful, Brett."

"Always." His voice was steady, reassuring.

"But if anything happened to you—"

"It won't. But even if it did, it's not on you, it's on him." He smiled rather wryly. "Well, and on me, if I let him get the upper hand."

"Still. I'd never forgive myself."

"Annalise," he said, and then stopped.

She stared at him, wide-eyed, unable to hide the fear she was feeling. And in that moment she felt something shift inside her, some final change in the slot he occupied in her mind, in her life. This wasn't just Ember's handler, a colleague, a man she liked and respected.

This was a man who made her breath catch, her pulse pound and her flesh heat, in a way no man ever had. And unlike the phantom they were trying to catch, she knew who and what this man was. Knew it down deep, with the kind of certainty she'd rarely felt about anyone.

"Don't." His voice was taut, almost strained.

"Don't what?" she whispered.

"Look at me like that."

"Like…what?"

"Like you want—"

He broke it off abruptly, started to look away. She could feel him withdrawing as if it was a physical pain. Something knotted up inside her and she reached out and put a hand over his. She needed to know. She had to know.

"I do want," she whispered. "Do you?"

His head snapped around and he stared at her. In those blue eyes she saw all the heat she could ever have imagined, and a need, a wanting that matched her own. And then he was holding her shoulders again, and for a moment she couldn't tell if he wanted to keep her away or pull her close. In the end, he did neither. He just moved, crossing the last distance between them in barely a single second. She knew the instant she saw his head move, lower, what was coming. And she tilted her head back, almost afraid to breathe, afraid if she did anything, even that, he would stop.

He didn't stop.

His mouth came down on hers hungrily. She gasped at

the feel of it, and the pressure instantly eased. He didn't break the kiss, merely lightened it, shifted to a slow, intense exploration that sent ripples of chill and heat through her at the same time, something she would have thought impossible were she not experiencing it firsthand.

She kissed him back just as hungrily. He tasted of warmth, a hint of coffee, but most of all just… Brett. And he was delicious. She wanted more, much more, and when his tongue lightly traced the line of her lips, she met it with her own. She heard him make a low, deep sound, and thrilled to the realization that he was feeling this as strongly as she was.

In the instant she wished he would, he pulled her closer. She felt the heat of his tall, strong body pressed against her, and wondered if her knees could hold out against the tide of sensation. He deepened the kiss, probing, tasting, and she clung to him as her knees indeed gave way. From head to knee they were pressed together, and Annalise felt a hum from somewhere deep inside, a feeling of rightness that took what little breath she had left away.

This, this was what she'd been looking for.

And it had been right in front of her all the time.

## Chapter 27

The last thing Brett wanted to do was let go of her.

The first thing he had to do was let go of her.

It took more resolve than he ever would have imagined to do. He felt suddenly chilled when her warmth was no longer pressed against him. And the moment he looked down into her face, the moment he saw the look in her eyes as they slowly opened to look back at him, he knew just letting go wasn't going to be enough.

He took a step back. Put more space between them. He was hearing an odd, rhythmic sound that he abruptly realized was his own breath coming in audible pants. She had literally taken his breath away.

And now she was just staring at him. Staring at him with those big, blue-gray eyes. Eyes that held a look of... wonder. A look that echoed what he was feeling, a bit of shock and awe right here in his kitchen.

And it suddenly descended upon him, the true size of the mistake he'd just made.

"That…shouldn't have happened," he said, unable to make his voice anything less than gruff, so tight was his throat.

"But it did," Annalise said softly, and the same wonder he'd seen in her eyes echoed in her voice. "And I'm glad."

He swallowed. Hard. "Glad?"

"Now I don't have to imagine what it would be like anymore."

He nearly groaned aloud. "I don't have that much imagination."

He regretted the words as soon as they were out. Somehow acknowledging the conflagration they'd nearly started made it even harder to think about stopping it right here and now. But he had to stop it. For all the reasons it never should have started in the first place.

"We're not doing this," he said, and this time his tone was sharp. "It's inappropriate, unwise and…and—"

"Unprofessional?" she suggested, and her tone was cooler now.

"That, too."

"I can see why you wouldn't want to…get involved with someone foolish enough to get sucked in by a—"

"That has nothing to do with this!" He snapped the words out, tired of her blaming herself for being the sweet, trusting soul she was. His hands came up as if to grab her shoulders again, and he had to stop himself. His fingers curled into fists as he forced them back down to his sides.

"You're not foolish. You're smart and kind and beautiful and sexy, and if your Dr. Rivers had been for real, he'd be a damned lucky guy to have you. Any man would be."

"Except you?" she asked quietly.

Brett realized abruptly that she had done this on purpose, maneuvered him into defending her in a way that betrayed what he thought of her. "Did I mention smart?" he muttered.

"First thing," she said.

Then she smiled. And there was something different about this smile. Something old and deep and very feminine. Warily he had the thought that she'd learned what she wanted, and now all he had to do was wait and see how she'd use it. Against him? Or should that be, for them? He didn't know anymore.

All he knew for sure was that kissing Annalise Colton had been a watershed moment for him, and that when this case was finally over, when she was safe—and she would be, he vowed silently—he would be looking at a very momentous decision.

Annalise sat on the edge of the bed. She'd retreated here because she had to think. And she couldn't seem to do that if she was in the same room with Brett. At least not in a rational way—her thoughts tended to stray in just one direction when he was anywhere in her line of sight. And if he was close…if he was close, her thoughts went haywire. Careened into imaginings like she'd never had before in her life. And she couldn't help wondering if this had been here all along, but had only been unleashed because of the circumstances and their enforced togetherness.

Which made her wonder again what would happen when this was over. And it would be over; Brett hadn't built his reputation and his clearance rate by giving up. He'd said he would get this catfish, and he meant it. And then what? If what had just happened was any indication, it was obvious. He was trying to friend-zone her. There wasn't any other answer for the way he kept retreating. And yet when she'd used his seemingly instinctive urge to defend her, to deny she was as big a fool as she felt over falling for the catfish, to prod out of him that declaration of what he really thought of her, his words had been balm to her battered ego.

The moment when they'd been talking about the other victims came back to her.

*They sound like me.*

*You mean, like kind, giving, caring people you'd be lucky to have in your life?*

That sounded quite like what he'd said just now. *You're smart and kind and beautiful…*

Kind. Why else would he keep emphasizing how kind she was? Kind was a generic sort of compliment, the kind of thing you said to or about a friend. And he probably didn't want to alienate Ember's trainer, knowing they'd have to continue to work together with the dog when this was over.

But he'd also said sexy. And that any man would be lucky to have her. Did a guy say that kind of thing if he was trying to push you away?

The other side of her, the side that seemed to heat up whenever she got close to the man, was hammering on her mind, demanding that she deal with the most obvious piece of evidence.

That kiss.

There was absolutely nothing friend-zone-ish about that kiss.

At least, there hadn't been for her. Had it not been that way for him?

*Now I don't have to imagine what it would be like anymore.*

*I don't have that much imagination.*

Oh, yes, it had been. And yet he was still pulling back.

And here she sat, in his bedroom, on his bed. The bed he'd insisted she take. Alone.

*And if he'd wanted to share it? If that kiss had led to where it obviously could have? Right here to this bed?*

The very thought took her breath away. And all the lecturing—telling herself that she was just on the rebound, that she'd been humiliated and wanted proof she was truly a desirable woman, that she was reacting and responding to him this way because of what had happened to her—didn't seem to be working.

Because that kiss had been real. Very, very real.

She jumped to her feet because she simply had to move. She started to pace for the same reason. The room wasn't huge, but there was some space despite the king-size bed. *His* bed.

She spun on her heel and started back the other way. Looked around rather desperately for something else, anything else to fixate on. The room was tidy, with only a shirt she thought she recognized tossed over a bedpost. She wondered if she picked it up, if she would get a touch of that piney scent she associated with him. Whether it was aftershave or just that he spent a lot of time out in the woods with Ember, she didn't know.

*And you're not going to pick it up.*

That demand made of herself, she looked around some more. Noticed the utilitarian-looking box attached to the side of the nightstand, realized it was a gun safe. She stared at that for a moment. It wasn't that she wasn't used to weapons. She'd been a teenager when Troy had become a cop, and it had seemed exciting. When she worked with officers and their K-9s it was her job and she mainly focused on the dogs. So somehow the sight of that safe brought home to her the daily reality of being a police officer; when something bad happened, you ran toward it, not away from it.

She turned away from it to look at the rest of the room. Found herself smiling now when she realized the messiest thing here was Ember's bed, with her toys strewn in the vicinity. That seemed right, somehow.

There were a couple of things on the dresser, what looked like a tray for things probably pulled out of his pockets at night, and a framed picture. A photo of him, down on one knee beside Ember, both posing nicely.

It made her smile. And then it made her breath catch. Because this photograph was very, very familiar.

She had taken this shot. She remembered the day; it had been after the clever dog had run a long, complex obstacle course, one that had thrown others off on a wrong track, perfectly. The Lab had never wavered, never lost track of her goal no matter what distractions, masking or camouflaging had been put in her way. She'd set a new record for success on that course, and Brett had been delighted. In fact, she realized as she stared at the image, he'd been happier than she'd ever seen him, before or since.

And it was familiar because it was one of her screen savers. One she rarely failed to pause and appreciate when it popped up. The others, other clients and trainees, made her smile, but this was the only one that made her stop what she was doing and simply look until it rotated off the screen.

Dear heaven, maybe she really had been lusting after him all this time and had just never acknowledged it—or been forced to acknowledge it—until now. Maybe this heat had always been there, maybe—

Something tickled the edge of her awareness, and she realized she could hear Brett talking, muffled by the closed door. It was late for some kind of friendly call, so maybe it was something official. Something she should know about.

She pulled the door open and stepped through.

"—know he's due to hit again any day now," she heard him say. "I think a sting's the best way to get a shot at him."

A pause, then, "I know that, Troy, but I don't think the guy would ever go for someone walking a dog like Bear. He practically screams police K-9. Ember's a Lab, like a million goofy pets. And I can fake his preferred target type."

What? As he paused again, clearly listening, she walked quietly down the hall. Then he spoke again. Rather sourly.

"If for no other reason than if it goes south and Davison gets away, I'll take less heat because my last name's not Colton. I'll do it."

Annalise stopped dead. Forgot to breathe.

Davison. It had to be Len Davison.

A chill rippled through her, unlike anything she'd ever felt before. Even when she'd seen that dart in the catfish's hand and realized she was in danger, she hadn't felt like this. No, this was an entirely different kind of fear. And the power of it made one thing perfectly and undeniably obvious.

She had fallen hard for Brett Shea.

She loved him, and he was going out there after a serial killer.

# Chapter 28

"What are you planning?"

Brett shoved his phone back into his pocket and turned around. His brow was slightly furrowed, as if he was thinking about all the ways that question could be answered just now. And she saw a trace of a grimace before he said, very neutrally, "Dinner. I thought I'd grill the chicken we bought—"

"So you do think I'm stupid." He'd no more been planning dinner than she'd been planning to swim across an entire lake.

He sighed, closing his eyes. Odd, she thought, that she was able to think a bit more clearly when he wasn't looking at her. At least, she was until her imagination took off again, and she found herself staring at him and…wondering. Wondering what it would be like to kiss him again, and this time let it proceed.

Then he was looking at her again. "As important as your case is, it's not the only one we have."

Well, that was nice and impersonal, in both words and tone. And she guessed he'd used that *we* intentionally, to drag the entire department into it. But the mere fact that he was doing that told her it was all deflection. She just wasn't sure if it was from what she'd overheard, or something else.

*Something like us? The very personal us?*

She shoved the idea out of her head. "Len Davison," she said flatly.

"Annalise—"

"You're going after him."

"We've been after him for—"

"I don't want the *we* obfuscation. Troy's obviously in on it—"

"And Bryce," he said, as if adding the name of her cousin, the FBI agent, made it all right.

"And whoever," she snapped, "but you're going to be the lure, aren't you?" She didn't really make it a question because she already knew the answer. "You're going to be bait, just like our fake schoolteacher. Did that inspire the idea?"

"Maybe," he said, sounding more than a little wary. "Same principle, anyway."

Great. So if anything happened to him, she was going to feel responsible. "Except the big difference is you're putting yourself in the path of a killer, not a thief."

He drew in a deep breath and said gently, "It's my job, Annalise."

The obvious effort to placate her had the opposite effect. "Your job? To try and get yourself killed?" Her tone was becoming strident but she couldn't seem to help it.

"Calm down. I'm not going to—"

"Don't tell me to calm down." She could see she wasn't

reaching him, so she changed tacks slightly. "You're going to use Ember as part of the trap?"

He seemed to relax a little. As if he thought her reaction was only because of the possible risk to a dog she loved. "It's part of his profile. But he never hurts the dogs. So it'll be fine. And Desiree is going to use aging makeup to make me look like I'm in my fifties, like his other targets."

*Except for you trying to get a serial killer to attack you.* She wanted to scream at him for his obtuseness. And it made her blurt out, "Are you even thinking about what that would do to…us?"

Brett went very still at her last word. He was looking at her with a sudden intensity that was almost unnerving. "You mean the Coltons having to deal with the death of a cop on top of everything else?" he suggested, giving it an interpretation she hadn't thought of. Giving her an out.

She didn't take it. Instead she exclaimed, "I mean me having to deal with your death!"

He was looking at her as if he'd heard everything she hadn't said, everything that had pushed her into making that undeniably passionate declaration. "Annalise," he whispered.

"Don't make me do that, Brett. Don't make me do that," she whispered back, not even caring how broken her voice sounded. "Not when I only just realized…how I feel about you."

He went rigidly still. Stared at her. Opened his mouth— parted those lips that kept drawing her gaze—then closed it. She just looked at him. She'd thrown her heart out there in what her grandfather had called a *damn the torpedoes* moment. She couldn't take the words back, and her gut was screaming that if she said anything more, she would only make it worse. He couldn't have made it any clearer that he didn't want this, didn't want her, and here she was forcing him into a situation that had to be beyond uncomfortable for him. She had to say something, do something. Pretend she hadn't said it? Turn it into something less, say that she'd meant it as a friend? Or that she didn't want Ember to lose him?

*You're a good friend, Brett, and I don't want to lose you.*

There, that could work. And had the advantage of also being true. It just wasn't the whole truth. But then, she'd just blurted out the whole truth, hadn't she? She'd just—

He kissed her.

He hadn't meant to do it.

He'd practically screamed at himself not to do it.

But as those words, those sweet, innocent, clearly genuine words had hung in the air between them, as he looked at her watching him with her heart in her eyes, he was lost. That she could still have that sweetness after what had happened to her wasn't just surprising to him it was... overwhelming. And he had moved before he thought, was probably beyond thought, pulling her to him and doing what he'd been aching to do again every hour since the first time.

He wouldn't have thought it possible, but she tasted sweeter, hotter than he'd even remembered. He stroked his tongue over her lips, and they parted willingly, even eagerly. And when the tip of her tongue brushed over his own, pure, hot fire sizzled through him. He nearly lost control right then, and plunged deeper, craving more. Craving everything.

The soft moan she let out against his mouth, a sound that echoed his own need, slammed into him. His body responded instantly, hardening in a rush that nearly left him dizzy. He could feel her name wanting to burst from him, but it was all he could do to simply keep breathing.

But finally he had to breathe, and lifted his head. Not away, just enough to catch some air.

"Brett…"

She murmured it as she held on to him, tightly, as if he were her anchor in a spinning world. Ironic, considering his own world—and his head—were spinning, and he felt as if she was the only solid thing left in it.

"Nothing can happen to you," she whispered. He wasn't sure if it was pronouncement or prayer, but either way the words clawed at him.

"It'll be all right," he said softly against her hair. "Troy will be there, and Grace, Bryce… I'll have Coltons at my back, so I'll be fine."

She pulled back just enough to look up at him. "You mean that? You really mean it? You trust them? You trust us?"

He looked into her eyes, although it was hard to drag his gaze away from her kiss-swollen mouth. And he realized with a little shock that he did mean it. "I do. Bryce is a good agent, Grace is already sharp as can be and Troy… there's no one I'd rather have as backup."

Her arms tightened fiercely around him and she laid her head against his chest, making his pulse kick up all over again. "Thank you," she whispered, as if he had given her some wonderful gift.

He marveled at that. It was so different from the way he'd grown up, he could only guess at what it must have been like to grow up as a Colton, and know that when the chips were down all of them would be there for you.

And then she stretched up and kissed him, tentatively at first, but the fire apparently lit as quickly for her as it did for him and in mere seconds it was again that fierce, burning thing. He felt her fingers digging into his shoulders, pulling at him as if she wanted him closer. That he understood, because more than anything at this moment he wanted her as close as he could get her. Preferably without the barrier of clothing between them.

He wasn't quite sure how his hands had slid down to her hips, but since they had he pulled her tightly against him. And again his body had reacted as it had even before that first kiss, in a way he hadn't experienced in a long time.

*Ever, you mean.*

Yeah. *Ever.* He nearly groaned aloud at the feel of her pressed to his hardened flesh, and in that moment he thought if they didn't pursue this to the inevitable end he would regret it for the rest of his life. And he practically groaned her name against her lips.

She broke the kiss and his every sense cried out in protest, but then she looked up at him and said simply, "Yes."

He went rigidly still. Yes? Yes to what? Because yes to everything he wanted right now was a very big yes. The biggest. He tried to find the words to ask, to make sure, because he had to be sure, he had to know she wanted this as much as he did, he had to—

A too familiar ringtone sounded from the phone in his back pocket. He'd forgotten, in that list of Coltons he trusted, that there was one more, one more he needed to be wary about, one who could easily hold any hurt he caused Annalise against him, both personally and professionally.

*Hail to the Chief.*

He couldn't do this. He shouldn't do this. He shouldn't even be thinking about going there, no matter how Annalise made him feel.

He let go of her and stepped back.

And it was likely the hardest thing he'd ever done in his life.

## Chapter 29

"How's my sister?"

Brett shot a sideways look at Annalise's sister Desiree, who had turned her considerable artistic skills to making him look twenty-five years older than he was.

*Which would be younger than I feel at the moment.*

He mentally brushed aside the thought. When Troy had mentioned this operation, she had volunteered to make him believably look in the target age range. She was proving as deft a hand with makeup and temporary hair dye as she was with her charcoal and pencils.

"I...she's fine," he finally said, rather lamely. When Desiree simply looked at him, waiting, he added, "A little rattled, still, but that's to be expected. All in all she's handled things amazingly well."

"Of course. She's a Colton."

His mouth twisted wryly. "Yeah. I noticed."

"She really likes your place."

He blinked. "What?"

"She said she loves all the outdoor space, the yard, and wants to see the coyote."

"Oh."

"And that your bedroom is nice and quiet, with all that open space behind it."

"It is," he said. Then, as she continued to stare at him, belatedly realized what she was getting at. "If you're asking if we're…sharing that room, we're not."

*Not that I wouldn't in an instant, if not for…so many things.*

"Why not?"

He blinked again, truly startled this time. And almost answered a blank *What?* again. He suddenly felt like he was back overseas, about to step into what he knew was a minefield.

"Are you really asking me why I'm not sleeping with your sister?"

Desiree smiled. "Aside from my little boy, she's been the most adorable, loving thing I've ever seen since the day she was born. I'm asking how, being in such close quarters, you can keep from falling head over heels for her."

He stared at the woman. The mention of her son reminded him of everything she had been through in the past few months, and he found himself marveling at her self-possession.

"You Coltons," he said, his tone a bit awed.

"We're a strong bunch," she agreed. Then, with a rather impish grin added, "Especially we women. So is that it? She's too strong for you?" He gave her the eye roll that deserved. "So it's that she's a Colton? That's what's holding you back?"

*Strong. Yeah, that's the word. So give her the truth.* "She's related to you, our guest FBI agent, one of our

CSIs, my frequent partner, a rookie I'm helping train and my boss," he said flatly. "What do you think?"

"Well, when you put it that way," she said wryly. "But I have to admit, I thought you had more nerve than to let that stop you."

"Sorry," he muttered, "all my nerves right now are focused on being a target."

"Point taken," she said, and thankfully dropped the subject.

And far too belatedly it occurred to him that he'd never contested her only half-teasing inquisition with the most effective answer. He'd never said he wasn't interested in Annalise.

He'd never said he wasn't sharing that bedroom—and bed—with her because he didn't want to.

When Desiree was done and he at last got the chance to look in a mirror before they headed out, he felt a jolt. He stared at his reflection, wondering if he was truly seeing himself in twenty-five years. Graying hair, more lined face, features succumbing a bit more to gravity. He tried to focus on her artwork—because there was no doubt that's what it was—but all he could do in that moment was wonder where he would be, what his life would be, when this really was the reflection he saw in the mirror.

And that his first thought was Annalise—simply because of those close quarters Desiree had mentioned. Not because he thought she might still be in his life by then. Nobody lasted in his life that long. And he'd never really cared about that.

But the thought of, when this was all over, going home every night to a house empty again except for Ember, seemed…crushingly depressing.

He shook it off. He had a job to do, and it was a job

that required his head be fully in the game. Because if he missed a cue, a clue, he could end up dead.

"Hey, Pops! You ready to roll?"

He snapped out of the bleak thoughts and turned to look at Troy, who was grinning at him.

Brett did his best old-voice imitation of one of his father's dressing downs. Troy laughed, and they headed for the unmarked van that held the communications equipment necessary for tonight's sting.

As it turned out, it wasn't necessary at all. Brett and Ember made several circuits through the park, carefully timed, Brett taking care to walk more slowly than he normally would, with nothing more happening than an occasional friendly wave from strangers passing by, and a couple of compliments for Ember. But none of them had expected to strike gold the first night of the sting, which he explained to Annalise when, makeup washed away, he got back well after midnight. And found her waiting up for him. As if she couldn't rest until he was home safe.

*Home.*

That's what it was. This was no longer just the place he lived, chosen for its functionality for Ember. It felt like home, in a way nowhere he'd lived before ever had. And there was only one reason for that. The woman who looked him up and down as if she needed to be sure he was truly all right.

*I'm asking how, being in such close quarters, you can keep from falling head over heels for her.*

Good question.

"No problems here?" he asked, trying for a diversion.

"No," she said. "And no action on the profile yet, either." He'd told her it would be okay for her to monitor it, while he was working the Davison case, but not to respond to anything.

"I didn't expect anything this fast. We only went live this morning."

Those few moments were difficult. Mostly because Brett didn't dare say much. And that was because his conversation with Desiree kept playing back in his mind.

*If you're asking if we're sharing that room, we're not.*

*Why not?*

And it was playing in his mind again when he told her to get some rest and watched her as she retreated back into that very room. And no amount of telling himself that going out as bait again when exhausted would be borderline suicidal seemed to work. He lay sleepless on the couch he was getting mightily tired of.

But adrenaline kicked in and did its job and he was awake and alert the next night when he and Ember strolled through the park again. He was glad it had cooled a bit tonight, maybe even dropped below sixty, given he had to wear a jacket to hide his sidearm. Ember was again having a great time, sniffing the wind, the ground, leaves, and not for the first time Brett smiled at the catalog of scents that must reside in her mind. Or nose. Wherever she kept it, it was a skill he both respected and admired.

And it was Ember who warned him. The dog's head came up rather sharply, and she swiveled around to face into the very slight breeze. Then she gave a low whuff of sound as she sat, looking up at him.

He spoke very quietly into the mic concealed under the collar of his jacket. "She's on a known scent."

"Copy." Troy's voice came back instantly through the nearly invisible earbud. "I'm on your six."

And he would be, Brett knew. *There's no one I'd rather have as backup.* He'd meant those words he'd said to Annalise. And it occurred to him that he should probably say them to Troy, too. He knew the man knew he had had reservations about the Colton presence on the department, but Troy had never pushed, had only said that made it their job to earn his trust.

Brett saw and heard movement in the trees to his left. It was too dark to discern much else, but he was still certain. Relayed it through the mic as he bent to pat Ember's head as if she were simply a recalcitrant pet who was tired of walking. And he turned slightly as he did it, so that he was almost facing the direction where he'd seen the movement.

And then a man stepped out onto the path. He was casually dressed, and wore a Tigers baseball cap, pulled low over his brow, casting his face into pure darkness.

*Fitting.*

Because it was Davison. He knew it, even if he couldn't fully see the murderer's face. He thought he would have sensed that himself, even if Ember hadn't told him in her own eloquent way. "Stay," he whispered to the dog.

The sting had worked. They had Grave Gulch's infamous serial killer within reach. And he wanted to end this now, toss the plan they'd all worked out and just take the guy down himself right here and now.

But that wasn't how it worked. He had to trust Troy and the others. *Trust.* The one thing that was hardest for him. But he had to do it, trust the team that was even now closing in for the capture and arrest.

All he had to do was stay alive until then.

# Chapter 30

"Sorry if I startled you," the man said pleasantly, conversationally, "but I was wondering if you had the time."

"For what?" Brett asked, pretending to misunderstand, stalling as his backup moved in.

It was a second before the other person responded, "Pretty dog." He said it as if he'd never asked the first question, and Brett knew he'd disconcerted him.

"She is," Brett said, taking advantage of the situation to give Ember, who was quivering with recognition of the scent she'd been set to track so many times filling her nose, a steadying pat. They were pushing the boundaries of her training, but all the work Annalise had done with her was paying off; she wasn't happy, but she was doing as ordered.

"She doesn't like strangers?" the man—Davison, he was sure now, shadowed face or not—asked with a note of wariness.

*You're no stranger to her.* "Do you like dogs?" Brett countered.

"Sometimes."

Brett heard a sound from behind him, the merest rustle of a branch. But it was enough to set Davison off, because in the next instant he spun around and was running. Back into the dark shadows of the trees.

"Rabbit!" Brett yelled into his mic as he started after the man at a dead run.

Troy's answering shout echoed in his ear, and the team abandoned any effort at stealth. They were all running now, following the fleeing suspect. Brett heard Bryce's voice in his ear acknowledging Troy's directions.

The terrain, the trees and the darkness were making it impossible to see, and the suspect was making no noise at all. Which seemed impossible, given the spreading branches and the underbrush. Unless Davison knew these woods well, Brett thought. Very, very well. That was worth remembering.

Ember tugged at the leash, wanting loose, but Brett held her back. He didn't want her in the line of fire during a foot pursuit of a killer. Black dog and black night were an invitation to a nasty accident. She could follow the scent easily enough later, if necessary, so he kept her close. And hoped that her prodigious tracking abilities wouldn't be necessary. This needed to be over, for the sake of possible future victims and the entire town of Grave Gulch. And the department that served it, but now was taking so much heat on so many fronts.

Not for the first time he had the thought that if he'd wanted a quieter, slower pace than the sometimes ugly big city, he hadn't gotten it. Not yet, anyway. But he was still happier here than he'd ever been in the capital. Hell, he'd been happier in the last few days than he'd been in his entire life. And that was a realization that slammed him in the gut like a sucker punch. Because there was only one reason he could think of why that was possible.

And it was the same reason every moment of those last few days.

Annalise.

He gave a sharp shake of his head. If he went down that path, even in his mind, he could practically step on Davison before he tuned back in to reality. And that was not a good place for a cop to be. Ever. But most especially when on the hunt for a serial killer.

He heard the chatter over the radio. Heard Grace's voice, higher than normal, clearly excited, and sent a silent warning to her to stay safe; he did not want to have to tell Annalise her little sister had been hurt. Moments later another exchange, this time Troy and Bryce, Troy sounding a bit fierce as he called a halt, for everyone to just stop, and listen.

Brett sat Ember as he halted. Listened. Barely breathed. Heard nothing. He was no woodsman, but it seemed too quiet. Not even the hoot of an owl broke the silence. As if even the wild things knew a wilder, much eviller thing had passed through their world.

"He slipped past us," Bryce said over the radio, his agitation clear.

Brett swore under his breath. This was the closest they'd ever gotten to Davison, and he'd somehow vanished?

"How'd he freaking do that?" Troy was not happy either.

"Dog in play," Brett said shortly, "hold fire." Ember knew those words, although as the well-trained K-9 she was, she waited for the order. Once the team had acknowledged his transmission, he gave her the full length of the heavy leash and said, "Ember, track."

The jolt to his arm and shoulder as the eager canine

took off never ceased to amaze him. His girl was on the job, and she would track that scent to the ends of the earth if he asked it of her.

*I'll settle for to Davison's door, wherever it may be.*

It was going to be a long night.

Annalise made another circuit of the living room floor. She'd given up trying to stop herself from pacing. She couldn't stop, not until Brett was safely back home. Apple and Jack were already convinced she was losing it, she was sure. She'd had them outside at least a half-dozen times in the last three hours. She had tired them out with games and fetch and anything else she could think of, never truly acknowledging even to herself that it wasn't the dogs she was trying to wear out.

If she could have done something stupider than fall in love with a cop, she couldn't think of it at the moment. Nor could she deny any longer that that was exactly what she'd done. Despite the stress and strain and worry she'd seen her family endure for loving someone in this intense but crucial profession, she'd gone and fallen for one.

The dogs didn't even lift their heads anymore as she turned on her heel in front of them and started back across the room. In fact, they barely twitched an ear. She tried to focus on the pair, and how much they'd progressed. Even being uprooted from her place to here, they'd settled in nicely. In fact, they were happier here than she'd ever seen them. Whether it was the huge yard, Ember's companionship or that there were two people here to provide them attention, she didn't know.

*Or maybe they fell for Brett the same way you did.*

Yeah, there was always that. And if that was true, then she was dreading the moment when the pups would have to go back to her place.

But then, she was dreading that herself.

As another hour rolled by on her phone's screen, she stared at it. Contemplated calling the station, to see what the status was. Told herself they had better things to do than answer her worried question. Not to mention she might as well run up a flag that declared she was in love with Brett Shea. She was not ready for that.

And she was certain he was not. Because she wasn't certain he felt the same way about her. She gave a shake of her head at the way her thoughts kept echoing each other, chasing each other, stirring up continuing chaos in her mind. And the longer this went on, the more chaotic her thoughts got. She started imagining all sorts of horrible scenarios, and she was close enough to the department to know just how horrible the scenarios could get in reality.

She'd worried about officers involved in dangerous situations before, especially those she worked with directly.

It had never been anything like this.

As dawn crept closer she dozed fitfully on the couch. The couch where Brett had been sleeping since she'd invaded his space. It was somehow comforting.

It was the dogs who stirred her to alertness with a couple of happy yips. The kind they reserved for their new buddy. Whether that was Ember or Brett, she wasn't sure. And since they were practically a unit, it didn't really matter. What mattered to her was they were home.

She was on her feet and had the door open before they even hit the porch. The only one who looked more dejected than Brett was Ember, who appeared beyond sad. Then Brett realized she was there, and his expression shifted to surprise.

"You're all right?" she asked anxiously. "Both of you?"

"Fine," he said. "Fuming, but fine. Why are you up?"

"I couldn't sleep." She didn't add *Because I love you and I was worried*.

"Everybody's fine," he assured her. "Troy, Bryce—"

"And Grace?" Annalise asked. He hesitated, as if wondering if he should answer that one. "It's safe to tell me, as long as she's all right."

"She is," he said, and headed inside.

She studied his face as they came in. He looked exhausted, but his jaw was set as if he was fighting anger. Still, he saw to Ember first, checking her bowls for water and kibble.

"I made sure they were ready," she said, and this time when he looked at her his expression was a little milder. She wasn't sure she should ask, but she needed to know. "Fuming?"

He ran his hand over his stubbled jaw, then through his hair. Then he let out a frustrated sigh. "We almost had him."

She nearly gasped. "Davison? He...took the bait?"

He nodded. "But he heard or sensed...something and took off running. Ember lost the scent deep into the woods." He frowned then. "It was weird. She sat like she does when the scent just ends, like when someone gets into a vehicle."

Annalise had to force herself to focus on what he was saying, even though she was hating every word of it. "In the middle of park?"

"Yes." He gave a weary shake of his head. "We've been searching since midnight. No trace. Ember went over the trail three times, and it always ends right there."

"Could he have had a vehicle there?"

"Nothing bigger than a bicycle," he muttered. "Which is possible, I suppose. But if he was able to do that in the dark, then he knows the park inside and out. He certainly knows it well enough to get away from us." He rubbed his hand over his face again. "They'll go over the scene again in daylight—maybe something will turn up. They'll try again, with someone else, different dog. Maybe Ember's just too big and scared him. The others have been smaller. And patrol will be focusing on the area, especially at night, but…"

He gave a half shrug and shook his head at the same time. She could only imagine how it must feel to have been that close only to have the killer slip away. And poor Ember—she knew the animal well enough to realize she felt as if she'd failed somehow. She'd done her job, tracked the scent to the end of the trail, but Brett's demeanor had to be telling her it wasn't enough.

"She's taking it hard," she said, bending to stroke Ember's head.

"My fault," Brett said instantly, warming her. "She did her part."

"She's a sensitive girl."

"I know. She reads my frustration." He rammed his fingers through his hair. "I could have grabbed him. He was that close."

Annalise's heart gave a funny little leap. And not a happy one. Brett had been within arm's length of a serial killer. She had spent a long time tonight thinking about it, repeatedly telling herself she could deal, that she'd grown up in a police-connected family, but this was different.

This was the man she loved. Not matter what his feelings were—or weren't—she couldn't deny her own.

"I'm not sure we'll ever have a better chance than we had tonight," Brett said. "And we blew it. I blew it."

"You didn't blow it. And you came home alive," she pointed out, a little shakily.

"That's not my job. My job was to catch this guy. Before he kills someone else."

And suddenly she was face-to-face with the reality of his work. The simple fact that part of his job was to put himself in harm's way. To risk injury, even death, so that someone he didn't even know, some citizen, did not have to. He obviously accepted that.

But now, as she stood there looking at him, she wasn't sure anymore if she was tough enough to accept it herself.

## Chapter 31

His house was too damned empty. And that was a thought Brett had never had before; it had never bothered him to live alone, and with Ember, he'd never really felt that way.

Until now.

When Annalise had insisted she needed to go home, he'd understood. Even though he felt better with her here, where he could keep her safe, she had her own life, her home, her routines, and wanted to get back to them. He would have preferred she stay until they had reeled in this catfish, but he understood.

What he hadn't understood was how could one woman and two dogs, who had only been here for three days, leave such a hole? Such an aching, empty place, not just in this house, but…in him?

He shoved aside the memory of coming home to this empty place and tried to concentrate on the laptop screen before him. Ellie had assured him she'd set things up so no matter where he checked the dating app from, it would appear the same. That that also made it possible for Annalise to do the same he was trying not to think about. It only made sense, after all, for her to have access, because she would probably be quicker than anyone to recognize the real catfish. He had the record of their text communications, and he'd read them several times—several because he'd had trouble staying objective, reading her excited and, face it, innocently optimistic posts—but that wasn't the same of having done it yourself in real time. Plus, it wasn't burned into his memory the way it no doubt was in hers. She still hadn't forgiven herself for falling for the guy's facade.

Which brought him back full circle again, thinking about Annalise and…missing her presence. And the dogs.

It was just too quiet. But how could he have gotten so used to the bustle and noise of the three of them so quickly? And why couldn't he shake the thought that it wasn't just wanting to go home that had made her insist on leaving? That it was, somehow…him?

He would have physically slapped himself upside the head, as his father had always said, if he thought it would do any good. He'd never had a problem with focus before, yet now he couldn't seem to go five minutes before his mind slid back into what was getting to be a rut.

It was simply that he was concerned for her safety. The catfish knew where she lived, and his gut was still telling him the guy wasn't going to take her catching him out lightly. Sure, patrol was keeping a close eye on her and her house but that wasn't the same as her being here, in a place the criminal didn't know about, and with him to watch over her.

But he hadn't been able to convince her to stay. And it was the way she'd looked at him when she'd doggedly insisted she needed to leave that had him thinking he was at least part of the reason.

Because he'd kissed her? Twice?

No, because she'd kissed him back. Eagerly. She'd wanted that.

So, because he'd wanted more, so much more, and it had been obvious?

*Face it, you wanted everything. You wanted her mouth, her hands, her body, everything.*

He threw down the pen he'd been toying with. Trying to hang on to that past tense was so much work he knew that proved it a lie. Proved he hadn't just wanted, he still did. Everything.

*And what about her heart? That sweet, giving heart?*

He didn't want that. He'd never wanted that from any woman. Hell, maybe that was what Annalise knew; maybe that was why she wanted out. Because to her, all the heat, all the need, all the wanting in the world didn't matter if it didn't come with the kind of love she was after. The forever kind. The kind he'd never known in his life.

The kind he didn't even believe in.

Or did he?

Ember nudged his elbow, startling him. Which told him how out of it he'd been, when the dog managed to sneak up on him. She didn't give him the "outside" signal, but instead simply leaned into him, encouraging him to pet her. He stroked her head, her impossibly soft ears, wondering what it was about dogs that enabled them to sense when their people were…what? Distracted? Unsettled? Confused?

He let out a long, audible sigh. He'd admit to all of those. It was the other ones he didn't want to admit to. The ones like empty. Lonely.

Hurting.

*What you should be obsessing about is that you had Len Davison within reach and let him get away.*

The fact that it wasn't anything he'd done that had set Davison off didn't matter; he was the one who had been close enough to grab him. That it had been the plan that he'd hold off until the others closed in didn't matter, either; he should have scrapped the plan the instant the guy was close enough. Except that he'd agreed to the plan.

All of which reduced him to wondering which was worse, obsessing about his empty house and Annalise's absence or the Davison fiasco. That he couldn't decide was just further evidence of how screwed up his mind was right now. He needed to concentrate. Their fictional schoolteacher had attracted a few hits on her profile, and he needed to go through them—

His phone signaled an incoming text. It was the generic tone, not work, so he finished calling up the profile to look at the hits before he looked.

When he did look, he froze for an instant.

*I should have assigned her a ringtone. Then at least I'd have some warning.*

Before he could veer off into trying to decide what tone would be suitable for her, he picked up the phone and opened his texting app. And denied that some part of him was hoping she was feeling a bit of what he was feeling. Maybe even that she wanted to come back.

I looked at the profile. I think he bit.

That blasted all else out of his mind.

Just opened it now. Which one?

The guy named Colin Stetler. Or calling himself that.

Checking.

He hit the icon to call her. He'd been resisting doing just that all evening, but this was business.

When she answered, he started as she had, no preamble, no niceties. "What makes you think it's him?"

She answered the same way, all business. "To start with, it's the same opening line, almost word for word. And has the same feel."

"The bit about her dog being cute, and how he's a fellow dog lover who wouldn't trust anyone who didn't love them?"

"Yes."

He remembered the catfish had done the same with her without having to look up the transcript. He practically had the interchanges they'd had memorized. How the catfish couldn't, because of his very busy schedule at the hospital, spend as much time with his dog as he wanted to, how much he missed little Charlie the beagle while at work, and on and on. The guy had played on her love for dogs perfectly.

*And counted on her warm, kind heart.*

He shoved the emotion aside, into that room in his mind it kept stubbornly breaking out of. He scanned the profile, noted the same sort of perfect, polished images of a good-looking, outdoorsy kind of guy with a big grin he supposed most women would like. The kind of images you might find in an ad campaign for some outdoor equipment store.

"This guy is even claiming he broke up with his last girlfriend because she and his dog didn't get along," she said.

"Search-and-rescue dog at that," Brett muttered as he looked at the profile.

"Yes. Nice and heroic. Just the type some women fall for."

The tiniest of edges had crept into her voice, making the words a bit too pointed. Was that aimed at herself? Falling for her fake doctor.

*Or you?*

He immediately tried to quash how that made him feel. Besides, that would mean she saw him as…heroic. Which he wasn't. He was just a cop, trying to do the best job he could.

He shoved the thoughts back in that room again, and this time he mentally locked the damned door.

"Anything else jump out at you?"

"Yes." Her voice seemed back to normal now. Or at least brisk and businesslike. "Look at the way he talks about his mother in the family section. Not that it might not be true, but it's another similarity."

He paged down. *She's the greatest.* He remembered the catfish profile. *Best mom in the world.*

"Dr. Masters thinks he probably has mommy issues," he murmured.

"And some guys know women look at how they treat their mothers to get a hint of how they might treat their wives."

He couldn't help it—the exchange made him smile despite what it told him about how she must look at him. "Guess I strike out on both counts, since I didn't know that, and my mother and I only talk on Mother's Day and her birthday."

"I call mine on my birthday. To thank her for having me, and for loving me."

For some reason that tore at him. And he barely stopped himself from blurting out something stupid like how easy it would be to love her.

"That's nice," he said instead, and it sounded incredibly lame even to him. "Anything else?" he asked, back to the matter at hand.

"I…"

"Annalise?"

"It just…feels the same. The way he uses words, the short sentences but big words."

"Like he's smart enough to have a big vocabulary, but too busy to spin out a long tale."

"Exactly," she said, sounding relieved. "And the pictures have the same feel, too. A bit too posed, too expert, no selfies, and the one he posted about a search-and-rescue mission he was involved in could be anyone at that distance."

He called up the image, which was indeed a distance shot of people combing through a thick stand of trees, one man in the background with a dog on a leash, obviously searching. "You're right. I'll have Ellie run an image match first thing, see if those other shots turn up on a stock photo site anywhere. And see if she can dig up a news story this photo might have gone with."

For a moment she didn't answer. Then, "Brett?"

"What?"

"I just noticed something. Look at that first picture of his dog."

He scrolled back up to the shot of a happy German shepherd with a tongue-lolling grin. "Yeah? Nice dog."

"Now look at the shot of the search again."

He went back to the other photo. There was something about the markings, the coloring of the German shepherd in the action shot… Then he sucked in a breath. "That's not the same dog."

"No. It's not. I know he doesn't say specifically that's him and his dog, but he certainly implies it."

"So it's either obfuscation, or…he's a fake."
"And if he's a fake…"
"He sure sounds like our fake."

# Chapter 32

*Our* fake.

How far gone was she that even him saying it like that, using those words, made her pulse kick up? *We. Our. Us.* Such simple, short words and yet they could have enough impact to change an entire life.

*He didn't mean it like that.*

And for one of the few times in her life she wished her last name wasn't Colton, since that seemed to be a big part of the barrier between them. But she immediately felt guilty and silently apologized to her parents. Besides, he had seemed to be getting past that. Just in time for her to realize she couldn't deal with him putting his life on the line, every day.

"I'll send this on to Ellie right now," he said, jolting her out of the recurring maelstrom of her thoughts. "Then a text to give her a heads-up. If I know her, she won't wait until morning to start searching."

"No wonder she and Mick barely see each other." But apparently the tech genius and her boyfriend made it work. Somehow.

"So now we need an answer for this guy."

She frowned instinctively, even though he couldn't see her. "Shouldn't we wait until Ellie finishes? To be sure?"

"I figured you'd be in a hurry."

"But what if he's a real person? It would sort of be like what the catfish does in reverse, wouldn't it? I'd hate to do that to some basically nice guy."

It was a moment before he said, sounding strangely bemused, "At least you think nice guys are still out there," he said.

"I do," she said. *I'm talking to one, even if he doesn't believe it.*

"All right. Why don't we make up a response now, but only send it if Ellie's able to prove our suspicions?"

So they spent a few minutes working up a casual yet friendly response to the man's query, with Brett agreeing to her additions and suggestions without hesitation. "It needs your touch," he told her. "I'm too down to business. You know, too get to the point and do it now."

"Too much a guy, you mean," she said, making sure her tone was teasing.

And she could almost see him smiling when he answered, "Exactly."

So the final version had the essentials Brett wanted, but with her own feminine touch. Then there was a long pause, and she wondered if he was trying to think of a way to just end the call. He'd been so…not quite brusque, but close. But then he spoke, softly, almost awkwardly.

"It's…really quiet here."

"I imagine you're enjoying the peace," she said, keeping her voice even with an effort.

"Not as much as I would have expected. The place feels empty." She suddenly couldn't speak. Found herself holding her breath. Then, his voice back to normal, he said, "Ember misses her friends."

"Do you?"

It was out before she could stop it. And when he answered, his voice had gone quiet again.

"Yes. I miss all of you."

Annalise clung to those words, and how he'd sounded saying them, long after the call ended. For Brett Shea, that was quite an admission.

It wasn't long before Ellie confirmed the photos on the account were faked; they were from a modeling agency. Which was a change from the stock photo sites, but they figured the catfish was being careful, switching things up a little. Otherwise he was following the script, with a few minor variations; he clearly wasn't stupid enough to just copy pictures. At least, not from himself; Ellie, being Ellie, had dug even deeper and found the guy sometimes did cut and paste sentences from other men's profiles.

"It's like he kept a file," she'd told them on a group call, "then tracked what he'd saved back to which guys took themselves off the app because they'd found 'the one.' Then he used the things they'd said."

"A real success model," Brett had said sourly.

And when Ellie had disconnected from the call, Annalise had said just as sourly, "So he uses real nice guys to pretend to be one himself. Charming."

"Yeah. But also a reminder. He's not stupid."

Brett sent the response they'd prepared. They had an answer within an hour, one full of enthusiasm and a charming humbleness that she'd answered. The same sort of feel she'd had from the catfish. She buried the humiliation that wanted to surge to the surface again and helped Brett craft an answer. And so it went over the next couple of days, back and forth between the predator and the bait, a slow, tantalizing game that would have seemed full of hope and promise, if she hadn't known how fake it all was.

On the work front, those couple of days were almost normal. Except for the time she spent looking at her session calendar and lingering on Ember's name, a full week away. Would she not see the sweet Lab before then?

Would she not see Brett before then?

True, she talked to him daily, usually more than once as they strung along the catfish. But it wasn't the same as being under the same roof. That had felt so... She wasn't sure what the word was. Wasn't sure there even was a word for that odd combination of unsettling and yet comfortable. Natural. Right.

But now his approach was all business. Their conversation was all business. His tone made that clear, and he never veered away from the case at hand. And that, she supposed, told her she was wasting her time wishing it was otherwise.

She tried to stay busy, to not think about it. She was grateful for the training sessions with her other clients. Each animal had its own personality, each handler their own way of working, and she adapted to each. The purpose of these eight-hour sessions was to keep the dog's skills sharp. Every two weeks they worked hard at it. Or every week in the case of a couple of dual-purpose canines she worked with, like Bear, the ones who were trained in not just tracking and searching, but protection and criminal apprehension.

But always in the back of her mind Brett lingered, Brett and the black Lab she'd come to love. She missed them, darn it. She missed them, she missed his cozy house with all the space for the dogs, she missed watching Jack and

Apple play with Ember, she missed sharing the kitchen tasks, missed cooking for them or watching him cook for them.

He'd said he missed them. All of them. Had he meant that, or was it just the dogs underfoot he missed?

Take him at his word, her heart said. *He meant all of us. He missed all of us; he liked the time you'd spent under his roof as much as you had. And he kissed you, like you've never been kissed before. He wanted more. He wanted everything you wanted. It was obvious when he had you pressed against him.*

*Don't be stupid again*, her brain said. *That was just a physical reaction. He's never said anything to indicate it's anything more than that for him. So yeah, he kissed you, but then he slammed the door. What does that tell you? And the last time, when it seemed like he'd opened that door again, his job came calling. And maybe that was a good thing, because do you really want to live in constant fear that one day he won't come back? Isn't that why you had to get out of his house? You know you're not tough enough for that.*

And right now that was the only thing she was truly certain of.

By Thursday of that week Brett was convinced he'd lost his mind. It was all he could do not to show up at Annalise's house and have it out with her. Make her tell him exactly why she'd bailed in such a hurry. The real reason.

And for the hundredth, maybe thousandth time, he wondered what would have happened if the chief hadn't called to give the go-ahead on the Davison op at that precise moment the other night. Would he have found out that breathy yes hadn't meant what he thought it had? Or would they have wound up in his bed, finding out just how fierce this need really was?

*Like you don't already know...*

But now that she was gone, now that his house echoed as if hollow, he was beginning to realize it wasn't just his house that was empty. He felt her absence like an entirely different kind of physical ache, one centered in his chest. A kind of ache he'd never felt before, one that could only be eased by her presence.

And he realized with a jolt that he wanted that presence, not just in his bed but in his life. He wanted the days to go on with them together, because it made him feel complete. He'd never realized what that would be like, and now that he had, it was gone.

She was gone.

And he didn't like it. He didn't like his life without her. Even though—or maybe because—she'd turned it upside down.

He didn't know what to call it. The only word that came to mind—love—scared the hell out of him.

But it was the only word that fit.

When a new message arrived, he didn't know whether to be glad of the distraction, or groan that it was from the dating app, which meant another return-message session with Annalise. At a moment when his thoughts were in chaos.

Almost reluctantly he looked. And went still, staring.

Not even a minute later his phone rang. And this time he knew without picking it up, because he'd finally assigned it a ringtone that fit. The pulse-pounding theme from one of those action movies she'd told him she loved. Although the music wasn't the only pulse pounding.

He took a breath, connected the call and before she

could speak—and maybe say something he wasn't ready for—he said, "I got it."

"This is too fast, isn't it? He's never gone this fast before, gotten to asking to meet so quickly, with me or with the others. Maybe it's not him after all."

She sounded distressed, and from what she'd said before he knew it was as much because she was afraid they'd strung along some nice, innocent guy as thinking they'd wasted time while the real catfish had maybe landed someone else. She really was one of the best people he'd ever met.

"Take it easy," he said reassuringly. "Don't forget the photos, and the thing with the dogs. Even if it wasn't him, he's still lying."

"Oh. Yeah."

"But I think it's him."

"But why so fast? It was a month before he pushed me to meet in person."

"Because that went south on him. He wouldn't take that well." He'd had another long talk with Dr. Masters, and they were in agreement on this.

"So you think he's hurrying to…what, make up for that?"

"I do."

He didn't elaborate, didn't tell her she'd humiliated the catfish more than he ever could have humiliated her, because his ego was fragile, much more fragile, and he would go to extremes to repair it, to be able to tell himself he'd gotten even. He didn't tell her because he didn't want to scare her, because he had a bad feeling about just how far this jerk would go.

Bottom line, this ruse had better work.

"So…do we say yes?" she asked.

"I think we say yes, but not for his day. He wants tomorrow night. Maybe for a reason, Friday, lots of people out and about he won't stand out as much."

"Not because it's *Friday the Thirteenth*?" she asked, her tone dry. He smiled, glad she could joke.

"Maybe that too. But let's offer him Saturday night instead."

"But that would mean you're working another weekend. You deserve a break."

He couldn't quite put a word on how it made him feel that that was her first thought.

"We're all sometimes working weekends until Davison is caught anyway," he said. Then, because he had to, added, "But thanks."

"Maybe we should make it Sunday afternoon, middle of the day, out in the sunlight. That way we can recognize him easily, because he'll be the worm drying out in the sun."

He laughed. And then, because she'd earned it, he said, "You're amazing, you know that?"

There was a moment of silence—a too long moment—before she said quietly, "I wish I could believe you believe that."

"I do believe it."

"Even though my name is Colton?"

Brett hesitated, then went for it, hoping he could get the real reason why she'd suddenly decided she had to go back home. He still didn't buy the routine explanation she'd given him. But he didn't know if it was something he'd said or done, or that what had nearly happened between them had scared her.

"The name doesn't trigger me as much as it used to."

"I'm glad of that," she said, in a tone so neutral he suspected it had to be purposeful. But before he could push the issue, she said, "So how shall we word her acceptance and alternate day?"

They worked it out and sent the response. Grave Gulch Coffee and Treats, Saturday night.

When the call ended, it was Brett sitting there not liking her all-business approach. The irony of that did not escape him.

*If this is how she felt with you, no wonder she left.*

Later, lying in the bed she had lain in, a fact that was more unsettling—and arousing—than he ever would have thought, he wondered if he'd ever be able to sleep here again.

And he was still restlessly and almost painfully awake when, just after closing time when the patrol officers would be on the lookout for drunk drivers leaving the bars, his phone rang. With the work ringtone.

He rolled over and grabbed the phone off the nightstand. Troy. Something was up. He grimaced at the date that glowed at the top of the screen; it was officially Friday the thirteenth.

"Go," he answered without preamble.

Troy answered the same way, but fury echoed in his voice. "It's Davison. Bastard hit again."

Brett smothered a vicious oath. He had no doubts Davison had chosen the day on purpose.

Friday the thirteenth, indeed.

# Chapter 33

"In the park?" Brett asked, although he suspected he already knew.

"Yes. But nowhere near where we were working the sting."

*Place was too damned big.* "Victim?"

"ID'd as Terence Parks, fifty-six-year-old male, married, no kids."

"Dog?"

"Yes. Little furball thing, unharmed. Belongs to the wife."

*The widow,* Brett thought grimly. "On the way," he said.

He rolled out of bed, flipping on a light as he did so. Ember looked at him curiously.

"We're on," he told her, and the dog leaped to her feet.

They were in the car and rolling five minutes later. Five hours of searching later, exhausted and far beyond frustrated, he was standing with Troy next to a marked unit parked at the entrance to one of the many hiking trails that meandered through Grave Gulch Park. The officer sitting inside, who had been the first one on the scene, was working on what would end up a very lengthy report.

The only clue they'd gained was from Ember. She had once more led them, although via a different path, to the same spot as the other night. The same place, up against the mossy rocks. And yet again she stopped, signaling the trail ended there, impossibly, amid the trees and underbrush.

They watched as the coroner's van left the scene, Brett thinking he was glad not to be the one who got to deliver the news to the man's wife. He'd done enough death notifications to never want to do another.

"This guy," Troy said, "is really, truly ticking me off."

"Amen," Brett agreed. "I want his ass on a platter, preferably skewered."

The radio in the marked unit crackled, and all heads swiveled toward the dispatcher's voice saying "All units, be advised…"

Brett sighed inwardly as the report he'd hoped he wouldn't hear quite yet came over the air; the protesters had arrived. It didn't even matter at this point how the word had gotten out; what mattered was the large crowd already gathered—and growing—in front of the station.

"At least they're not here, screwing up the crime scene," he muttered.

"Yet," Troy said sourly.

"Good point. Let's get it wound up, then," Brett agreed.

A couple of hours later, after the beleaguered CSI team had gone over every blade of grass and speck of dirt one last time, Troy and Brett finally cleared the scene. By then the report was not only that the crowd of protesters had grown, they were getting nastier, so Brett decided to drop Ember off at the training center. She wasn't trained for crowd control, nor did she have the intimidating appearance and demeanor that would make people think twice before approaching her. He didn't want her hurt, so she'd be better off there.

With Annalise.

He braced himself to see her again, for the first time in more than four days. Decided to monitor the radio as distraction, and heard the crowd was getting more and more unruly, becoming more of a mob than concerned citizens.

Sergeant Kenwood met him near the entrance. "Sounding pretty bad over there," he said as Ember padded over to greet him familiarly.

Brett nodded. "Why I'm leaving her here before I head over."

Kenwood took the leash with an answering nod. "Good call. Was thinking of heading there myself."

Brett shook his head. "You've got civilians and animals here, and if that mob gets a wild hair to go after anything police related, they'll need you."

Kenwood sighed. "You're right. It just goes against the grain."

"I know, Sarge. I know."

Brett heard the door behind him open and knew who it was instantly. A sort of tingle hit the back of his neck and shivered down his spine.

"Hell of a mess," Kenwood said. "You take care over there."

"I will." He heard quick, light steps, headed toward them and tried to brace.

"I just saw a news report. You're going to the station?" Annalise almost demanded. He finally turned to look at her, and the worry in her expression, in eyes more gray then blue today, quashed the tension he was feeling.

"Yes."

"I'm coming with you."

"No. There's no—"

"They're screaming for my cousin's blood, my family's blood. I'm going," she insisted, "with or without you. I just thought one less car in the mess might be better."

She meant it. He could see that. She was afraid, but for her family she would stand in the face of potential danger. And when it came down to having her go there by herself, or with him so he could watch out for her, there was no contest. No contest at all.

"All right," he said. "But you do what I say when I say it." He practically snapped it out, because the thought of her being hurt made him shiver inside.

"Yes, sir," she answered, with nearly as much snap.

The mob was even bigger than he'd expected. It filled Grave Gulch Boulevard, and in fact had two fronts. One side was facing the police department, shouting about incompetence and how many more people had to die, while the other half was aiming at city hall across the street, demanding Chief Colton resign.

He turned off the boulevard well before they reached the angry crowd and headed for the back entrance. He was counting on the fact that the media was out front to keep the protesters there, who sometimes measured success, or at least the impact they were having, by the number of reporters present. But even behind the big stone building the sounds, the yelling, the chants, all the ugliness was clearly audible. The refrain "Chief Colton has got to go!" was repeated over and over, and in one moment a single yell about getting rid of every Colton like the rats they were rang out.

Annalise was shaking by the time they got inside, her bravado fading in the face of such hatred for her cousin, her entire family.

"Try not to let it get to you," he said once they were safely inside.

"They hate her so much. They hate all of us, and all we've ever done was try to protect them, keep them safe."

"They're scared and angry," he said as they walked down the hallway toward the chief's office. "People do unusual things under either of those conditions. Both together is a recipe for…what's happening out there."

She stopped dead and looked up at him. "This is my *family* they're threatening!"

He didn't know what to say so said nothing, although his jaw tightened. And as if she'd noticed, her expression changed, softened. And to his shock she reached up and cupped his face with a slender hand.

"And I wish you knew what it feels like, to at least have a family you love and who love you."

He stared at her, stunned that in the middle of all this she could even think of that. And suddenly everything seemed to shift, and the crowd outside, the antagonism and downright hate, felt very, very personal. As it must to her. He'd never felt anything quite like this sensation, and it was both startling and disconcerting. And he realized that he was feeling as if the threat to the Coltons was a threat to him.

Because it was a threat to the woman he loved.

Heat flashed through him, not the heat of need but of shock as he realized what it was he was feeling, as he finally admitted it in so many words.

He loved her.

He loved Annalise Colton.

He was still a bit shaken when the door to the chief's office opened and a man came out. Brett glanced over and went still as he recognized him. Camden Kingsley, internal-affairs investigator for the county. This wasn't the first time he'd seen the tall, deadly serious man nosing around; he'd spotted him here in the station a few times over the last couple of days. And while the man himself might be okay, Brett didn't know him well enough to say otherwise, just his position and the job he did was enough to set any cop's teeth on edge. Thankfully the guy kept going.

Then the chief, her top aide and the department PIO—not a job Brett would wish on anyone right now, not that public information officer had ever been a position he'd envied—stepped out. They were clearly finishing whatever conversation had been going on inside, but Brett saw Chief Colton register their presence and gesture them toward her. The two other officers left with silent nods as they approached, and Brett thought he'd seen expressions less grim at murder scenes. And as she turned toward them he saw that the chief herself looked exhausted.

Once the others were out of sight Annalise ran the last few steps to her cousin and hugged her fiercely.

"Thanks," Melissa Colton said. "I needed that."

She wasn't joking, and again Brett marveled at the strength this family took from each other. What must it be like, to be part of a unit like that? He'd always figured it was sort of like being a cop, but connected by blood instead of uniform. But this was different. This was more. And he felt a powerful jab of something it took him a moment to recognize as longing.

When the chief looked at him, he wasn't sure what to say. Settled on "I'm sorry, Chief." He nodded toward the front of the building and by inference the crowd outside. "You don't deserve any of that."

"But maybe I do." She sighed. "I'm thinking it might be best all around if I step down, for the good of the department. And Grave Gulch."

"No!" He startled himself with his own vehemence.

"No way. You're the best I've ever worked for. This'll calm down once we get Len Davison and Randall Bowe, and in the meantime we've got your back."

He meant it. He hadn't really crystallized it into words until this moment, but he meant it. It was a rather startling realization after all his wariness about the pack of Coltons threaded throughout the department, but he couldn't deny he'd meant every word.

Annalise was staring at him. Then she smiled, so warm and sweet it was all he could do not to grab her and kiss right there in front of her cousin, his boss.

The chief asked for an update on the catfish. Brett was surprised she'd even thought of it, given what was going on outside. But it only proved what he'd said was true; she was the best he'd ever worked for.

And he'd do anything he could to see that the mob outside didn't get their way.

# Chapter 34

"Who was that guy, the one who walked out first?" Annalise asked as she came to a halt beside Brett's desk, where he'd gone to check in while she stayed with Melissa to give moral support. "Melissa just waved me off when I asked."

She knew she hadn't been wrong about his reaction to that man and hoped he didn't try to deny it. Or brush it off as nothing, as Melissa had.

He didn't.

"Internal Affairs," he said shortly.

She felt a chill. "Oh."

"Yeah."

"He's investigating—"

"Everything," Brett said, in a tone that matched his dour expression. "They're watching us, all of us, like a hawk. One foot wrong, and they'll come down on us hard."

"You mean about Bowe?"

"Yes." He reached out and shut down his computer, grabbed up his phone and stood up. "Asking did we know what he was doing with evidence and look the other way, like some of that mob outside claim? Can any of us be trusted?"

"That's so unfair. It was Bowe, no one else. Especially not Jillian!"

"I…admire how you all stick together."

That was a change, and her breath caught, because she understood so much better now. "Because you've never had family like that."

It wasn't really a question, but he answered anyway. "Never."

"Well, you do now. Melissa told me you have the complete respect of everybody on the department, starting with her."

Her cousin had also told her, with a too-knowing look, that she couldn't do any better if she was looking for a man to build a life with.

*I'm not tough enough to be with a cop.*

*You're a Colton. You'll cope.*

*But he's not looking for that.*

Her cousin had smiled softly then; for a moment her troubled expression was replaced with something much softer, a look Annalise had only seen on her face since she'd met her fiancé, Antonio. *Sometimes men don't know exactly what they're looking for until you show them.*

Brett was staring at her now, as if he'd had to process what she'd told him. "She said that?"

"An exact quote." He looked almost embarrassed. But he also looked pleased, which pleased her in turn. "Do you have to stay here?"

He shook his head. "I just needed to check in on some

things. Troy's handling the Davison case for the moment, so I can prep for the catfish tomorrow night."

"We're really sure this is him?"

"My gut says it is."

"All right."

He gave her a sideways look. "That's it? No doubts?"

She had complete faith in him, and she let it ring in her voice. "Not if you say it is."

"Annalise," he said.

He stopped, but something had changed in his voice, something that reminded her of how he'd said her name before he kissed her the first time. Her pulse kicked up a little and stayed there. But it wasn't until they were back outside in his car that he really looked at her.

"Tell me why you left."

That caught her off guard and she stalled. "You want a list?"

"Fine."

"It was time."

"Try again."

That pricked her temper. He wanted honesty? She'd give him honesty. "All right. I was starting to care about you. And you made it quite clear you don't want what I want—"

"Annalise—"

"Don't interrupt me. You're the one who wanted a list. As I said, you made it clear, so staying hoping you'd change your mind would be stupid. And I've had enough of being stupid about men."

"You're not—"

"I'm not finished." He was looking at her rather oddly now, but she was on a roll and wanted it all out in the open before she lost her nerve. Which thought brought her to the final, most compelling reason. "Most importantly, I was afraid," she said honestly. "That I'm not tough enough to be with a cop."

Even as she said it, her cousin's voice rang in her head. *You're a Colton. You'll cope.*

And as she said it, something flared in his eyes. "Does that mean…you wanted to be?"

"Does it matter? You don't want the same thing I want. I'm not looking for a fling, and you don't want anything else."

"Maybe I've changed my mind."

"You're going to have to be more definite about that."

He drew in a deep breath. "Come home with me," he said abruptly.

She stared at him, her heart truly beginning to race. The heart that wanted her to jump at the hope in those words. But for once her common sense, still a bit battered by the catfish, reined her in.

"Why?"

"That house is too damned empty without you." His mouth twisted at one corner, into a wry half smile. "All of you."

"So, it's my dogs you want?" she asked, determined to make him say it. And as if he'd understood the intent, he turned in the driver's seat to face her.

"Cut me some slack. I've never been here before. I've never fallen for anybody like this before. But it's you I want. Any way I can have you. Any way you'll give me." He took in a deep breath and added, "For as long as you want."

For Brett Shea, for Mr. I'm-Not-Looking-For-What-You're-Looking-For, Mr. You-Have-To-Believe-In-Love-Before-You-Can-Give-Up-On-It, that was quite a declaration.

And for stars-in-her-eyes, believes-in-the-fairy-tale Annalise Colton, it was enough for now.

\* \* \*

Apple and Jack scampered around in delight, clearly glad to be back. Ember seemed happy as well, to have her new canine friends back with her. Brett was letting the excited dogs out back, and as he watched them go Annalise saw him grin and say, "Let the romping begin."

She felt her cheeks heat as she thought of the other ways those words could be interpreted. She knew perfectly well what that brief stop at the drug store in town had been for. She appreciated the precaution, and not having to deal with it herself. Especially right now. She was not quite in the same state of mind as the dogs. It wasn't that she was having second thoughts, but now that they were here, she felt a bit awkward. On the few occasions she'd spent the night with someone, it had been a spontaneous sort of thing. This was not that. This was planned, intentional, a conscious decision.

*And exactly what you wanted. What you've wanted long before you ever realized it.*

And shouldn't it be a conscious decision? More often than not, she regretted impulse moves she'd made in her life.

He bent down to unlatch the doggie door so the trio could get back in on their own. And her cheeks heated all over again as she admired how his backside curved those back pockets.

"Brett?"

He turned around, still smiling. And she realized she'd never seen him look quite this way. Lighter. Happier. Despite everything going on around him and the department, happier. And as she looked at him she felt herself start to smile, because it seemed impossible not to.

*It's you I want. Any way I can have you. Any way you'll give me. For as long as you want.*

All her doubts, her awkwardness vanished. And she decided to voice that other interpretation of his words.

"Speaking of romping," she said. "Maybe we should take advantage of their absence."

Instantly heat flared in his eyes, and his entire demeanor changed. He crossed the space between them in two long strides, and when he pulled her into his arms she felt as if she was coming home after a long, stormy journey.

He kissed her, long, deep and hot, and for the first time in her life she truly realized how intimate a kiss could be. With others it had been a testing, an experiment. With Brett, there was no testing necessary; she already knew the effect he had on her, the places in her he reached that had never been awakened before.

*I don't know if this is love because I've never been there before.*

His words had seemed almost sad to her when he'd said them, but she suddenly realized that part of them was true for her, too. Because she had never been here before. But she knew what it was, because unlike him, she'd grown up with it, seeing it every day between her parents.

Love.

And it made her realize how amazing it was that the child, the boy who had never known what she had, had become the man he had. It told her more than anything else could about the heart, the core of Brett Shea.

And suddenly she wanted to make it all up to him, to show him what it could and should really be like.

She kissed him back, more than eager, more than hungry. She kissed him with all the longing, all the need she'd ever felt, probing, tasting, savoring. She heard him groan, low and deep in his chest, in fact she thought she felt the sound of it. His hands slid up over her rib cage and she felt a light caress over the sides of her breasts. Tentative, as if asking permission.

Speaking would require breaking the kiss and she didn't want that. So she instead slid her own hands down and pulled at his shirt, yanking it free of his belt. Then she slipped underneath it and stroked bare, sleek skin over his taut abdomen, loving the way that he sucked in his breath, the way she could feel that reaction under her fingers.

She wanted to whimper when he broke the kiss, but then she heard him suck in a breath so deep she thought he had, as she had, forgotten to breathe. Or perhaps forgotten how. And then he whispered her name, and the way he said it made her forget how to think. This was a time for feeling, and new and exhilarating sensations were flooding her.

"Now?" he asked, in that same shaky voice.

"Right now," she answered, sounding much the same.

He swept her up into his arms and carried her to the bedroom, to the bed he'd surrendered to her before. The only surrender she was interested in now was to the sensations overtaking her, awakening every nerve, every muscle, every inch of skin. She moved to help him when he started to tug at her clothes, or maybe it was her tugging at his; she wasn't sure anymore, and it didn't matter anyway. She wanted him naked, and she wanted to be naked with him. More new territory.

Clothes shed, they went down to the bed together, his hands on her and hers on him, stroking, searching, finding, memorizing. She wanted to know everything about him, everything he liked, so she could lure him to these moments again and again, prove to him it could last, even forever. At the same time he seemed to somehow know her, intimately, already. He trailed his hands, his mouth over her, waking up every nerve until she was nearly crying out with the feel of it. He rubbed, flicked, then suckled her nipples until she did cry out, her body practically rippling with fierce sensation.

His hands slipped over her, lingering a moment at the curve of her hip, then moving downward to stroke the very core of her. She didn't need the way his fingers slid over that knot of nerves to know that she was slick and ready, because she already knew it. But the bright, hot flash of fire that shot through her was new, breath-stealing, and again her body rippled under his touch.

He paused only to grab one of the newly bought condoms, but once he had it open she took it from him. He stared at her. "Let me," she whispered, wanting to touch him more than she wanted her next breath. She savored the look on his face at her words, the way his jaw clenched, as if he was assessing whether he would survive. Then he closed his eyes and she reached out. The groan that broke from him as she sheathed him was the most wonderful sound she'd ever heard.

He truly was beautiful. Tall, lean, powerful and purely male. She was certain he would laugh again if she said it, so she didn't. But later she would tell him, in no uncertain terms, just how beautiful she found him. And she wouldn't let him deny it.

And then she had no time to think. Or any desire to. Her desires had narrowed down to one thing. She wanted him, now, hot and hard and inside her. And when he moved to slide into her she welcomed him with a cry of his name. He groaned out her name in turn, and it was the most beautiful sound she'd ever heard.

And as if a dam had broken, all the months of denying how much he appealed to her, all the stolen glances, the telling herself it couldn't be, burst through. And as her body gathered itself, the impossible sensations building, she felt an unusual kind of gratitude for the circumstances that had brought them here. And then all thought was blasted out of her mind as her every nerve seemed to convulse at once, sending heat searing through her as her body clenched around him, and the only thing she heard was him saying her name like an oath, and her own voice moaning his over and over.

# Chapter 35

"Ember's not going to like you three going home," Brett said as he dished up the scrambled eggs he'd just finished cooking.

Annalise looked at him as he slid her plate across to her. "Oh?"

"Neither am I."

"They do like it here." She met his gaze, held it steadily. "I like it here."

Memories raced through his mind of all the times they'd come together. It had been the most astonishing, incredible, damned-near miraculous night of his life. Of any life, even one he could only have imagined. And the times in between, when he simply held her, when she snuggled up against him in utter contentment, had made him feel something he'd never felt before. An urge, a need, a demand entirely apart from the physical wonder he'd found with her.

He'd meant it when he'd told her he'd never been here

before. And because of that, he'd had no idea. No idea what it would feel like to want, to need someone so compulsively it was almost unbearable not to have them. Not just sexually, but always, quiet moments like now, together, a unit, stronger together than the sum of the parts...

And he realized this was what his parents had never had, had never known. And he felt suddenly sorry for them, because this...this was the most amazing thing ever. And he smiled as he thought of all the time ahead, time he wanted to spend learning about her, every bit of her heart and mind.

The smile she gave him now, as if she knew exactly what he'd been thinking and felt the same way, gave him the nerve. He leaned forward, planted both palms on the cool stone of the counter and said it, the words he'd never expected to say.

"Then stay."

She stared at him. "What?"

"I know it's a little farther from the training center, but the extra room is worth it, isn't it? For the dogs, I mean? I know this house is smaller than yours, but we can expand, there's plenty of room, and we can update a few things—"

"Brett Shea, are you asking me—us—to move in with you?"

He'd thought that was obvious. "I... Yeah."

"One night together and you want us to move in."

"Actually, it's been several nights," he pointed out. "And we've known each other for nearly a year. This is just the first night we..." He trailed off, not sure how to describe it. His mornings after had never really mattered before.

"Had mind-blowing sex? Screwed our brains out? Nearly set the house on fire?"

By the time she got to *fire*, he was grinning despite himself. He walked around the counter to her and took her hands. "All of that." But then, with one of the greatest efforts of his life, he made himself add, "But something even more important happened last night."

"It did?"

"You made a guy who never has and never thought he would, believe in love."

She stared at him. Waited, silently. And he realized she wanted the words. Maybe needed the words. Deserved them, for sure. And suddenly he wanted to give them to her.

"I have to believe in it now," he said softly, "because I love you."

She threw her arms around him and gave him a kiss that had an effect on him that, until about ten days ago, he would have denied was even possible.

The eggs were cold by the time they got to them, but neither of them cared.

Late that morning Brett took her back to the training center to pick up her car. Then he would head to the station for the final briefing on the operation tonight, date night for the catfish and the schoolteacher. They wanted everything and everyone in place well before the appointed time, just in case the guy was watching.

As he drove, Brett was pondering how he could expand the garage so there would be room for her car as well as his unit and gear, listening to the rustling in the back as her dogs scrambled for the best position to look out the windows, while a glance back showed Ember looking on with what he'd swear was amusement.

"She's like an elder sibling, watching the younger ones be silly," Annalise said when she saw his look.

He laughed. He'd thought he'd laughed more since he'd been with her than he ever had in his life. "And she will be, soon." He reached out and put a hand over hers. "If you're sure?" he asked.

"I am. I'll start packing the minute I get home." She turned her hand over so she could grasp his. "Now you have to really, truly be careful tonight."

"Assuming it all happens as planned. He's a pretty smart guy, or he wouldn't have gotten away with this for so long."

She smiled at him. "You don't have to keep saying that anymore. Yes, I was foolish, but I know I'm not really stupid. I fell for you, didn't I?"

He had no words for how that made him feel, so he didn't even try. And at the station he carried those words around in his mind as they ran through the plan once more, then began to put it into action. One by one so they wouldn't draw attention, his backup team headed for the staged house. They would take up predetermined positions around the house, up and down the street, most in civilian clothes and vehicles. Two, in uniform and fully armed and armored, would be the actual takedown team if necessary.

Brett was determined it would not be, because he wanted to take down this scrawny little imposter of a man himself. More now than ever.

In place inside the house, Brett secured Ember with commands to stay and for silence; he'd considered not bringing her for this, but she was his partner and he might need her. Then he again inspected all the possible points of entry, did a final test on communications with the team, made sure the phone they'd rigged as the teacher's was charged and on, then settled in to wait.

He supposed it was a measure of how things had changed—how he had changed—that instead of the usual calm, patient attitude he usually managed on a stakeout, he was edgy, pacing and forever thinking. And not about what he should be thinking about. He was personalizing this. Because, damn it, it *was* personal now. He was antsy to have this done, to take down this clown who had hurt Annalise, to put an end to this unpleasant event in her life. He wanted it over and done with and in the past, so they could start into the future.

Their future. Something he'd never had before or never expected to look forward to in this way.

He was just glad the rest of the team was outside, so he didn't have to explain the silly grin that broke loose far too often. Which led him down another path—what he was going to do when, as it inevitably would, news got out about them.

Them.

Annalise and him.

Him and Annalise.

A couple.

A long-term couple.

Forever? He hoped so. For the first time in his life, he hoped so. No, not just hope, he was determined it would be. He'd have to make that clear up front, to…all of them.

The chief. Troy. Desiree. Grace. Jillian. FBI Bryce. The other Coltons he'd never met. The list was incredibly daunting for a guy used to being alone, on his own, for nearly fifteen years, since he'd been eighteen and his parents had pronounced their duty done.

*Those Coltons would never do that. For better or worse, they are a unit and stand together. Have each other's backs.*

Driven by an urge that was as new to him as the rest, he called up the website for the K-9 training center on his own phone, just so he could look at her picture. He should take a better one, so he could have it with him. The official portrait was fine, but she looked so formal and…well, official. He wanted a picture of the smiling Annalise, the laughing one, the soft one. Hell, he wanted the angry one, too, with her chin set as she faced down whatever it was. When the chips were down, she was as tough as she had to be. And despite her doubts—*I'm not tough enough to be with a cop*—he knew she would always be.

The text came in as expected, just before the teacher would have had to leave to meet at the coffee shop. Brett read it, a sour grimace on his face. *Figures.* Of course that would be the excuse, something dramatic, laudable. A search and rescue for a missing little boy was his excuse. *I'm so sorry.*

Brett typed in the response he and Annalise had prepared, expressing the teacher's disappointment but understanding, and a compliment on his heroic vocation. And then came the rest of it, the vow to make up for it later, and in the meantime for her to expect something to make up for the forced cancellation. The delivery of her favorite drink—and some special treats—from Grave Gulch Coffee and Treats would arrive shortly.

Brett sent out the signal that it was a go, putting the team on high alert. They all reported back, in position and ready. And Brett was back to pacing again. And all his self-lecturing that it wasn't good to be this edgy, that that was when you made mistakes, wasn't helping. He wanted this over, wanted Annalise out from under this cloud, and he wanted it now.

"Incoming white van. Southbound from Hilltop. Slow."

The announcement came through loud and clear. Officer Fulton, he thought, the quiet but dogged patrol cop who had volunteered for this because she'd been at Annalise's the night the catfish had struck.

"Copy," he returned.

It was a minute later before the southern lookout spoke. "Got him under obs. He's slowing. Looking at houses. Or addresses."

"Copy," Brett repeated. "All units?"

Each reported in turn. They were as ready as they could be.

*Come on, come on, come on...*

"Heading for the driveway!"

A split second after he heard the words Brett saw the sweep of light across the front windows as the headlights of the van raked the house. He moved to where he could see through the big front window but would be far enough back not to be seen by the suspect. They'd agreed on radio silence starting the moment the suspect got out of the vehicle until Brett gave the signal to move in by turning on the porch light.

The man who got out of the white van looked right. Short, thin, at least, it was impossible to see more from here in the dark. He walked to the back of the van and unloaded a cart. This time it was a more casual affair, no linen tablecloth, but what Brett guessed from his visits to the place for morning coffee was a festively colored paper mat. The suspect then set several items on the cart, including some sort of machine like Brett had seen in the shop, he guessed to make the cappuccino as promised.

The catfish spared no detail, obviously. And Brett felt a twitch of misgiving, wondering if they really had covered all the bases. Once more he reminded himself this guy was not stupid. But he was here, and in moments he'd be cuffed and on his way to where he belonged.

The man wheeled the cart up to the front door and knocked. Brett waited a three count, then walked over. Weapon drawn now, he stood with his left shoulder to the wall, keeping his gun arm free. He reached with his left hand to open the door while in the same motion he flipped the light switch beside it with his elbow. Light flooded the porch from the high-power bulb he'd installed the first day he'd come here to check the site.

"Don't move. You're covered on four sides."

The shorter man's head came up. His face was now as clear as if spotlighted. And wide-eyed fear was just as clear in his expression. "What?" he practically squeaked.

Brett swore violently as the team closed in. "Stand down!" he snapped out.

"What's up?" Officer Fulton asked as she neared the front door.

"It's not him," Brett said disgustedly.

"What?" the young cop asked. "But he's got the van, the cart—"

"I saw him that night. This isn't him."

The former suspect realized he'd been absolved, although he likely had no idea for what.

"But…does that mean some regular guy just happened to use the same MO?" Fulton asked, sounding bewildered.

"I don't know." But he doubted it. The catfish had to be connected to this, somehow.

"I wonder where he really is," Fulton said, looking around as if she expected the real criminal to just walk out of the dark and into their hands.

"So do—"

Realization slammed into Brett as hard as if that van in the driveway had hit him at sixty. The little differences, the rush, the photos—he'd written them off to the catfish changing things up so he wouldn't get caught… But they weren't for that. They were because, for the catfish, this *was* different. This was to make up for the last time, to salve his ego, to show no one, but no one foiled him. Especially not his target, his mark.

*Soon enough, my sweet. I'll be coming for you.*

Annalise.

Annalise, at home alone, with just her dogs, because they'd assumed she'd be safe tonight.

He'd assumed.

And now he ran.

## Chapter 36

Apple and Jack barked and howled in an odd sort of accompaniment that made Annalise laugh. She'd been working since the moment she and the dogs had gotten home, packing, organizing, and probably ridiculously, singing the entire time. But she couldn't help it, her heart was soaring, so full of happiness it couldn't be contained.

She was going to have the future she'd always dreamed of. Well, minus the loving a cop part. That, with all its accompanying stress and danger had never been part of her dreams, but she would simply have to deal. She would talk to Evangeline, and they could compare notes, coping strategies. Her future sister-in-law was tougher than she was to begin with, and her time as a prosecutor had honed that, but Annalise was certain she could learn. She had to learn, because there was no way she was giving up Brett.

She was using the opportunity to set aside some things she no longer used or wore—and a couple of bad choices that had never been off the hanger or out of the box—to be donated. It was making a bit of a mess, but that was okay. Because she wasn't going to be here much longer.

She was going to need boxes. There was a moving company in the next town that sold them, she knew, and mentally added that to the list of chores that was growing rapidly.

And then there was the other list. The people list. People she would have to tell she was moving. Where she was moving. And why. Starting with her parents. And she had no idea how they were going to take it.

Maybe she'd start with her siblings. Grace and Desiree, they'd understand. Heck, they'd practically already guessed anyway, at least that she was attracted to him. And Troy would be okay with it, she knew, because she knew he liked and respected Brett. Or would he? Sometimes liking and respecting a colleague was different than accepting them as the lover and boyfriend of your sister. She hoped—

The sound of the doorbell startled her off the merry-go-round of thoughts and sent the dogs into a cacophony of noise.

"A little late, guys," she teased them as she started that way. "Did my glorious singing drown out the sound of someone coming to the door?"

She'd been in the bedroom at the back of the house. So aside from a bit of barking at a car that had parked in the alley a little while ago, she hadn't heard anything but the dogs. They had been more interested in what she was doing and—apparently, from their dancing around— her wonderful mood.

Not so long ago she would have just opened the door, but no longer, sadly. She felt a little pang as she realized she might never feel that safe again. But she smiled as she remembered soon she would both feel and be safer than she had ever been, because Brett would be there for her.

She stopped at the door and leaned forward.

"Pizza?" Annalise stared through the peephole at the box from Paola's the delivery man was holding up. "I didn't order any pizza."

That wasn't to say it didn't sound wonderful.

"It says it's a gift," the voice came through the door. "So somebody thought you need it."

Brett. She grinned sillily. It had to be Brett. Even while he was working, he was thinking of her.

She unlocked the door and pulled it open.

And gasped in horror.

Brett's plan was to come in from the alley, so he'd slowed to a crawl before making the turn off the street. His mind was racing so fast he was surprised he couldn't hear it whir. They'd have to be careful, startle the guy and who knew what he might do? Have to assume he was armed in some way. Knife, maybe. Because this was personal. She'd scared the catfish, so he wanted her scared. He wanted to make her pay.

The thought of her hurt, cut, bleeding, made a cool, calculating sort of anger rise in him. The bastard would not get away with this. Not with Annalise.

His SUV edged forward, and he looked down the alley. The first thing he saw was the white van, which had stood out by size alone even at this distance.

Two people behind it.

A man, short, thin, wearing a shirt as white as the paint job.

A woman.

Wrestling with him. Fighting.

Annalise.

He couldn't really see the woman from the far end of the alley, but he knew.

A jolt of pure fear shot through him, spiking his adrenaline level. It was all he could do to keep himself from ramming his foot on the accelerator, making a tire-screeching turn and giving away the game.

He registered everything, assessing in split seconds. She was fighting him, so she was conscious. But even as he thought it, she went limp. Which answered the dart question. The man shoved her into the van. Jumped in after her. And the door slammed shut.

He knew it had only been a couple of seconds, but it felt like a lifetime. He put out the info, not caring if what he was feeling was obvious in his voice.

"He's got her. In the alley. White panel van. Fulton, take the north end."

"Copy. I'm less than a minute out."

The sound of the van's engine cut through the night. Less than a minute wasn't going to be fast enough. Brett yanked the wheel around and jammed the accelerator to the floor. His SUV leaped forward, just as the van pulled away. The other driver realized quickly he was in trouble, and both van and police vehicle headed through the alley at far too high a speed.

The chase through the night was harrowing. For the first time since he'd left the city Brett missed something: the ability to call for air support. He could use a helicopter with a nice, bright spotlight. It was clear the catfish knew the area. He made turns down narrow streets that looked as if they should be dead ends but weren't. Cut through the parking lot of a small local grocery to come out on a bigger street. Increased his speed, dodging through Saturday-night traffic. And twice not dodging quite enough.

Brett managed to avoid the collisions himself. Barely. And that gave the van a few precious seconds to pull ahead.

And to make a last instant turn. Brett followed. Ember let out a yelp as the SUV careened around the corner.

The van was nowhere in sight. Gone.

Annalise was gone.

He would find her. If he had to cover every inch of Grave Gulch on foot, he would find her. He would walk his feet bloody if he had to.

He'd been driving up and down every street, not just looking for the van but for anyplace it could hide. But there were houses with garages everywhere, and if the catfish had rented one, he could be out of sight altogether.

*Fine. So we do a damned door-to-door.*

His jaw tightened even more. He should have known. He never should have let her stay at her place, but he'd been so happy she wanted to move in as quickly as possible he hadn't protested. And now she was caught, trapped, in the hands of a piece of human debris who, in his way, was as bad as Bowe. Always blaming everything on someone else, in Bowe's case his wife, in the catfish's probably every woman who'd ever turned him down.

He was not going to lose her. Not when he'd only just found her, when he'd only just found out what it was all about, not just love but life itself. He'd finally—

His foot hit the brake almost before his conscious mind registered what his peripheral vision had caught. A block of white. He backed up to look. And saw a sliver of the back of a white van, barely visible behind a tall fence.

He stopped his SUV on the cross street, out of sight. Leashed Ember, who was already at a high pitch, feeding off his fierce state. They started toward the spot, using the fence hiding the van to hide themselves and proceeding a few feet off the sidewalk.

Ember told him several feet before they got there that she had the scent. Her head came up, and even in the dark he could see her nose working, pulsing as she sorted the smells. Annalise, he thought. Wouldn't it be something if that work she'd been putting in with his dog ended up saving her?

He put the location and call for backup out in a whisper. He barely noticed the responses and didn't care. This was his to do. He'd made the monumental screwup of not realizing what the catfish would do.

Ember paused, clearly uncertain. She was onto something, but looked at him in puzzlement. Yet her tail was wagging slightly. She was getting both her quarry and Annalise.

"Track," Brett ordered quietly.

Ember led him to the back of the run-down cottage. Not to the door of the cottage itself, but to a separate shed behind it, a small building with a door and a broken window beside it. Ember danced, still not sure if she should be proud she'd found Annalise or worried about The Other.

Then her head came up and turned, as if she'd scented something—or someone- -new. Her signal wasn't alarm, so Brett figured it had to be someone she knew. A yell came out of the darkness to his right.

"Duck!"

Instinctively he dropped. Heard something go over his head and land with a metallic clatter behind him. A glance told me it was a lethal, curved blade that looked like nothing less than a machete. Flung full force through the broken window in the moment when he'd been checking Ember's reactions. And it could easily have hit him and done some serious damage. If not for the warning.

He spun to his right and Troy Colton materialized out of the darkness.

"Heard your backup call," his fellow detective whispered.

"It's the catfish. He's got Annalise."

Troy went very still. "Then let's take his ass."

No questions, no doubts, no hesitation and full confidence. They really did have his back. Not just Grave Gulch PD, but the Coltons.

"I saw a door on the back side. You want to try talking him out, while I go in from there?" Troy whispered. At Brett's look, his grin flashed. The grin that had become so frequent since Troy and Evangeline had connected. Which Brett finally understood. "Hey, I blend in at night better than your pasty Irish face, bro."

"Can't argue that. I practically glow in the dark." And he felt the kind of connection he'd only felt with compatriots he literally trusted with his life.

"Let's do this," Troy said.

Brett called up every hostage-negotiation tactic he'd ever been taught. Pretended he was reluctant to take lethal action. Pretended he was perfectly willing to wait out here until the catfish decided, as if ceding control to him. And pretended—to himself, because he had to—that he was certain the man wouldn't kill Annalise because he wanted to torment her for insulting him.

The first time the guy called out an answer, demanding he leave, Brett knew they were on. Troy would know the suspect's attention was on Brett and make his move. And staying here, letting it happen that way, was the hardest thing he'd ever done. But it was the best chance for Annalise, and right now that was all that mattered. And Troy would see that it went down right, that she stayed safe. Because that's what Colton cops did. And in a way, he was one of them now. They didn't know it yet, but he'd make sure they did. He wouldn't accept any less, for Annalise's sake.

Brett started to move when he heard a shout from inside. Then the door on this side burst open and the catfish bolted out, looking back over his shoulder as if terrified.

Brett reached out with his right foot and caught him on his next stride, right above the ankle. The guy went down like the flailing bag of scum he was. Flushed out like a quivering quail and tripped up like a graceless freak.

And Brett couldn't think of a more appropriate ending for him.

# Chapter 37

Annalise listened for a moment before she opened her eyes. The last image in her mind, so vivid, so ugly, was that slimy monster with his hands on her, trying to force her into that van. He had to have used one of his stolen darts on her.

But now she was lying on a bed, in a place where there were other people, because she could hear distant voices and footsteps. And someone was here, because she could feel the warmth of a hand wrapped around hers. And that scent… Like the forest, like the pine trees she loved.

Like Brett.

Her eyes snapped open. Hospital? She was in a hospital? But in the next instant even that didn't matter. Because Brett was there, he was the one holding her hand, and looking at her with as much love as she ever could have hoped for in his bright blue eyes.

"Welcome back," he said softly.

"You figured it out," she said. "You found me. Saved me."

"With some help from Ember. And Troy." Her brows rose. "He was there when I needed him," was all he said, but she read much more in his eyes.

"You caught him though?"

He nodded. "Name's Ben Toomey. He played along several women on the app, hoping we'd be on one of them, instead of you."

"So it wasn't your fault."

"Less my fault than I first thought," he amended. "I was afraid I'd done something to tip him off."

"Of course you didn't."

"Turns out he lost most of what he had in a nasty divorce. Dr. Masters thinks he's stealing from women as payback."

"Better than some things he could have done, I guess." She frowned. "But I don't remember—"

He squeezed her hand gently. "They said you'll probably remember most of it, once the drug's completely out of your system."

"I do remember that when everything went blank I was in hell, but—" she squeezed his fingers and smiled at him "—now I wake up in heaven."

He actually blushed. Which pleased her to no end. And when he lifted her hand to his lips and kissed it, she felt her pulse leap. Curious, she glanced at the monitor near the bed and laughed. He looked up, appearing a bit startled. She pointed with her other hand to the screen, to the suddenly higher number that was slowly decreasing.

"I guess there's no denying what you do to me now, is there?" she teased.

His gaze locked with hers. "If I was hooked up to one of those, mine would do the same thing. Every time you look at me."

She drew in a deep breath. She could have died last night, if Brett was a little less brave, a little less determined. She could have died without ever saying it. And so she said it now.

"I love you."

The expression of wonder and relief that came over his face then said more than even his words did. "I never really knew what love was. I do now. It's what I feel for you."

Warmth flooded her, but she had a single reservation left. "I should never have opened the door to him. But I thought you'd sent him."

"It doesn't matter. He's locked up, and he's going to stay there for a long time."

"But I was fooled again. I should have learned by now never to trust—"

"No," he said, stopping her. "Please, Annalise, don't ever lose that sweetness, that warmth." He took an audible breath before adding softly, "Sometimes it may be the only thing that keeps me going, knowing that there are people in the world like you. And your family. I won't deny I had my doubts, but I see now who the Coltons really are. And I know they'll have my back if I need it."

She held those words close to her for the next few days. They helped her get through giving her statement to the patrol officer who came to her room. Once she was released from the hospital she returned to packing, feeling a shiver of relief that she would be leaving this place that had once been a home but was now simply the place where the worst things in her life had happened. Brett had taken a couple of days off to help, and it was a joy to hear him telling her recklessly to bring everything she wanted, and they'd figure out where it all would go later.

He even talked about his plans to expand the house, in such detail she knew he had to have been thinking about it for a while. Which removed her last fear that he might have just said those wonderful words because she'd been lying in a hospital bed. The dogs were deliriously happy, which she completely understood since she was, too. They'd be even more happy if they knew Brett had suggested they just adopt them themselves, so they would always stay together.

And her joy bubbled over when he took her on an elaborate, elegant weekend date at the historic Grand Hotel up on Mackinac Island, an elaborate meal and two nights alone in a luxury room. When she asked why, it was so expensive, he'd said simply, "I want you to remember this date, not the bad ones."

But two weeks later it hit a peak she'd never thought possible when he came home—a phrase she loved, saying it or thinking it—with a rather tentative expression on his face.

"What?" she asked immediately.

"This is only so you can see it," he said, almost warningly. "It has to go back. I had to get the chief's and the prosecutor's permission to take it. But I wanted you to know I kept my promise."

"You always keep your promises, Brett Shea."

The smile he gave her then sent her pulse flying all over again. Then he pulled a small plastic bag out of his pocket. She frowned, recognizing an evidence bag. But then she saw what was in it.

Her grandmother's bracelet.

Moisture gathered in her eyes, and she flung her arms around him. She couldn't find a single word to say, so she just hugged him, holding on as if…well, as if she was holding on to the rest of her life. And he hugged her back in the same way.

"I was thinking," he said against her hair, his voice

sounding oddly thick, "that since you can't really have this back until the trial's over that maybe we should get you…something else with diamonds."

She went very still. Became aware of his heart hammering in his chest, almost in time with her own.

"Brett?" she whispered.

"A ring. Would you wear my ring, Annalise? Will you marry me?"

She stared up at him. Was vaguely aware there were three dogs sitting near their feet, the clever Ember, who realized something important was up, keeping the smaller two in line. Their family. For now. Swallowed tightly, found her voice.

"I'll want kids," she warned.

For the first time doubt flashed in his expression. "I don't mind but I don't know how to be—"

She lifted a hand, put a finger to his lips. "Sure you do. Just do the opposite of what yours did."

He laughed, and she felt his tension ease. Then his brow furrowed slightly. "Does that mean…yes?"

"Yes, yes, a thousand times yes."

And Annalise Colton looked up into the blue, blue eyes of her future husband, and realized she truly had been holding on to the rest of her life.

\* \* \* \* \*

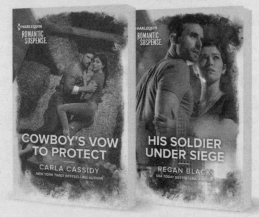

## #2151 COLTON 911: FORGED IN FIRE
*Colton 911: Chicago*
### by Linda Warren

While Carter Finch is trying to investigate a potential forgery, Lila Colton's art gallery is set on fire. As a result, Lila becomes the main suspect. Carter stays by her side and they're drawn into multiple mysteries that threaten a possible future they could have together...

## #2152 A COLTON INTERNAL AFFAIR
*The Coltons of Grave Gulch*
### by Jennifer D. Bokal

Police officer Grace Colton is being investigated for unlawful use of force. Internal Affairs investigator Camden Kingsley is charged with finding out what happened—but there's more to this case than meets the eye...and romance is the last thing either of them expected.

## #2153 STALKED IN SILVER VALLEY
*Silver Valley P.D.*
### by Geri Krotow

Former FBI and current undercover agent Luther Darby needs linguist Kit Danilenko's talents to bring down Russian Organized Crime in Silver Valley, and Kit needs Luther's law enforcement expertise. Neither wants any part of their sizzling attraction, especially when it becomes a liability against the two most powerful ROC operatives.

## #2154 COLD CASE WITNESS
### by Melinda Di Lorenzo

When Warren Wright is caught witnessing several armed men unearthing a body, he has no choice but to run or be killed. His flight leads him to seek cover, and he inadvertently draws Jeannette Renfrew into his escape plan. The two of them must work together to solve a mystery with connections to Warren's past.

---

HRSCNM0921

"Kit, you misunderstood me. Let me try again."

He saw her shake her head vigorously in his peripheral
vision. If he could grab her hand, look her in the eyes, he
would. So that she'd see his sincerity. But they'd started
to climb and the highway had gone down to two lanes,
winding around the first cluster of mountain foothills.

"No need. Just take me back home." This version of
Kit was not the woman who'd greeted him this morning.
Great, just great. It'd taken him, what, fifteen minutes to
make mincemeat of her self-confidence? He felt like the
lowest bird on the food chain, unable to escape the raptor
that was his big mouth.

"I'm not taking you home, Kit. We're going on this mission, together. I'm sorry if I pushed too hard on your history—it's none of my business. None of it." He needed to hear the words as much as say them. The reminder that she was a mob operative's spouse, albeit an ex, would keep him from seeing her as anything but his work colleague.

She was nothing like Evalina.

The memory of how the ROC mob honcho's wife had used him, how stupidly he'd fallen for her charms, made his self-disgust all the greater. It was one thing that he'd allowed himself to be duped and his heart dragged through the ROC crap. It was another to cause Kit, a true victim of her circumstances, any pain.

"Are you sure you can trust me, Luther?"

*Don't miss*
Stalked in Silver Valley *by Geri Krotow,*
*available October 2021 wherever*
*Harlequin Romantic Suspense*
*books and ebooks are sold.*

Harlequin.com

# Get 4 FREE REWARDS!

## We'll send you 2 FREE Books plus 2 FREE Mystery Gifts.

**Harlequin Romantic Suspense** books are heart-racing page-turners with unexpected plot twists and irresistible chemistry that will keep you guessing to the very end.

**FREE** Value Over **$20**

# *Love Harlequin romance?*

## DISCOVER.

Be the first to find out about promotions, news and exclusive content!

 Facebook.com/HarlequinBooks

Twitter.com/HarlequinBooks

Instagram.com/HarlequinBooks

Pinterest.com/HarlequinBooks

YouTube.com/HarlequinBooks

ReaderService.com

## EXPLORE.

Sign up for the Harlequin e-newsletter and download a free book from any series at
**TryHarlequin.com**

## CONNECT.

Join our Harlequin community to share your thoughts and connect with other romance readers!
**Facebook.com/groups/HarlequinConnection**